TAMING THE WLF

THE NOBLE NORSEMEN

VIRGINIE MARCONATO

OLIVERHEBERBOOKS

PROLOGUE
EAST ANGLIA WINTER 1036

The girl opened her eyes.

It was obvious from the way she blinked that she had no idea where she was. Perhaps she had been beaten or someone had slipped her a sleeping draught before the sale started, perhaps both.

Wolf frowned. Her face was unmarred but that didn't mean her body was not covered in cuts and bruises and anyway, the man offering her for sale did not deserve praise for not hurting her. If he had not mistreated her it was only because he had not wanted to diminish his profit by presenting her in less than the full glory of her beauty.

For the girl was exquisite.

Wolf understood why she had been kept last. She stood out from the other slaves as surely as a finely chiseled piece of jewelry amongst rough iron collars. One of her braids had come undone and luscious hair covered her left shoulder in a cascade of shimmering copper. Her eyes, framed by long, velvety lashes, appeared dark, almost black, an unusual trait in someone so fair of complexion. Her face and throat were pale as a swan's plumage, and looked just as temptingly soft. As to her body...

Her body was perfection, a beguiling combination of soft curves and elegant limbs barely hidden under a delicate shift. It was a body made for hot, passionate lovemaking. The woman was temptation, sensuality personified. Where on earth had the slave trader found such a jewel?

As if he'd heard his inner musings, the man spoke, addressing the crowd in front of him.

"Well, what say you? You will not have seen the like of her often. That beautiful hair is softer than silk, and smells like flowers." He took a handful of the copper tresses and brought it to his nose, making a point of rolling his eyes as he inhaled its scent. The woman jerked her head but there was nothing she could do to prevent him from rubbing it against his cheek. "Pale skin, dark eyes, and a body any man would give his right arm to possess. You don't believe me? See for yourself!"

Without any warning, he reached out to her shift and ripped it open from throat to navel, revealing two perfect ivory breasts and a soft stomach. The men jeered. Wolf clenched his jaw.

Unsurprisingly, the girl let out a cry of outrage at this new provocation but, bound as she was, she could not do anything. Or...

To Wolf's intense surprise, she spat in the man's face and cursed him. A feisty one then... His interest in her increased tenfold. Spirit was always something to enjoy. The man, however, was less impressed. He lifted a hand, ready to strike in retaliation.

Immediately, Wolf called out an extravagant sum of money, diverting his attention away from the rebellious girl. The slave trader turned to him, a slow grin on his face. Clearly, he was not a man to miss an opportunity.

"Sold," he said in a dark voice.

CHAPTER ONE

A strange coldness invaded Wolf.

He had just bought himself a slave.

How on earth had this happened? He had not come to town with the intention of doing such a thing. In fact, his whole body rebelled at the idea of owning another human being but his attention had been caught on the way back from the port by a cheering crowd and he had arrived in time to see the slave trader uncover his last offering, the beautiful Saxon woman. Up until then her face had been hidden under a rough cloth bag, presumably in the hope of raising the men's expectations and stir them into offering wild sums for her, just as he had done. Why had he been pushed into such an act as buying another person?

Because there had not been any other choice, that was why.

As soon as he had set eyes on her Wolf had known he would buy her. It was not her extraordinary beauty that had decided him, even if he had been just as stunned as the rest of the men by her looks. It was the air of defiance about her. Although she was plainly bewildered and afraid, she was standing up for herself, or at least trying to. Well, *he* was not tied up and helpless. He would come to her aid. No one else would have her, touch her or even leer at her for a moment longer.

If she was to be sold then he would be the one to buy her.

He walked to the platform, wondering if his purse even held the promised sum. In the heat of the moment he had not stopped to check how much coin he had on him.

"Wait!" a voice from the other side of the crowd shouted. "I will bid on the girl as well."

A moment later a blond man came to stand in front of him.

"No, you won't," Wolf growled, straightening up to his full height. "Not unless you want to spend the rest of your life sipping gruel like an old man, that is. I will fight you for her and what's more, I will win."

The man instantly recoiled. Evidently he had not seen who he was dealing with and he could not help being impressed by his opponent's stature. Wolf knew many a man found him forbidding and never had he been more grateful for his physique than now. He wouldn't have to lift a finger to ensure the girl left the place as his.

"Well?" the slave trader enquired, hoping to get even more money for the sale.

"Well nothing. The girl is mine," Wolf answered with decision, keeping his eyes on the man in front of him. He did not seem ready to challenge him but it was best to leave no doubt in his mind.

"Let the man name his price first."

"It's not a question of price. If anyone wants her they will have to get through me first." Wolf drew a knife from the sheath at his belt and waited, knowing the man would never dare challenge him now. He had gone a sickly shade of gray at the sight of the blade.

Without a word he faded back into the crowd. Unsurprisingly, no one else came forward.

Wolf had won. Grunting, he threw his purse at the slave trader. Then he turned his attention back to the girl.

———

THROUGH HALF-OPENED eyelids Merewen saw a man walk up to her. No, not a man but something much worse, a giant armed with a knife and snarling at her. Her whole body lurched in terror.

Merciful heavens, was he going to kill her?

Forgetting for a moment that she was tied to the post, she made to flee, only to be stopped by the rope digging painfully into her wrists. She forced herself to take a deep, steadying breath. This was a nightmare and she was about to wake up. It was the only thing that made sense. Why else would she be here, trussed up like an animal, exposed to a crowd of leering men and about to be killed by a scowling demon?

Her head was swimming, yet another proof that she was not in her normal sate. The last thing she remembered was attending her brother's funeral and wishing she could retire to her chamber to finally allow herself to grieve. Evidently she had fallen asleep crying and, in her sorrow, had conjured up a frightful nightmare. But if it was a dream, why was she conscious of dreaming? Why was she so cold? Why could she hear the men speaking in languages she wasn't even aware existed?

Another tug at the rope at her wrists confirmed it. This was no dream. It was all too real.

With a moan of powerlessness she closed her eyes and stopped moving. If the man wanted to kill her there was nothing she could do to stop him. She might as well try to preserve the last scrap of dignity a half-naked, tied up woman could possess.

The sound of coins being passed from hand to hand reached her ears, followed by a wheezy voice she didn't recognize.

"She's yours."

A moment later an arm wrapped around her waist and she found herself pressed against a rock hard body. The pleasure of that contact took her by surprise. She had been about to collapse in terror and the support the man provided was highly welcome, as was the heat emanating from his chest and the fact that he was now hiding her exposed breasts to the crowd of onlookers. She felt him raise his arm above her head to cut the bonds tying her to the post.

So that was why he had drawn his knife... He had not intended to kill her, but to free her.

Her arms fell down, and her body instantly sagged. The man tightened his hold around her and grunted, the sound of someone dissatisfied more than really angry. She opened her eyes and stared into a pair of blue irises that despite the icy color seemed to burn her with their heat. Something unfurled within her, a kind of blooming sensation originating somewhere in her chest and spreading through her whole body with alarming speed. The man's jaw tightened, as if he experienced the exact same thing and did not know what to make of it either. For a moment time suspended its flight and she forgot the cold.

Then he put his knife away in his belt and, before she could say or do anything, swept her into his arms.

It was only when he walked down the platform that Merewen understood that she had been bought as a slave.

At first she had been too relieved to see that the man was not going to kill her, too comforted by his strength and warmth to realize the full implications of what had happened. But now it hit her with the force of a lightening bolt splitting a tree in two.

She had been bought by a stranger and that stranger was carrying her away to... to where exactly?

She shook her head. Where mattered little. What mattered was what would happen once they got there. Her new owner was impossibly strong – how else would he be able to carry her as easily as if she was a child? – and determined to have her in his bed – why else would he have bought a woman whose breasts had been exposed?

Against such a man she wouldn't stand a chance.

Her only option was to escape. Now, before he had taken her to wherever he intended to take her. She instantly started kicking and writhing.

"No!" she cried out. "Let me go, put me down!"

The hold around her only tightened. "I won't put you down. You are barely able to stand," the man said calmly. "And I won't let you go. You are half-naked. Trust me, it wouldn't be in your best interest to wander the streets in such a state. Now, stop wriggling or I will have to throw you over my shoulder. It will be more comfortable for me, but not for you."

This answer left Merewen speechless, so much so that she indeed stopped struggling and allowed the stranger to carry her away. He was right, in a half-torn shift and with her head swimming, she was in no state to do anything. Night was falling fast. Where would she go, alone and with no money? She had no idea where they were. Evidently, a large town, but that hardly signified, as she did not recognize it. Besides, she needed to understand how she could have ended up being sold as a slave, and the man was the only one who might answer her questions. He spoke her language well enough, even if she detected an accent in the way he spoke, an accent that gave his words a hard edge that was not unpleasant.

Soon they walked past a group of men laughing by a fire. One of them called out in their direction.

"Wolf! There you are! Come join us for a drink!"

The man did not even slow down. "Not now. Go and tell Eirik he can ride without me. I can't come tonight."

Someone answered in a foreign tongue and all the men laughed, nodding toward Merewen in understanding. Her cheeks flamed red. They thought her owner was carrying her away somewhere to have his way with her, just as she had feared. Before she could panic anew, a deep rumble resonated in her captor's chest and he answered in the same language, something sharp and biting, evidently a rebuke. The men lowered their eyes to the floor and looked contrite. Merewen shivered. What sort of a man had she been sold to? Impossibly strong, forbidding enough to silence five jeering men with a few words, and called... *Wolf?*

Perhaps she should try to escape, torn shift or not.

A moment later, the man entered a hut that, judging from what she could smell, had housed more animals than humans but by then she was so overwhelmed, so exhausted, so confused that when he laid her down onto a pile of sheepskins that looked surprisingly clean, she did not protest. Odd as it was, being carried against his warm chest had lulled her into sleep, made her almost subdued. She could not be in her normal state because in a distant corner of her mind she was sure she should be terrified by the man, not soothed. The trader must have slipped her a sleeping potion before the sale. That would explain her sluggishness and the fact that she could not remember how she had arrived in this town and in the hands of a slave trader.

When she had woken up she had found herself tied up to a post, her face hidden by a sack of cloth. She had heard what was going on but understood little, and seen nothing. It had not occurred to her that she was being sold as a slave until a long moment later, for how could she have thought such a thing? But been sold she had, sold *and* bought.

She looked around in surprise. The blond giant had disappeared through the door after placing her on the makeshift bed and she was now alone in the room. Frozen to the bone, she picked up one of the sheepskins to try and cover herself but quickly saw that her only option was to lie down and pile them all on top of her. No wonder her captor had not thought it necessary to ensure she could not escape. Half-naked and freezing, all she wanted to do was burrow under the covers.

A moment later the man was back and Merewen stood back up, not wanting him to get any ideas when he saw her lying down.

"You need to get dressed," he said in a deep resonant voice that was further enhanced by the accent she still could not quite place. "It is too cold for you to remain in just your shift."

"Yes. Not to mention humiliating and indecent!" she snapped back, clutching at the torn shift. Holding it close was the only way she could hide her breasts. "What's this?"

He cocked an eyebrow when she pointed at the dress in his hand. "It's a turnip," he answered, looking at her straight in the eye. "As you can see."

His lips quivered and his whole face was transformed when he smiled. Merewen refused to acknowledge that without his jaw set in granite, he was even more striking. The man was now not only handsome but devilishly appealing and an odd thought crossed her mind. A man who smiled like he did could not be dangerous.

She shook her head. Not dangerous! What was she thinking! Evidently the trader's potion still had not cleared from her mind. The man was her captor, easily twice her size and strong as an ox, it mattered not what he looked like or how he smiled!

As if it was not enough that he had bought her like an animal, he was now mocking her!

"I know what it is!" she snapped. "I mean, where did you find it?"

"I didn't find it. I bought it for you. You cannot remain in such a humiliating, indecent attire."

He had used her previous words she noticed, yet another way of mocking her.

"My... A slave and now a dress! At this rate, you will be broke before the end of the day," she jeered, determined to hide her fear behind a façade of confidence. "You really shouldn't have gone to such expense. From what I understand, slaves are not usually given the choice of how they—"

"I didn't buy you to be my slave," Wolf cut in. He could not bear the idea of the girl believing such a thing of him. He did *not* own slaves, whatever she thought, never would. "I won't hurt you, I swear."

"Oh. And I suppose I should just believe you? Your name is Wolf, you bought me at a slave auction, you live like a..." She gestured wildly around her, as if the reasons for her to think him an ill-educated, dangerous savage were too numerous to mention.

He lifted his chin, none too pleased at the accusations. "I am not a barbarian, whatever you might think. I bought you at the auction to spare you a fate as a real slave, nothing more! I thought you would have understood it by now. And my name is not really Wolf. It's Ulf. But when I arrived here people misheard it and started calling me Wolf. I did not correct them and it stuck. Now all my friends call me Wolf."

"Your friends, or your enemies?"

"My friends," he asserted. "And I repeat, you are not here to be my slave. You will come to no harm."

She blinked a few times, as if she wasn't sure what to make

of this promise, as if she didn't dare hope he had bought her to set her free. Which was a good thing for he had not, not exactly.

"Why did you buy me then?" she asked in a whisper.

He shrugged, unsure of how to explain an impulse he did not quite understand. It was wiser not to mention the appeal she exerted on him as a woman, and he wasn't sure she would believe him if he said that his curiosity had been piqued when she had spat in the slave trader's face. She didn't seem too well disposed toward him to say the least, and it was hard to blame her. She was so small and delicate that it would be a miracle if his sheer size didn't frighten her.

Or...

Was she frightened? Suddenly he was not so certain. She wasn't cowering in a corner or refusing to meet his gaze and she had just provoked him. Frightened women did not behave thus, they simply tried to melt into the background. He should know. He had never been able to forget the look on Solveig's face every time he raised his voice or made a brusque gesture. She seemed to disappear within herself. The idea that this woman was made of sterner stuff pleased him. He never wanted to see diffidence in a woman's eyes when she looked at him for as long as he lived.

"Put the dress on," he said, bringing the discussion to an end by throwing her the garment.

She caught it deftly but after one sniff, threw it back to him. "It reeks of sweat. I am not putting it on."

And with those words she turned to face the wall, effectively dismissing him.

Wolf arched an eyebrow. Well, that answered his question at least. The girl was definitely not frightened of him. Either the slave trader's draught had given her a sense of false security or she was a woman of uncommon spirit. He smiled to himself. Of course, she was. It was practically the first thing he had noticed about her, what had urged him to buy her. A woman like that would be nothing but trouble. Wouldn't it be wiser to send her on her way? Yes. Perhaps. But he did not want to. It was not just a question of honor. True, he had bought her only so that he could protect her from the crowd of men, but if he were honest with himself, he did not *want* to send her away.

He wanted to get to know her, and make her see that they did not need to be enemies.

He wanted... well. It was best not to dwell on what else he wanted from her.

"I guess I will go and buy another dress then," he murmured to himself, marveling that he should do her bidding. He *never* allowed anyone to dictate his behavior. "Keep yourself warm in the meantime. I'll get the fire going when I return."

As soon as the door closed, Merewen ran back to the sheep-skins and tried to make sense of what had just happened. Where was she? And how was she going to get out of this nightmare?

It was only when the sound of the door opening jolted her awake that she realized she had fallen asleep instead of coming up with a plan. Ignoring the cold, she forced herself to stand up and face whoever had walked in. If it wasn't the man she was expecting then what would she say? *How* would she say it? The intruder might be another foreigner who didn't speak her tongue and would make the most of his discovery. A half-naked, powerless woman lying on sheepskins would undeniably be a temptation for anyone.

Her relief at seeing the blond giant enter annoyed her. Why did she feel so strongly about this man she didn't know and could not trust? He owned her, had paid money for her, as if she were a mere possession. He had carried her away without even offering a word of reassurance. Merewen refused to remember that the heat of his body had been welcome, or to acknowledge that he had not swung her over his shoulder like a bag of grain, instead holding her in a way that was comfortable for her. She refused to think of his smile or his efforts at seeing her decently dressed because the last thing she wanted to feel toward him was gratefulness.

Outrage was a much more appropriate reaction.

Besides, if he saw any signs of softening on her part he might interpret it as an agreement to make her his in every way a man could possess a woman. Although he had told her that he had not bought her to be his slave, she did not believe a word of it. It was better not to lower her guard just yet.

"Here," he said, throwing her a different dress. "Put this one on."

By now Merewen was so cold that she would have agreed to wear the dress he had first brought her, despite the smell. Fortunately she didn't have to, for he handed her a soft woolen gown that would have cost a lot more than he no doubt wanted to pay for a slave.

Hiding her surprise at the quality of the garment, she shrugged it on and had to bite her lip not to sigh in relief. The gown was as warm as it was beautiful.

"I see that the color meets your approval," he said with a smirk.

She did not reply.

Nodding, he went to the firepit and set about stoking it with the pieces of wood he had brought in with him to set it alight. Merewen watched on, fascinated. His gestures were precise and surprisingly elegant for a man of his stature. But then everything he did betrayed the same grace. His gait was supple, his words measured, even his voice was soft as velvet, nothing like the gravel you expected to come from his mouth.

Before long, a welcome fire was roaring in the middle of the room.

Wolf hid his grin when the girl came closer, as timid as a

wild animal refusing to be tamed but unable to resist the lure of man. Now that she was dressed, his little guest seemed to have lost some of her diffidence. Once she had been fed she might even be amiable. He shook his head, amused. He would no doubt have to wait a little longer for that to happen.

"Are you hungry? I am," he said without waiting for her answer. He guessed she would be, but would never admit to it.

She was standing on unsteady legs, and though she didn't want to betray the fact, it was obvious that she was not feeling well. Her eyes were still unfocused, her lips had yet to lose their blue tinge and she was shivering violently.

For all that, she was unutterably beautiful, and nothing like the women he was used to meeting. Her shift, damaged as it was, appeared to be of the best quality. It was doubtful the slave trader had provided it for her. No. This was no farmer's daughter.

So who was she, how had she ended up being sold—and what in the name of Odin was he to do with her?

He had no intention of owning a slave, be it a man or a woman. All he knew was that he had seen red when he had seen her treated so appallingly by the scoundrel who had exposed her to the lust of the men present. He could no more have walked away than offer himself up as a slave. He could not regret the impulse but the fact remained.

He was now saddled with a woman who was nothing to him and did not seem in the least disposed to be grateful.

Oh, well, finding a role for her could wait. For now, they would eat.

In the bag Ingegard had given him he found some smoked eel, half a loaf of bread, a piece of cheese and a flagon of ale. At least this feast had not cost him anything. The woman had been only too happy to provide 'her savior', as she always called him, with everything he needed to feed him and a woman half his size. This was one of the most rewarding aspects of offering his help to the villagers. Everywhere he went he was sure to meet with a grateful friend who remembered the assistance he had given them and wanted to repay him for the favor.

Tonight it was more welcome than ever. He and the girl would be warm and fed.

Merewen's stomach started to rumble at the sight of the food. She had no idea when she had last eaten. It could be days, depending on how long ago she had been given the sleeping potion. Eating might help her clear her head.

Without looking her way, as if he trusted her to ask for food if she needed it, Wolf placed everything on the table and started to eat. After a brief hesitation she reached out for the bread, daring him to comment on her surrender. He smiled faintly but said nothing. Instead he handed her the flagon of ale.

"Would you prefer to drink first? I have no cup, I'm afraid."

She wasn't sure if he was mocking her for what he assumed were delicate manners or he was just being thoughtful because that was what came naturally to him. It amazed her that she should even entertain that second possibility, but she had to own that he was being very attentive to her needs. He had clothed her and was now feeding her when she had neither asked for it nor expected it.

"Thank you." She took the flagon and drank deep, knowing she would not dare drink again once he had placed his lips on it.

"Get yourself settled for the night," Wolf instructed once they had finished the last of the cheese. "I will be back shortly."

Alone again, Merewen wondered once more if she had not dreamed the whole episode. Had she really been offered for sale to a crowd of leering men earlier that afternoon and afraid of being killed? It all seemed like a lifetime away. Now that she was properly dressed, not hungry or cold anymore, now that her indignation had melted away she could feel herself falling back into a delicious torpor. She could not detach her eyes from the fire burning in the pit as it spread its warmth throughout her body. Clumsily, she reached out for the flagon of ale and took such a big swig that she poured the rest of the contents all over the front of her dress.

"Oh, no!" she mumbled. Now this dress would reek too!

Refusing to sleep in wet clothes smelling of ale, she hastily disrobed and rinsed it off with the water Wolf had placed into a bowl on the table, presumably for her to wash with. Finally she draped the dress on the stool in front of the fire to dry and went to bed. Now that the fire was warming the room, she would not be cold in her shift.

It was not long before Merewen succumbed to a deep sleep.

CHAPTER TWO

The girl was growing increasingly agitated.

In the bright moonlight Wolf watched her writhe and moan on the sheepskins. She had been sound asleep when he had returned to the hut earlier but had been getting uneasy for quite some time now. She had kicked her covers and would not lie still. At first he had tried to ignore her and get the sleep he needed but he was now getting concerned.

Was something ailing her?

Frowning, Wolf took a few tentative steps toward her, expecting her to bark at him, ordering him to stay away. But she was still asleep and, he could see now, all but naked. A beam of moonlight, strategically placed, allowed him to see her from neck to navel. She had discarded her dress before going to sleep and her torn shift was gaping open over her chest, exposing the two perfect breasts he had not been able to get out of his mind. White in the silver light, crowned with dark red berries, they called out to a primal part of him. The sight affected him so much that he overturned to stool in front of him. He stilled, bracing himself for her reaction. It never came.

Either she could still feel the effects of the draught or she was exhausted, for she did not even flinch at the noise.

Forcing himself to ignore her nakedness, he focused on the source of her discomfort. What was wrong with her? Stomach upset? Fever? He had not checked her body for injuries earlier and she had not appeared to be bleeding but perhaps she was hurt all the same. Had it been a mistake to favor her modesty over her health? Perhaps he should have at least asked if the trader had harmed her in any way.

While he was debating what to do she snaked one hand between her thighs and wrapped the other around her left breast, giving it a squeeze. A feral growl escaped Wolf's lips.

Oh, she was prey to a fever, but not one caused by a festering wound! The girl writhing on the bed in front of him was caught in a licentious dream and trying to reach her pleasure.

His blood surged so fast that he had to sit on the stool he had kicked earlier for fear of collapsing. Never had he seen anything half as arousing as this girl with her hair fanned around her like living fire stroking herself and he did not even consider for a moment averting his gaze.

At first she seemed satisfied by her caresses but it quickly became obvious that she was doing little more than stoking her desire without managing to bring about the release she so desperately craved.

Hitting the floor with her flat palm, she let out a grunt of frustration.

"Ah, please," she moaned, turning her head toward him. With her face in the shadows he couldn't be sure her eyes were opened. But it sounded as if she had awoken and was begging him. "I need..."

Wolf didn't think, he didn't even blink. A heartbeat later he was by her side, ready to take over if she asked.

"What do you need?" he rasped, even though he had a fair idea of the answer.

"You." That one word sent shards of need through his veins. Before he could answer she pulled him by the neck to shove her breast into his mouth. Well. It did not get any clearer than that and Wolf was not one to deny a woman her pleasure.

When his lips closed over her erect nipple she cried out and arched her back so much he feared she would injured herself.

"Yes!" she panted.

In answer to his growl she buried her fingers into his hair to anchor him in place and spread her legs, the invitation clear. Fighting the urge to bite her, Wolf extended a hand to gather the hem of her shift to her waist and was shocked to touch only silken skin. The girl had already bared herself in readiness for his touch.

Oh, she *was* awake, and demanding to be pleasured.

He didn't even try to resist. With a possessive groan he closed his hand over her soft curls. Wet heat burned his fingers, wrenching another groan out of him, causing him to suckle her harder. By the gods, how was he going to give her the pleasure she needed and then find the strength to leave it at that?

The girl was so desperate for release that her body started to pulse as soon as he moved to stroke her most sensitive flesh. A raw cry escaped her lips and the hands at his neck tensed, while she dug her nails deep into his scalp. A series of shudders rocked through her, then finally she went limp.

Releasing her nipple Wolf sat up, feeling drained himself. That, without a doubt, had been the most erotic moment of his life. For a long moment he contemplated her in the moonlight, ignoring the raging need throbbing in his body. She was so beautiful! He could not recall ever seeing a woman who appealed to him more. Even his wife had not been as alluring because she had possessed no inner fire. In bed Solveig had been as cold as the ice covering the lakes of his native land in winter but this girl was as hot as the water spewing from its geysers when you least excepted it.

The thought of what they could do together almost caused him to erupt with the same force.

After a while she started writhing again. Her release had been too quick, and had left her unsatisfied. She wanted more.

"Again?" he murmured, more than ready to give it to her.

"Again," she whispered back, her dark eyes fastened on him.

Teasing her hard nipple with his thumb he watched, transfixed as her face transformed under his caress. Her lips parted, her cheeks reddened, her eyes closed, her breathing grew more and more labored. Moaning, she started to move her hips in an evocative, rhythmic movement that left no doubt about what she wanted. Unable to resist the silent plea, Wolf slowly eased a finger inside of her and let out a harsh curse. This would be the death of him. She was so hot, so wet, so tight! Perhaps he could ask...

No.

Wolf stilled, for suddenly he felt the proof that the girl had not known any man. The sobering realisation brought him back to his senses. He could not take an innocent, not like this, without talking about it first. He would do what she had asked, help her and bring about the pleasure she had tried to find by herself but he would not breach her maidenhead, not now, not in this way. With her senses on fire she would not be thinking clearly. That she wanted pleasure did not mean that she wanted to be taken, much less deflowered.

"I won't take you tonight," he said quietly. "But I can give you what you need."

She sighed, as in relief, and placed her hand on top of his.

Obeying the silent instruction, he stroked her gently, careful of not going too deep and compromise her innocence. In no time, he heard a long rasp that almost caused him to come undone himself.

Bending down over her, he trailed his tongue along her bottom lip. At the same time he curled the finger that was still inside her. She erupted, crying out her pleasure into his mouth. It was too much.

With his free hand Wolf tore at his braies and brought about his own release with frightening speed, feeling as if his whole body was bursting at the seams. Panting, he raised his head to the ceiling and groaned. Never in his life had he felt such explosive pleasure. And he had not been inside her, not even felt her hands on him. What would he feel if they made love properly one day? He could not begin to imagine.

By the time he had recovered, the girl was peacefully asleep once more, her small hand draped over the one that was still cupped over her sex.

Something was different.

Whether it was good or bad Merewen wasn't sure but she had never felt that way before. There was a strange languor in her body and a pleasant peace in her mind. Then she understood.

The dream! Of course!

The dream that had pursued her for months had come to her last night. She bit her lip when she remembered the extraordinary feeling that had flowed through her veins, the final explosion. All this time she had tried to achieve such a release, without ever succeeding. And finally last night, she had.

It had been glorious, breathtaking.

With a contented smile, she stretched. Soft fur met her hands and her shift fell open, revealing her breasts. She sat up in shock as it all came back to her. The slave market, the torn shift, the potion!

She was not at home in her bed, waking up after a sensual dream. She was in a miserable hut with a man who had bought her like an animal! Immediately her hands went to cover her breasts but a quick glance around assured her that, mercifully, she was alone.

Merewen stood up on shaky legs and hastily got dressed. The last thing she wanted was for anyone to walk in on her while she was so exposed. Of course Wolf had already seen more of her than was decent, but she did not intend to show him an inch of flesh that was not on her face or on her hands. From now on, even her hair would be tightly bound.

It was imperative that she guard herself against him and the temptation he represented because she suddenly realized that the face she had seen in her dream when her body had exploded in pleasure was none other than his. Usually the men she pictured were only vague images that bore no resemblance to anyone she knew but the piercing blue eyes and sensual mouth she had seen poised over her last night had definitely been those of the tall Norseman.

And this observation was not reassuring in the least, because that dream had been particularly vivid, particularly shocking. He'd asked her what she needed and she'd said: 'you', as if it were the most normal thing in the world that she should give herself to him, as if he had every right to touch her. She had opened her legs to him willingly, and almost forced him to plea-sure her. And because it had been dream, instead of protesting or taking his place between her thighs to reach his release as a man would do in real life, he had done as she requested and given her what she needed, without asking for anything in return.

He had made her body shatter.

Twice.

When Wolf pushed the door of the hut open later that morning there was only one thing on his mind.

Please, let the girl be up and dressed already. I won't be able to deal with seeing her half-naked and writhing on the bed.

Thankfully, he found her in the middle of the room attending to the fire.

Relief swept through him. He wasn't sure he would have been able to stay in control if he had seen as much as her collar bone. Virgin or not, he might well have tumbled her onto the sheepskins and employed all his seduction skills to convince her to surrender her innocence to him. But she was dressed and her hair was not only tied in a neat plait but coiled at her nape as well. She was too beautiful to be ever called demure but it was the best he could have hoped for. Determined to keep a clear head, Wolf forced himself to ignore the way the dress molded her curves when she bent over the fire to stoke it with a poker.

"We are leaving," he announced gruffly, not trusting himself to remain alone with her in a such a private place. It would be better to be out in the open, in full view of everyone. Then there would be no danger of him losing his mind and doing something neither of them wanted him to do.

"L-leaving?" she stammered, turning to face him.

When their eyes met Wolf received the full beauty of the girl like a physical blow to the gut. He could see now that she had not been quite herself the day before, dazed and confused because of the trader's draught. Now, clear-eyed, rested from her sleep and glowing from the pleasure he had given her in the night, she was simply dazzling.

He cleared his throat and remembered that she had asked him a question.

"Yes, of course we are leaving. I assume you do not wish to stay in this pig sty? I only brought you here so you did not have to sleep out on the open last night but it is not where I live," he added, appalled that she might have thought him coarse enough to live in such a place.

From the way she looked at him, it was clear that she had. He swallowed back a curse. A tormentor, hardly more civilized than an animal, is that what she thought of him?

When Wolf scowled at her, Merewen bit her lip in shame because she *had* thought the place was his home. Evidently she had been doing him a disservice. He had just called it a pig sty and seemed offended that she had assumed he lived in such squalor. But what else could she have thought?

"Where are you taking me?" she asked, lifting her chin. After all, what did it matter if she had offended him? It was not as if they were going to spend their lives together.

"Home," he said, making that one word sound impossibly husky. Her eyes widened. Surely he didn't mean what she thought he meant?

"You're not taking me—"

"No." He gave a faint smile at the horror that must be painted in her face. Evidently he had understood she was worried he would bundle her on a ship sailing to wherever he came from. "I am not taking you across seas to a land of barbarians. I mean my house in the village beyond the valley."

She frowned, trying to establish where that might be, and then nodded. What choice did she have anyway? If he intended to take her with him she would be unable to stop him.

"Let's go, then," she said, following him out of the hut.

Waiting by the door, all saddled and ready to go, was an enormous stallion that could have carried three women like her without flinching. Merewen gulped. Seeing the enormous animal only served to remind her of its master's imposing stature. Of course, a man like him would not own a pony. The poor beast would have crumbled under his weight.

"This is Demon."

"Well chosen name," she muttered, not quietly enough that Wolf didn't hear. She saw his lips curl but he did not pass any comment.

"Now, I do not intend to buy another horse just for this one journey," he said, patting the beast on the rump.

"No. You have spent far too much on your slave already," she sneered, gesturing at her dress.

"As you say." He tightened the girth on the saddle, ignoring the pique. "So you are going to have to either ride with me or follow on foot."

"Follow on foot! I could not do that!" she gasped. Was he mad? How was she supposed to run behind such a powerful animal? She would have found it taxing to walk behind a donkey.

"No, probably not," Wolf agreed easily. "So I suggest you climb on."

He would never relent. She could tell that his intention had been to ride with her all along, only he had thought it better to present her with an alternative to make it appear less like an order. That thoughtfulness surprised her and she could only conclude that he truly meant not to treat her as a slave. Still, the idea of being seated on a horse in front of him, with his arm wrapped around her, made her heart flutter, which was perhaps understandable, and heat flood her veins, which was less so.

Her only option to avoid the unseemly contact was to flee. But how? She would never outrun him. Unless...

Unless she was on a horse. An enormous, presumably inde-fatigable horse.

Her eyes landed on Demon. Could she master such a beast? Perhaps not in normal circumstances, but to escape captivity she would have tried her luck with the Devil itself. After all, even if she fell after a mile it did not matter, she would be free.

Or dead, she reflected grimly, her neck broken. Still, between a demon and a wolf she would take her chances with the former. Merewen lifted her foot, wondering how she was going to reach the stirrup that hovered in front of her navel.

"Wait." Two hands closed around her waist before she could solve that problem. "I think not. I will climb on first," Wolf purred in her ear, looming over her. "Just in case."

Merewen forced herself not to move or protest in any way. The last thing she wanted was to add to his satisfaction. He had seen right through her plans of escaping and was taking pleasure in unsettling her with his sheer physical presence. She would not admit that it was working, that she was feeling herself weaken and wanted nothing more than to mold herself into his embrace, close her eyes and allow him to carry her away wherever he wanted.

It was hard to understand why a man who had bought her in a slave market could make her feel so safe but it was undeniable all the same.

"Can I release you now?" he drawled after a while.

"Do you often wait for permission you don't need from people who cannot contravene you?" she snapped, walking away from him in annoyance. There was no excuse for such weakness. Unlike the day before, today her mind was clear. She should *not* be melting into his embrace.

"No. Just with you."

There were a great many things he only did with this woman, Wolf mused. Allowing her to give him orders for one, stirring his blood so much that he behaved like a lust-crazed fool for another. To his surprise, a smile bloomed on his lips. Not once in the two years since he had arrived here had he felt so alive and no one had intrigued him half as much as this vexing Saxon did.

He knew many a man who would be amazed to hear the

way he allowed this girl to talk to him and many a woman who would envy her for being given pleasure without having to lift a finger in return. In truth he barely recognized himself. Not that he was an aggressive man, not by long shot, but he was no meek lamb either, and he definitely did not allow anyone to order him about. Neither was he a selfish lover but when he made love to a woman, he usually expected them to take an active part in it and ensure his satisfaction in some way.

This was all new, and he wasn't sure what to make of it, or even if he liked it. He snorted, deciding it was better not to dwell on it and carry on as if everything were normal. Surely once the novelty had worn off, he would be able to revert to more sensible behavior.

Then, of course, he would have to decide what to do with his new acquisition.

Uncertainty flickered in his chest. For the first time since Solveig's death he was going to bring a woman into his house to live with, something he had absolutely refused to do since he'd left Iceland. Of course, the arrangement would be different. The girl was not his wife, his lover or even a guest but the result would be the same. She would eat, sleep, wash under his roof. How would he deal with it?

It would be torture. There was no denying it. She appealed to his senses too much for him to be able to pretend she wasn't in the room. Still, there was no helping it. He could not abandon her to her fate now, not before they had established what had happened to her and that she had a safe place to return to.

He vaulted on top of Demon.

Merewen watched Wolf swing his leg over the horse's back as easily as if it had been a mere pony and extend his arm out to her. There was no choice but to comply. Once again, escaping would have to wait.

As she placed her hand into his, she could not help but

blush. In the saddle, they would be pressed close to each other, the heat of their bodies mingling... If he knew what she had done the night before under the cover of darkness, the nature of her very vivid dream, what would he think? Panic invaded her. *Was* Wolf aware she had dreamed of him pleasuring her? He would have slept in the hut with her, even if she had no recollection of him coming back after the meal. What if he had awoken to her moaning? Although she could not be certain, she could well imagine she had cried out at the height of her pleasure. It had been so intense she might well have screamed and panted. What would he have made of it all?

Nothing.

He had made nothing of it, she realized, shaking her head at her own stupidity. If a man as virile as he was had really heard her moan or caught her pleasuring herself he would have jumped on her and made the most of the opportunity. At the very least he would have alluded to it this morning, if not outright mocked her for her wantonness. But he was behaving as if nothing out of the ordinary had happened. Merewen allowed herself to relax.

Yes, she was safe. By some miracle, Wolf was unaware of what she had done, and he could not guess what a wanton creature she was.

"What are you waiting for?" he asked, arching an eyebrow. Her hand was still in his but she had made no move to climb onto the horse.

"Nothing," she answered, before hoisting herself up in front of him.

She most definitely was not waiting for him or anyone. She had spent her whole life relying on herself alone. She had no intention of changing her habits now.

By the gods, this was going to be one long, unbearable journey.

Wolf gritted his teeth. Perhaps he should have gotten another horse for the girl, he reflected as they rode out of the town gates a moment later. Every time she moved, her perfectly formed backside rubbed against his groin, a most cruel, if refined form of torture, because he knew there would be no release even after they had dismounted, except by his own hand. The woman in his arms was out of bounds. He had bought her but she did not belong to him. He wanted her but there were too many reasons why he should not entertain any ideas about her.

He muffled a curse and shifted his position in the saddle. Riding while as hard as stone was not something he would recommend to anyone. To add to his discomfort, he did not want her to notice the effect her proximity was having on him so he forced himself into all sorts of unnatural positions, none of which made any difference. Every time Demon made the slightest movement he felt her nudge at his hardness.

To his surprise, she had not shown any indication that she remembered the events of the previous night. The fact that she had not alluded to it, betrayed any discomfort or shame in his presence, made it obvious. It seemed that, contrary to what he had thought, she had not been fully conscious of asking him anything. That or the draught had made her forget everything... Either way, he did not believe for one moment she would be acting the way she was if she knew what had happened. Whether she would be more outraged or mortified he wasn't sure, but one thing was sure, she wouldn't be able or willing to keep her feelings to herself and she would never have agreed to sit with him on the horse. Rather, she would have given him a dressing down to remember.

The worst of it was, he would probably enjoy it if she chose to shred him into ribbons with her sharp tongue, something that puzzled him. The desire she provoked in him, inconvenient as it was, had come as no surprise, considering how beautiful she was but the pleasure he got out of their heated exchanges was not so easily explained. All in all, it was probably for the best if they could behave as if nothing had happened, because if they started discussing it, he would not resist admitting that seeing, hearing, feeling her pleasure had been the most satisfying experience of his life and that he wanted to do it again.

What was wrong with him? How could he think things like that about someone he had only just met, someone who most likely saw him as a tormentor and wanted nothing more than to escape as soon as possible?

Hiding his irritation, Wolf kicked his horse into a gallop.

The sooner they arrived and he could get her off his burning lap, the better.

CHAPTER THREE

"Wolf, you've returned! You need to speak to Hannah. She won't listen to me!"

"Do you remember the name of the man who makes ropes in the next village?"

"Magnus is still missing, we need to—"

"Wait. I will attend to you all, I promise," Wolf said, raising a hand to interrupt the flow of words threatening to overwhelm him. Demon had scarce placed a hoof in the village and already he was assaulted by questions and demands. For the first time, it irritated him. Usually he didn't mind his own needs coming second to those of the community but it was not just about him anymore. "Let me get the woman settled first."

The woman.

Wolf cringed inwardly. He had not found a more satisfactory way of referring to her but the two words sounded like an insult. Mercifully she didn't speak Norse for he guessed she would have flared up.

The villagers all turned their attention to her at the same time, the expression on their faces ranging from disbelief and irritation to curiosity and admiration. He cursed himself for having drawn unnecessary attention to her, for she would no doubt be uncomfortable being the focus of attention when she did not understand a word of what had been said.

What had he been thinking, bringing her here, when everyone in the village knew just how adverse to taking another wife he was? In view of this they would not know what to make of the fact that she was to live with him. Not once in two years had they seen him share more than a night of passion with anyone. They would not fail to read more than he was comfortable with in the arrangement but what was he to do? He could not prevent speculation by introducing her as his slave, or worse the woman he had just bought! It would be even worse.

Oh, well, it was too late now, but a solution would have to be found, and fast.

When a dozen curious faces turned toward her Merewen had to grab hold of the horse's mane to steady herself. Who were these men and why had they jumped on Wolf as soon as he had stepped down from his mount? What had they been told to make them look at her thus? It seemed the answer to these questions would have to wait, for Wolf was holding out his hand to her in unmistakable command. She was to dismount without further ado.

Not trusting herself not to tumble to the ground if she did so unaided, she allowed him to lift her down from Demon, which he did with disconcerting ease. Merewen gritted her teeth. That she should relish the heat of his hands around her waist was perhaps understandable. After all, it was devilishly cold outside and she wore no cloak, but the urge to nestle herself into his arms was less easily explained—or forgiven.

Hadn't she had enough of him after a day of riding in his arms? What was wrong with her? This man was not her lover, and would never be!

Without a word, she followed him to a small but clean and

well-appointed hut. A pang of guilt assaulted her when she remembered the pig sty in town. How had she thought he lived in such a hovel? No wonder he had seemed put out. She felt herself flush but, mercifully, Wolf was too busy unpacking the contents of a large bag to pay any attention to her.

"Wait here," he instructed tersely once he had finished. "I will be back soon."

A moment later he was gone.

Merewen looked around her, trying to get a better understanding of the man who had bought her. What she saw reassured her. This was no barbarian who paid no heed to cleanliness and material comfort. The hut appeared tidy and, as far as she could see, everything a person needed to cook, eat, sleep and dress was here. It even smelled good, thanks to the bunches of dried herbs suspended from the roof.

She shook her head. As clean and welcoming as the hut was, it was not her home, would never be. Then it hit her.

Did she still have a home?

Even if she managed to escape from the village, where would she go? No one was waiting for her. With her parents both gone and her brother dead, the prospect of returning to the house where she would only find memories of a happy time and no one to talk to was not a cheerful prospect to say the least.

One by one the people she had loved had been taken away from her, until there was no one left who wanted her.

Swallowing back a sob she sat on the stool and started to shell some nuts she had spotted in a bowl by the window. No doubt Wolf would come back to give her some task or other soon but she preferred to look occupied rather than as a slave awaiting her master's orders when he did.

"WHO WERE these people and what did they want?"

At first Merewen didn't understand why Wolf smiled when she asked the question but then she winced when she realized that she sounded as jealous and possessive as a wife—and that instead of annoying him, it amused him, precisely because she was *not* his wife and had no reason to worry about what he did.

"You wanted me all to yourself, didn't you?" he drawled, confirming her suspicions.

"Yes," she snapped, annoyed at her foolishness. "I simply could not have lasted another moment without you!"

The sarcasm fell on deaf ears and the smile widened further. "As I thought. Worry not, I am back now, and I won't be leaving until tomorrow."

Ignoring this infuriating response she carried on shelling nuts. To her surprise, Wolf sat down next to her to help. It was odd seeing a man with the physique of a warrior do such a mundane task, as odd as it would have been seeing a child wield an axe in battle. Of course the *way* he was doing it was more warrior-like than childish... He simply crushed two walnuts together in his fist.

Something in her shivered at the demonstration of strength.

"These people are Danes or Icelanders, like me, and they were asking for my help," he offered when she thought the discussion closed.

"All of them?" She was astounded. There had been a dozen men at the very least. They could not all have been asking for his help!

"All of them. I was absent for three days, you see, and I have become a sort of pillar of the community, someone to turn to in times of need."

"Well, if it isn't ironic. To me you're a tormentor and yet to these people you're a savior..."

"A tormentor? Is that really how you see me?" This was said

in a low voice, as if he hated the idea. Unexpectedly, it tugged at her heart to think she had hurt his feelings. Even worse was the realization that she had lied. She had simply spoken out of spite, for she did not see him as a tormentor anymore. At first, when she had seen him towering over her with a knife in his hand she had been afraid, undeniably, but since then he had bought her clothes, fed her, treated her decently and, of course, there had been the dream...

It was hard to be afraid of a man who had touched you so intimately, even if deep down you knew it was not real.

The pleasure had been real enough, though...

"What else could I think?" she mumbled, determined to hide her change of heart. Besides, it was better if he thought she resented him. It might help her to keep her unwelcome feelings at bay. "You bought me at a slave market and brought me home on your horse like a possession."

"I do not consider you a possession," he said slowly. "And I did not buy you to be my slave. I told you so already. You need to believe me."

She did. But that still did not explain his actions. "Why then? Why did you buy me?"

He shrugged as if he did not quite understand himself why he might have done such a thing. "If I hadn't you would have been sold off to one of the lecherous swines drooling after you. Isn't that reason enough? How did a woman like you end up being sold at a slave market anyway?" he asked, popping one of the shelled nuts into his mouth. "You do not look as if you belonged there."

"Does anyone look as if they belong to a place where they are sold as cattle?"

"A fair question, I will admit." He let out a small, appreciative laugh. "You're right. I don't think anyone belongs there. Now. Would you mind answering my question?"

"I do not know how I ended up with the slave trader," Merewen sighed. The same question had plagued her all day, and no wonder.

People did not find themselves put to sleep and tied up to a pole with a bag over their heads, ready to be sold to leering strangers by accident. It was simply not a hazard of life. She needed to understand how such a thing could have happened to her and, like it or not, Wolf was the only person who could help her. He might have some answers for her. Instead of aggravating him, she had better glean as much information as possible from him.

The last thing she remembered was attending her brother's funeral. Leofric had died aged only fifteen. A sickly youth, he had suffered from ill health all his life before a bloody flux had finally carried him off in a few days. Their mother had died in childbirth twelve years ago, along with her baby sister and their father, a wealthy landowner, had died two summers ago. Merewen was now alone, with no family left, no one who would care about her disappearance, come to her rescue or even offer her shelter if she managed to escape the man who—

She blinked when the rest of the thought refused to take form, as if her mind was physically preventing her from thinking ill of the man because it knew he didn't deserve it. Only the day before she would have been uncompromising, called him a tormentor and meant it. But everything seemed to have changed since then. Maybe she had truly started to believe that he was not just her captor... True to his promise, he had not hurt her. He was not even holding her captive. She was free to come in and out of the hut, leave if she wanted. He had not tied her up, or threatened to come after her.

Her stomach sank because, as reassuring as that thought was, it was not a comforting one. If even the man who had spent an extravagant sum of money for her did not care if she stayed with him or disappeared into thin air, then she truly did not matter to anyone.

"Anything you can tell me?" she asked, pushing the uncomfortable notion to the side.

"It seemed to me that you had been given a sleeping draught," Wolf said, indicating he was at least willing to help her. She realized he had moved only when he lifted her chin with his finger, forcing her to meet his gaze. Heavens, but he really had the most incredible eyes, clear but deep, intense, mysterious, intimidating all at once.

And the most entrancing smell. From where she was she could not miss it.

"What gave you that impression?" she croaked, suddenly unable to breathe properly. She had reached the same conclusion but she did not recall having shared her thoughts with him.

"There was this odd gleam in your eyes and your words were slurred," Wolf explained, not releasing his hold on the girl. She seemed utterly entranced by his proximity—as much as he was by hers. "You also don't seem to remember all that happened on that first day."

That first *night*, he should perhaps say. She had no recollection of telling him she wanted him before shoving her breast into his mouth in clear invitation or how she had opened her legs for him and begged him to bring her relief.

A growl started to build at the back of his throat at the memory. He clenched his teeth to stop it from erupting.

"You don't remember anything from the night at the pig sty, do you?" he forced himself to ask. He would certainly remember it as long as he lived.

It seemed to him that she flushed slightly but she shook her head. "No."

Wolf didn't know whether to be reassured or put out by the admission. Even if it was probably for the best she didn't remember, it had been the most entrancing moment of his life. It was galling to see that she did not even seem to know it had taken place!

Tilting her head up to him he looked deep into the abyss of her incredible eyes. They were of a color never seen in his native country and drew him in with their sheer magnetism. From such close proximity he saw that her irises were not just black, as he had first thought. A dark swirl of gray made the outer rim appear about to dissolve into smoke. The effect was captivating, like peering into wisps of fog for some elusive form to appear and seeing nothing.

Even more satisfying, she seemed to enjoy looking at him as much as he was enjoying looking at her.

They stared at each other in that manner for a long time.

After while the girl frowned at his forwardness but made no move to slap his hand away or even draw back. This was encouraging, for he knew she was not above spitting on men if she felt the need to. She would not hesitate in pushing him away if she felt threatened. Perhaps this odd compliance was due to the fact that she thought he was only trying to ascertain whether he could still detect the effect of the sleeping draught in her eyes. Well, it mattered not what she thought as long as she allowed him to touch her.

He wondered briefly if he should not take advantage of her unusual stillness to kiss her before deciding it was best not to. If he kissed her, he might not be able to stop at that and they were in the middle of a conversation that was clearly important to her. She would not thank him for distracting her, even if he had no doubt she would respond to his touch.

Besides, he did want to get to the bottom of what had happened. How could a woman like her have ended up at the hands of a slave trader? Her safety might well depend on the answer to that question and he was determined to protect her.

Buying her to prevent her from ending up in the hands of a lecher had only been the first step.

"It did feel like I had been given a sleeping potion," she agreed eventually. "Presumably so that I could be abducted more easily."

"Yes." He had no doubt she would have fought tooth and nail had she been able to, and her attacker had known it. This was perhaps a clue, pointing to someone who knew her fiery nature well enough to take precautions beforehand. "And mayhap your abductor would have wanted to make sure you did not recognize him."

Her eyes widened as if she had not thought of that before. He hated himself for showing her just how dire her situation was but Wolf was of the opinion that being forearmed was always preferable. The person who had sold her into slavery was no doubt someone she knew.

"What else can you tell me?" she asked, recovering with commendable swiftness. "Was I with others, were they all women? Which direction did we arrive from?"

He shook his head, regretting that he could not help her more. "I don't know. I have only been to that town once before, and it was purely by chance that I ended up seeing you. I am not wont to wander around slave markets, if you must know. I only went to the port to see a ship just come from Iceland."

A silence. Then she took another walnut and asked again.

"So you have no idea who the slave trader is or where he came from? I had never seen him before and he was not at my brother's funeral, of that I am certain."

This raised Wolf's hair on end. "Funeral?"

There was a pause during which she cracked a nut open. Wolf could tell she was buying time. He waited patiently. This would be a difficult discussion.

"The last thing I remember before waking up on that platform is attending my brother Leofric's funeral," she admitted eventually, looking as if she would have preferred not to tell him anything about her life. "He... He had died in my arms the day before."

Wolf saw her bite her bottom lip as if to try and keep tears at bay. Suddenly there was a bitter taste in his mouth. He had not realized just how traumatic the whole thing would have been for her. Not only had she been sold into slavery but the last thing she had done before that was deal with a terrible loss... No wonder she had been confused and angry when he had taken her.

"Were you and your brother close?" he asked quietly, bracing himself for a rebuke. No doubt he would be told that it was not his place to ask such a personal question.

"Yes," the girl answered unexpectedly. "Leofric was six years younger than me and I had been the one looking after him after our father's death. He had always suffered from ill health but lately I had started to hope he was getting better, to think that perhaps he would live to see his twentieth summer. I was wrong, of course, for he..."

Her voice broke, betraying a depth of emotion she had hitherto managed to keep under a tight leash. This first glimpse of vulnerability took Wolf by surprise. He had come to think of her as a strong, defiant woman who faced her enemies and her problems head on. This unexpected side of her made her even more irresistible, for now all he wanted to do was wrap her in his arms and offer her the comfort she clearly needed. But he knew she would only push him away if he tried anything, not because she didn't need it, but because she would be mortified to know he had seen her helplessness.

The girl had just as much pride as he had and he ought to respect her feelings.

He bunched his fists and kept very still, waiting for the rest of her explanation.

"Anyway," she carried on once she had herself under control. "During the meal that night I started to feel odd. I assumed it was the grief and the lack of sleep getting to me but now I understand that the potion was starting to take effect. Someone would have poured it in my drink, I imagine, so that they could hand me over to the slave trader with no questions asked. After that I do not remember a thing until I woke up tied up to the pole where you found me."

There was the usual note of accusation in her voice but Wolf merely smiled. She had said 'found', not 'bought' this time. It was a progress of sorts. When she looked at him her eyes held no rancor, only questions.

Yes, they were definitely making progress. She did not see him as her captor anymore. It was a first step. In time, she would come to see that she was lucky to have ended up with him rather than one of the scoundrels leering after her naked body.

"Being sold into slavery is an extreme situation for someone to find themselves in," he told her, refusing to dwell on the image that was already branded in his mind. "The men present at the sale were all Danes returning home on a merchant ship that same afternoon. If I hadn't bought you, you would, in all likelihood, have ended up leaving the country with your new owner, as a slave with no name or past. In other words, you would have disappeared off the face of the earth, no one would have been able to trace your whereabouts. Do you have any enemies that would wish you out of the way?"

"None than I can think of. I told you, I am all alone, no one cares what happens to me."

Merewen fought back a sob at the depressing situation. But Wolf was right. She must have an enemy she didn't know about. It was the only explanation for what had happened to her. How had she not thought of that before? This had not been an accident but done to her on purpose, and premeditated. The sleeping potion proved it.

As a young girl she had thought herself well-loved and happy. Now all the members of her family were dead and she was finding out that someone wanted her dead, or at least hated her enough to hand her over to a man who would sell her into slavery, who wished for her never to be seen again. How was she supposed to accept the frightening notion, or feel safe again?

For the first time, the full horror of what her fate could have been hit her. No matter how much she had ranted against him at first, Wolf had not hurt her, raped her, taken her away on a ship to a foreign land or even asked her to do anything in the hut. Instead he was talking to her as he would to a guest, he had clothed and fed her, offered his protection and was now trying to understand who could want to harm her.

It was more than she had a right to expect and she had no idea how to react. What did he expect from her if not to be his slave?

She took another nut from the bowl. The pile of shells by her elbow was getting impressively big. When she reached out to the nutcracker her hand brushed against Wolf's. Warm. Hard. So much bigger than her own. His fingers were long and elegant, his nails neatly trimmed. These strong, beautiful hands had been at her core only the night before, coaxing indescribable pleasure out of her. No, she reminded herself, they hadn't, not really, only in her dream!

Still, her body responded as if it had all been real. Under the table she squeezed her thighs together and clenched her teeth at the same time to prevent a moan from escaping her lips. Heavens, was she going to think of the eruption of pleasure in her body every time they touched, every time her eyes landed on his hands? It would be torture!

"What is your name?" Wolf asked, holding her gaze.

Mercifully he didn't seem aware of the lewd direction her thoughts had taken. Still, confusion made her bristle. "Why do you want to know?"

A faint smile curled Wolf's lips. How had he ever imagined that the stubborn woman would answer him without first making him feel the sting of her venom? And why did he like it so much?

"Do I need a reason other than common politeness to want to know your name?"

She glared at him, as he knew she would. His smile widened. Teasing her was quickly becoming his favorite pastime, and smiling felt good. Perhaps living with someone was not so bad—as long as feelings and responsibility did not get in the way, of course. But although he did not want to get married again, being with the girl had brought home how alone he had been for the last two years. He had missed the comfort of having someone to talk to.

It seemed that with the Saxon he would get the advantages of a life companion without having to deal with the inconvenience. He would also get the excitement that had been cruelly lacking in his marriage.

All in all he could not regret the money he had spent on her. It seemed he'd purchased much more than a slave. He'd found what had been missing in his life.

"Let us say I have no desire to call you 'woman' when I address you," Wolf told her, crossing his arms over his chest.

"You need not call me anything. I will be gone before the end of the week."

The smile was instantly wiped off his face. Imagining her on her own in the wild made his insides contract in anguish. No, she was not going anywhere until they knew who was after her and why. He would not fail another woman and endure being told she had died because of him. The burden he was carrying was already too heavy for one man.

This little captive would not come to any harm, not while she was under his roof.

"You're not going anywhere if I have anything to say about it," he growled.

CHAPTER FOUR

"Time for bed," Wolf announced as soon as they had finished a frugal meal of bread, nuts and cheese.

Merewen looked to the corner by the window where a massive pallet was covered with furs. It looked soft and inviting, a haven in which to burrow and escape the cold. It was also the only sleeping place in the hut, a consideration that could not fail to send her heartbeat into a fierce drum—of anguish, she assured herself, *not* anticipation.

"This is your bed," she stated, facing Wolf once more.

"It is."

"Where am I to sleep?"

"In it."

She immediately recoiled. "No!"

His lips twisted, as if he'd guessed she was not protesting at the idea of sleeping close to him, but rather did not want to risk throwing herself at him while she did. "Let me be clearer. You will sleep in it, but alone. I'll sleep somewhere else."

Her eyes widened. "Somewhere else?" Though she hated to admit it, the idea that he was about to leave her made her heartbeat increase another notch. Of course she told herself that it was only because she could rely on him to ward off any potential attackers, not because she wanted... well... to take advantage of being tucked in bed next to a man in possession of such an impressive physique.

"No one will enter the hut while I'm gone, I swear," Wolf assured her, cutting through her musings. Evidently he had seen her worry. She nodded, knowing that if his decision had already been made there was nothing she could do, save beg him to stay, something she absolutely refused to do. A woman, even one who had been bought, had her dignity.

"Very well."

Merewen refused to ask him where or, more pointedly, with whom he would spend the night. She would not act the jealous harpy and give him any more reasons to tease her than she already had. After all, she didn't know anything about him. He might well have a sweetheart in the village, or even just an accommodating widow who kept a place warm in her bed for him for whenever he wanted to indulge his masculine urges. Why would he stay to protect her when a night of passion was waiting for him?

Her thoughts must have shown on her face for he smiled crookedly.

"I will not sleep with a woman tonight," he told her, eyeing her up and down, the heat in his gaze causing her blood to race in her veins.

"Won't you?" she asked in her best unconcerned voice.

"No."

Wolf took a step toward the girl, then another, wanting to gauge her reaction.

When she did not recoil, he knew he was making the right decision in leaving the hut. He could not sleep in the same room as her tonight, least of all in the same pallet, not when she was fully conscious and unsettled by his proximity. This time if she started to touch herself in her sleep he would not be able to stop himself from taking her and giving them *both* pleasure. He was already hard and ready, dangerously close to surrender. After a morning in the saddle with her curves pressed against him and then a whole afternoon watching her as she moved about with the grace of a doe he would not have the strength to resist if he felt any part of her luscious body brush against his.

He would rip her already damaged shift and plunge inside her delicious flesh before she had time to say anything.

But doing such a thing was out of the question. She was a virgin, she knew nothing of men's base urges, so he would only frighten her with the urgency of his need. Besides, he had promised not to hurt her and it was important to him she believed him. She had barely come to trust his word. He could not undo all his hard work now. Not that he would hurt her of course, but he knew he would not manage to be gentle either.

If he ever bedded this girl, he would do so with all the impetuosity he had kept in check with Solveig. The two women's contrasting personalities made it inevitable that he would unleash the wildest part of him. When he mounted Demon, he did not behave in the same way as he did when he rode a plodding rouncey. He did not take the same precautions because he knew the stallion was as spirited a mount as he was a fierce rider and could handle it. The two of them were a match made for relentless, satisfying rides. And he sensed that bedding this girl would be just as exhilarating and leave him breathless.

But it would not happen tonight. Tonight he would have to be reasonable.

"Sleep soundly," he growled. "I will be back at dawn."

"I SLEPT WITH MY FRIEND SIGURD."

Merewen did her best to hide her relief at seeing Wolf walk into the hut shortly after dawn the next morning. Despite his promise that no one would bother her, she had spent an agitated night, expecting the door to open at any moment on a lust-crazed villager or a drunken maniac foolish enough to brave Wolf's ire for a moment in her arms. Not that she thought herself irresistible, but you never knew.

"I see," she answered breezily. "Now I understand why you admitted of your own accord you would not sleep with a woman. The promise will have cost you little if you prefer the company of men."

Wolf's perfect lips twisted in a now familiar smile. How quickly one could become accustomed to someone's little quirks, she reflected. They had known each other for less than two days.

"I slept in Sigurd's hut if you prefer, on the floor. *Alone,*" he added, his eyes lighting up in amusement.

"I prefer nothing," she answered dampeningly, even though the idea of such a man being lost to womankind had provoked in her a pang of regret she preferred not to dwell upon.

"And I assure you that I prefer women to men," he insisted, making her blush further. "I like everything about them, their softness, their smell, their—"

"Very well," she blurted out. "You prefer women. I believe you."

Thinking it best to drop the matter before he became too specific, she set out to making some bread to break their fast. Perhaps the kneading would alleviate some of her frustration. If she punched the dough with enough force she might actually manage to ignore the maddening man in front of her.

With more anger than efficiency, she placed flour into a bowl and threw herself into the task. She was not here to discuss Wolf's preferences in bed.

The sight of the woman making bread on his table made Wolf's insides constrict in an emotion he was not at pains to identify, having experienced it time and time again in the last few months.

Longing.

Tossing and turning on Sigurd's floor all night, he had tried to convince himself that he had exaggerated the comfort her presence in his hut brought him, that it was just the inevitable reaction of someone feeling too lonely for his own good, that it was not her who appealed to him but rather the fact that he was not on his own with his grim thoughts anymore. As for the unfortunate lust she stirred in him, he had hoped it would have disappeared after an uncomfortable night spent on hard ground.

It had not, and he could not fool himself any longer.

The fiery Saxon appealed to him because of who she was, not just because she happened to be here. No one else would have made him smile by suggesting he'd spent the night in Sigurd's arms. No other woman would have made him hard just by blushing like a maid when he knew her to harbor wild feminine urges.

He watched her make bread for him with a hunger that had nothing to do with the rumbling in his stomach. The scene was oddly domestic and put dangerous ideas into his head. Wolf knew he could not afford to marry again after what had happened to him but that did not mean he did not wish things could be different. He knew he did not deserve a family but that didn't mean deep down he did not crave one.

A blinded warrior might know he would not be able to see again but that did not mean he did not miss watching the sun rise on a bright summer's day. The heart did not always heed what reason told it. Wolf wanted the very thing he could not afford to have and having the girl in his home only made more glaring all the things he would never get.

Her gestures were assured and efficient, and the way her small fingers sank into the dough and massaged it created all sorts of lewd images in his mind. When his manhood jerked he did not even blink. It seemed he would have to resign himself to the fact that he could not be in her presence without sooner or later becoming as lust-filled as an untried youth.

What was certain was that he would not be bored as long as she was under his roof. How long that would be he didn't know. She had told him only the night before she did not intend to stay for long.

Well, we'll see about that.

"You still haven't told me your name... *woman.*" Wolf smiled when she winced. "I see that you do not like me calling you 'woman' any more than I do," he carried on when she remained silent. "Perhaps it will convince you to give in and tell me how I should call you instead. You can even choose a name if you like. It doesn't have to be your real one. I don't mind. After all, no one here uses mine. Pick an animal."

"Why does it have to be an animal?"

He let out a bark of a laugh. He had not meant to insult her but the affronted look on her face was priceless. "You're right. You should go for something a lot more feminine and delicate. A flower perhaps."

Merewen had never been the kind of person to persevere when the situation was lost and she was always able to recognize when she was beaten. As she would never win against this man, she decided she might as well give in graciously.

"My name is Merewen." Suddenly she wanted him to know it, wanted to be a real person to him, not just a woman he had bought like an object, someone without even a name. Now that she believed he did not mean to keep her as a slave, he ought to be able to call her something other than 'woman'. Her real name was the best option. She didn't want to hide under a flower or anything else.

"Merewen. It's beautiful," he surprised her by saying. Receiving a compliment when she had been ready for a cutting remark for how easily she had given in rendered her speechless.

As if he thought he had better take advantage of her unusual passivity, Wolf placed his two hands flat on the table opposite her and leaned in, stopping only when their foreheads were almost touching. In that moment she had the absurd notion that he was about to kiss her.

Her heart started to beat wildly.

How many times had she dreamed of such a moment? Of seeing desire in a man's eyes when he looked at her and knowing he felt the same longing for her as she did for him? Why it had to happen now with a man who had bought her and not with a man who loved and respected her was beyond her.

Although, perhaps it was not so odd, seeing as she had yet to meet a man who loved and respected her.

After her mother's death Merewen had been the one looking after Leofric, and the task had left little time for herself or dalliances. At the age where a young woman should have known her first flirtations, she had been confined to a role resembling more that of a mother or a nurse and all but cooped indoors. She hadn't minded it but, undeniably, it had taken a toll on her personal life. The few men who had taken an interest in her had quickly grown tired of seeing her run to her brother's sickbed dozens of times a day.

As a consequence, not only had she never been considered as a potential conquest, but she had never even been kissed. Either her suitors had not been brazen enough to take the liberty or they had been interrupted before they could act on the impulse.

There had been no other choice but to take refuge in her

imagination, and invent what real life did not provide her. In her increasingly more vivid dreams, men looked at her as if they wanted nothing more than to devour her, they kissed her with all the force of their pent up passion, and they made love with equal fire.

She had always thought that nothing could ever come close to these wild imaginings.

Until she had met Wolf...

Right now he was looking at her with that look of hunger she had imagined a thousand times and she suddenly wondered if she had not bitten off more than she could chew by wishing to be ravished by an untamed man. Being stared at by a real wolf about to pounce would not feel more disturbing.

Should he kiss Merewen, Wolf wondered for the second time in as many days? It was a very bad idea, just as it had been yesterday. They seemed to have reached an agreement of sorts. He did not want to compromise it by acting too rashly too soon. If he kissed her now, it would be a fiery, uncompromising kiss that would scare her. As she was untouched, it was reasonable to imagine that she had never been kissed either, or if she had, he doubted it was by a man half-crazed with need, who already knew the taste of her nipple and the heat of her core.

If he kissed her there would be no stopping him from devouring the rest of her and she was not ready for such shocking intimacy. He had already taken what he had no right to take once, and felt guilty enough about it. He could not do so again.

She was a virgin. Making love would have more serious consequence to her than to a widow used to having lovers. Worse, she might start expecting things from him he would never be able—or willing—to give her.

What a fool he really was! He had refused to bring any of his conquests in the hut even for one night for fear of giving them false hope and now he had brought in a woman who had nowhere else to go, whom he could not send away.

Was he determined to make things harder for himself than they already were?

Gritting his teeth, he took a step back, then another. Why had he come so close to her? What did he hope to gain by playing with fire so? Did he really think she would throw herself into his arms? He needed to focus on something other than her luscious lips and liquid heat if he was to regain some mastery over his body.

Sewing. Yes. That ought to do it.

"I almost forgot," he told her, reaching to the bag hanging from his belt. "Sigurd lent me this this morning."

Merewen was thrown off by the sudden change in Wolf's demeanour. In the blink of an eye he had gone from burning hot to coolly detached. Evidently kissing had been the last thing on his mind. She had been the only one affected by their unseemly proximity.

Swallowing her disappointment, she took the leather pouch he was handing her. In it she found two needles and some thread. Before she could ask why his friend had lent him such a feminine item, he took out a tunic from the chest by the door.

"You expect me to mend your clothes?" she cried out, as understanding dawned.

What a return to reality! He hadn't meant to kiss her at all, only thought to flatter her by telling her her name was beautiful, to mollify her so he could start making demands! *That* certainly never happened in her dreams! Men did not hand her tools when she had been expecting passionate embraces!

Wolf arched an eyebrow. "I have no intention of asking you to mend my clothes but even if I did, I do not see how it would be such a slight to presume that you would do a better job than me, who can barely hold delicate needles."

He looked genuinely puzzled by her reaction, as if he had meant no offence and in truth she knew that her reaction had been motivated more by the humiliation she'd just suffered than any wrong doing on his part. One moment he had looked as if he wanted nothing more than to ravish her on the spot and now they were discussing the mending of his clothes... No wonder she had been disconcerted.

"So what is the shirt for, if not for mending?" she asked more calmly.

"It is for you to put on while you sew the front of your shift," he explained. "I thought you would feel more comfortable if you weren't naked while you did it. There is no other choice but to mend it for I could not find a shift your size that did not reek of tallow or onions and besides, yours is too fine to be wasted."

Merewen was so stunned by his answer that when he threw her the undershirt she didn't catch it in time. He had hunted around for clothes to replace her damaged ones and he was now offering her the means of repairing her shift, the only item of her old life left to her. Tears burned her eyes and she feared for a moment that she would start crying.

It suddenly seemed the most thoughtful thing anyone had ever done for her.

"Thank you," she said slowly, picking the shirt from the floor. "While I am at it, do you have anything that requires sewing?"

Something like satisfaction gleamed in the blue eyes. "Actually I think there's a rip in the sleeve of the tunic you're holding. Perhaps you could see to it. Do you know, I could get used to having someone cook and mend my clothes for me during the day."

And warm my bed at night.

Though he did not actually say the words, devastating

desire had replaced amusement in his eyes. Heat instantly flooded her body.

Oh! Was there ever a more insufferable man! Why could he not just answer her and be done with it! Why did he have to reduce her insides to a puddle with a well-aimed glance?

"Forget it!" she snapped, throwing him the tunic. "I will wear my dress while I sew the shift. It will do just as well."

If he was going to be such a rogue, then he could mend his own clothes with his own massive, clumsy hands.

CHAPTER FIVE

For almost a sennight, they lived together side by side and, as Sigurd was the only person Wolf had told how they had really met, the villagers assumed Merewen was a woman from town with whom he'd been having an affair and that he'd finally decided to make things official between them. He could understand why they might think such a thing and, indeed, living with her felt just like living with a wife. With the notable exceptions that they did not share a bed or kiss or even touch of course.

It was constant torture, every bit as bad as he had feared, and tested his control to the limit.

Nevertheless, he had stopped going to Sigurd's at night, having found it impossible to close an eye while Merewen was alone in the hut. Her safety was more important than his peace of mind. So he'd gone back to the hut, sleeping on a makeshift pallet by the door, as far away from her as possible. To his relief, she had not raised any objection to having him so close to her at night. She had even seemed relieved to see him keep guard.

This mark of trust was the best gift anyone had ever given him. He'd been so shaken in his belief in his ability to protect a woman efficiently that he was grateful to Merewen for making him feel reliable.

Just as he was finishing shaving she walked back inside, her hands full of herbs and vegetables. With a nod in his direction she threw everything in the pot boiling over the fire pit and just like that, the idea that had been whirring in his mind for days took hold of him with unprecedented force.

I could marry this woman. I like her and she already lives with me. In fact, I should marry her. It is the only honorable thing to do, considering what everyone thinks.

His resolution not to marry again had been made before he had been forced to live as husband and wife with someone who could legitimately resent the situation. Now that he was openly living with Merewen, he should ensure she felt comfortable with the arrangement.

And as much as he had thought never to take a wife again, there were a number of reasons for which marrying *her* would be a good idea.

Not only was she alone with nowhere or no one to go back to, but an enemy wanted her disposed of. She needed protection and a place to live. If she were his wife, he could look after her properly, he could give her a home, a home where she would be protected and valued.

Because he would value her. He already did.

His decision to keep her was not just one based on lust, even if it undeniably played a part. If he had simply wanted her body, he would have seduced her. There would be no need to marry her afterward. But Wolf wanted more than her body. He wanted everything she had to offer. Marriage to a woman who piqued his interest would allow him to put his past behind and start anew in this place he had never really chosen.

His hopes of returning to his own country had never looked more distant. That was what he had learnt in town the other day. He'd heard about a ship coming in from Iceland and he had gone to meet the merchants in the hope of hearing news of his home town from someone on board. What he had been told had not been encouraging. His name hadn't been cleared and his home had been taken over. It seemed he would have to remain here in for a while longer, if not for the rest of his life. In these circumstances, uniting himself to a Saxon made sense. She would help him fit in, explain customs that were still strange to him... and warm his bed at night.

Undeniably, this was an aspect of marriage to Merewen he was keen to explore.

Last but by no means least in the list of reasons why he should remarry was that with a woman legally bound to him, he would be able to enjoy lovemaking to the full, as the children from their joining would be legitimate. With the few conquests he had seduced in East Anglia he had always stayed in control, not wanting to father children he would not be allowed to raise.

Married to Merewen, he would be able to lose himself in pleasure. In fact, there would be no choice. He suspected a lover like her would make it impossible for him to exercise restraint.

A responsive, sensual woman perhaps did not fit every man's description of a suitable wife, but it fit his. Wolf was not afraid that her passionate nature might lead her to other men's beds as he was confident in his ability to satisfy her needs.

As to her fiery personality, far from daunting him, it actually reassured him. A wife who did not cower in front of him would not render him mad with frustration and therefore expose herself to his ire like Solveig had. Wolf had learnt long ago not to allow rage to overpower him. But he had found to his cost that he did not handle frustration well. A spirited stallion could prove a challenge but you did not despair of him in the way you did of an unresponsive nag, you did not shout at it in exasperation. Every man had his snapping point and there was nothing more unbearable to Wolf than passivity and lack of spirit. With a woman who had spat into the slave trader's face while tied up to a post, then forced her buyer to procure a dress that didn't smell of sweat when she was half-naked and freezing, he was in no danger of tearing his hair out at her lack of responsiveness.

He could deal with any challenge his wife presented him as long as she was not submissive and he already knew there wasn't a submissive bone in Merewen's gorgeous body.

And if he married her, she would have no reason to leave. They had never discussed the future but he could well imagine it would not be long before she questioned the reason for her presence under his roof.

As he would never keep her as a prisoner or worse, a slave, and since an innocent, proud virgin would never accept being anyone's lover, she had no reason to stay. But Wolf wanted her under his roof—and in his bed.

Marrying her was the only way to make this happen.

There was no denying that the circumstances of their meeting would not make things easy for him to convince her to accept his offer but it was no use bemoaning the fact now. Like it or not, she was here and he could not consider letting her go.

And so his decision was made.

He had bought her, which meant that she belonged to him. He might as well marry her and belong to her as well.

"You asked why I bought you that day," he started, smoothing a hand ovee his freshly-shaven jaw.

"Yes?" Merewen dropped the knife she had picked up to give him the attention such a declaration deserved.

"Well. I bought you to be my wife," he announced slowly, deciding it was better not to tell her the decision had been reached *after* he had paid an extravagant sum of money for her, and for reasons that were best kept to himself. She had found the fact that he had bought her hard to accept. If she thought his intentions toward her had been honorable from the first, she might well be relieved.

As soon as the words had left his mouth, however, he understood that it wouldn't be that easy. She'd blanched.

"But I... I cannot be your *wife*!"

Merewen stared at Wolf in disbelief. He wanted to marry her? Had she heard that right? It seemed she had because he frowned, as if he had expected her to comply without question.

"Why not?"

She blinked. Was he being deliberately provocative?

Because I don't know you, because you bought me, and you haven't even asked *me to marry you, you* told *me I was to marry you after a week during which I kept wondering what would become of me! Because my life has just been turned upside down and I don't know what to do. Because I don't understand why you set my blood on fire every time we look at each other and it frightens me.*

The list of reasons was endless but somehow she felt he would dismiss them all with a flick of his wrist. There was only one thing he would not be able to ignore, whether he wanted to or not.

"Because I'm already married," she improvised.

This was a reasonable claim to make. After all, why shouldn't she be married? She was certainly old enough to have a husband. Wolf didn't know anything about her and there was no way he could guess she was unmarried and untouched.

"Oh. You're married," he said, crossing his arms over his massive chest. "Really?"

"Really. Does it seem so impossible to believe?" she answered, piqued that he should doubt her word. Was she that unattractive? His answer proved the question had shown clearly in her eyes.

"Don't get me wrong, you are certainly appealing enough to have caught a man's attention, despite your challenging ways." She could have sworn he was amused, and not at all ruffled. "But it is awfully convenient that you should only mention it now, don't you think? You have been at the village for a week and yet you never said anything about having to return home. You never said anything about a husband having a claim on you when I took you away either. It seems to me that the first thing you would have done was threaten me with retaliation if I did not let you go."

Merewen mentally kicked herself. He was right, that was what any married woman would have done. How had she not thought of that? Still, she could not back down so easily.

"I...I wasn't thinking clearly when you took me away from the trader," she told him, willing herself not to blush. "I was still under the influence of the potion, if you recall, and in a state of shock."

"Ah. Yes, of course. The shock. It will no doubt account for this extraordinary lapse in judgment." He nodded slowly. "Of course, that was a week ago. I'd say you've had time to recover since then, and remember that a man was waiting for you at home."

This time she stayed silent for there was nothing she could answer.

So the vexing little Saxon wanted him to believe she was married? Wolf allowed a smile to bloom on his lips. Would he have believed her claim if he had not felt the proof of her innocence that night at the pig sty? Probably not. It just seemed improbable that she had not alluded to it before. Nevertheless, he needed to make sure, for indeed he could only marry her if she did not have a husband already. The fact that she was still untouched proved little. She might have been abducted straight after the wedding ceremony by the groom's family, people who did not approve of the union and had tried to dispose of her by selling her into slavery.

It was a stretch, but not impossible, and would even explain why a refined woman like her had ended up at the hands of a slave trader and why she wouldn't want to return to a man whose family frightened her. After all, he'd already decided she had been abducted by someone who knew her and wanted her gone.

"So tell me, how long have you been married?" he asked, leaning casually against the wall. As he'd predicted, she flushed, betraying her discomfort.

"Two years," she said with a commendable effort at breeziness.

Two years... Wolf smiled inwardly. Now he had her. She had just ruled out the only explanation for her virginal state. No man would resist a wife as delectable as she was for so long, even if he had not desired their union.

"And what's wrong with your husband?"

"W-what do you mean, wrong?" she stammered.

"Is he an old man? Or perhaps he was injured in battle, rendering him incapable of fulfilling his marital duties?" He rubbed his chin in mock consideration. "I am trying to understand the reason for his impotence, you see."

"Impotence?"

Well, the little vixen had lost her infamous tongue, it seemed. All she could do was repeat what he said.

"Yes," he leaned in confidentially. "Because, married as you are, you are a maid untouched. And I don't know many men who would live for two years next to a wife as alluring as you without making love to her time and time again."

"I—"

"I think this husband of yours doesn't exist," Wolf cut in before she could mumble an explanation. "I think you made him up as an excuse to refuse my offer. And it's not going to work."

"I am married!" Merewen retorted instantly, desperately wishing it was the case, that she was not alone in the world, that someone, somewhere, was worried about her. Never had she felt more dejected. She'd had to resort to dreaming her lovers to alleviate solitude, and now she had to make up a husband to protect herself. How pathetic.

"Very well. Let's have it your way. What's your husband's name?"

"Æthelred."

She did her best to sound assured but her mind had gone to mush the moment Wolf had called her alluring while looking at her with his amazing eyes. How was a woman supposed to think in front of such a man?

"And how did you two meet?"

"He... was a friend of my brother's." It seemed a reasonable enough explanation.

It was not, as Wolf's next comment made clear.

"Right. The same brother who was several years younger than you?" His lips quivered. "You are telling me that you married a boy barely out of his mother's skirts?"

"He is a bit older than Leofric," she mumbled.

"Still, you apparently married him two years ago, when he will have been no older than fourteen summers." Wolf laughed. "Well, that could certainly explain why you didn't have a proper wedding night. Perhaps the boy was so inept then he didn't know where everything was supposed to go! But we both know that an excitable sixteen-year old would not be able to keep his hands to himself when in bed with a woman. And so we are back to my original question. What's wrong with him that he could not work out what to do with you?"

Merewen bit her lip. Why did he have to remember how old

Leofric had been? And why had she forgotten that she had mentioned it to him? He was unsettling her, that was why! Another few questions and she would crumple, admit she was not married—and his for the taking.

While she was hesitating, Wolf uncrossed his arms and came closer. "Tell me one last thing so I may know that you are not just making it all up. What do you like your husband to do to you in bed?"

Merewen's mouth fell open. Had he really just asked her such an intimate question? One look at his smirk confirmed that, yes, he had, and he would not leave off until he'd had an answer.

"You... How could I even answer that question?" she gasped.

He smiled as if she had said precisely what he had expected her to say. "You could not, that's my point. Because you have never known any man."

His words hit her square in the chest. How on earth did he know she was untouched? He sounded so sure of himself! Was he a mind reader?

"How could you possibly know that?" She flushed when she realized she had just admitted that he was right. Now not only would he know she was not married, he would know she had not managed to attract any man despite being well past twenty summers.

Oh, this had to be the single most embarrassing moment of her life!

Wolf stared down at Merewen. Her eyes had gone wide with a mixture of worry, embarrassment, and guilt.

The same guilt invaded him. How could he admit that he had taken advantage of her dream to touch her naked body? True, she had asked him to, and he had not hurt her. He had only given her pleasure but still it was clear that she had no recollection of what had happened that night, no knowledge that for the sweetest, most delectable moment, one of his fingers had been inside her.

It was better that way. She already thought him unbearably high-handed, there was no telling what her reaction would be if she knew what he had done. She might well flee in horror.

But if he didn't admit to it, how would he explain the knowledge that she was a virgin?

He could not.

"You flush whenever a man comes near you. You cannot be used to lovemaking if a simple caress is new to you," he said, coming closer. Once he was within touching distance, he brushed the tip of his fingers over her velvety cheek and saw her inhale sharply. That simple sound set him hard as a rock. "Look at you. You are untouched."

"I..."

She lowered her gaze but not before he saw something flash in her dark eyes, replacing the shame and embarrassment. Desire.

She wanted him, too.

His groin tightened further.

"You don't have to remain an innocent," he growled, wondering how long he would resist before he snapped. "As your husband, I could show you what happens when a man and a woman come together."

Merewen could not move. Yes, she was flustered. Yes, she was untouched. But she was not innocent, far from it. Mercifully, though, Wolf could never have guessed what dark desires she entertained, what shameful caresses she had given herself under the cover of darkness, what vivid dreams plagued her at night, what blinding pleasure she had experienced only the other night, when she had imagined him poised over her, suckling her breast. It was her secret; no one could ever know, for fear they would condemn her as a shameful wanton.

Women were not supposed to feel such things, to crave a man's touch.

And she was not supposed to melt under this particular man's caresses, especially when he was only mocking her!

But, oh, how she wanted him to show her what happened when a man and a woman came together, or rather when *he* made love to *her*! It would be explosive, too intense for words, she was sure of it, even if she based this belief on what had only been a dream. But what a dream! Her body started to heat up at the memory. Without a doubt Wolf would be as skilled in the art of lovemaking in real life as he had been in her imaginings—and she would respond just as wildly.

If he could make her blood pound hard in her veins with a simple brush to the cheek, what could he do if he decided to explore other parts of her body with intent?

"Do not touch me," she said, taking a step backward. If they touched, she wasn't sure how long she would resist. She might well wrap her arms and legs around him and beg him to take her. "You have no right!"

"I know, we are not married. And your pup of a husband, whose voice has likely not broken yet, will kill me if I touch you," he drawled, not in the least impressed.

"No, *I* will."

With those words, she stormed out of the hut.

Wolf bit back an incredulous laugh. Had she just threatened him? Really his little Saxon was irresistible. She was also impossibly contrary and defiant. Did he really want such a wife? Life with her would be...

Thrilling.

He had smiled more in a week with her than he had in two years. He wanted more of her. More of her sharp tongue, more of the silky softness between her thighs, more of her passionate nature, more of the complicity that had started to grow between them. He wanted to taste her lips, feel her warmth wrap around him, hear her moans of pleasure when he plunged inside her. He wanted to laugh with her, argue with her, be silent with her.

He had bought her moved by a selfless urge, even though he had not wanted a slave, for her benefit.

Now he wanted her to be truly his.

Due to unforeseen circumstances, he had become Merewen's protector. He had already saved her once, and he was now looking after her. Marrying her would not change what he was in effect already doing; it was not going to cost him more effort. The only difference was that he wouldn't have to fight his desire for her anymore.

Yes, impossible as she was, he wanted this woman to be his wife. He had already concluded that if he married again it would have to be to a woman of spirit, one who would not elicit his boredom, one who would be able to face the dangers she might face with courage and determination, one who would not lie passively in his bed and be afraid of her womanly desires.

In short, the opposite of Solveig.

And no one fitted that description better than the quick-tempered, sensual minx he had saved from a miserable fate. Even physically, with her dark eyes and fiery hair, she was nothing like the fair, sweet Solveig. Of course, he did not love her, like he had once loved his wife, but it was not a problem, quite the opposite. It would be easier to keep a cool head that way. He was not even sure it was possible for him to love again anyway. As a youth, he had fallen in love with Solveig, only to be disillusioned when her true nature had been revealed. It had been a sobering experience, one that had shattered any illusions he might have once entertained about love.

There was no danger of such a thing happening to him with Merewen. She wore her heart on her sleeve, and hid nothing of her thoughts, which guaranteed he would not wake up one morning and wonder how he had not seen the truth of her.

So it was decided. He would marry this woman who had seemingly been placed on his path by the gods.

All he needed to do now was to convince her to accept him.

CHAPTER SIX

A swirl of icy air and a burst of light heralded Wolf's return into the hut as dusk started to fall over the land, making Merewen both shiver and lift her head at the welcome respite from the gloom. It was such an apt metaphor for the ambivalent feelings he provoked in her that she could not help a sigh. Why could things not be simple where this man was concerned? All day long she had agonized about his unexpected offer of marriage.

Could she marry Wolf?

On the one hand, she saw no reason not to. On the other, it seemed like folly.

Women did not marry men they had only known for a week, men who had bought them, rather than chosen them, men they lusted after. Well... that might actually happen more often than one suspected, only no one talked about it. No, they didn't, because the purpose of marriage was not to indulge one's senses, Merewen reminded herself sternly! She had better not lose sight of that fact, even if the stranger who wanted to marry her did look like a Norse deity. There were more important things to consider than his looks in this affair.

Determined not to appear as if she had been waiting for him all day, she turned around and returned to her meal.

"Don't worry about me," Wolf said with a smile, coming to face her.

Merewen shrugged and dipped another piece of bread into her broth. Perhaps she should have waited for him to start eating but, considering she was not his slave, much less his wife, she had no reason to pander to him.

"I was hungry and had no idea when you would return. I didn't see why I should wait. And why are you laughing now?" she asked, eyes narrowing. He had thrown his head back and was indulging in a hearty bout of laughter. He laughed like a man who had not laughed in a long time and was discovering anew the pleasure it brought him. And, annoying as it was, she could not tear her eyes from the column of his neck, pulsing with strength and vitality.

Heavens, she really was in trouble if even the sight of his neck had the power of sending her heart into a flutter... Perhaps she should leave before her senses overpowered her mind and caused her to make a decision she would regret.

"I'm laughing because I feel as ridiculous as a farmer who, after years complaining he doesn't get enough water for his crops, has to watch his fields being submerged under a deluge of rain," he answered enigmatically.

"What is that supposed to mean?"

"Nothing. Are you comfortable? Warm enough?" he enquired, sitting opposite her.

"Actually, no," she answered, while he ripped a chunk of bread out of the freshly baked loaf. "I couldn't find enough wood to get a decent fire going. You might want to start cutting the logs at the side of the hut into chunks manageable for a normal-sized person. The ones I found were all the size of trees."

Wolf tried very hard not to laugh again but he only managed to choke on his bread. He had heard more complaints out of that woman's mouth in days than he had from Solveig in years. His wife would never have eaten without first ensuring that he was served, she would have turned blue before admitting she was cold, and as to even suggesting that he liked to take his pleasure with men or contradict him in any way...

He could not recall a single occasion when she had expressed an opinion that was not the same as his. It had always annoyed him and many a time he had wished she could find the courage to admit to whatever was bothering her, or even just share her thoughts. Her timidity made him feel like a constant threat, not a pleasant feeling for a man who was already worried that his size gave people the wrong impression about him.

Wolf smiled to himself. Now that he had met someone who was not afraid to tell him just what she thought and point out his failings, he had to concede that staying silent was not always the worst choice a woman could make.

Oh, well, at least he didn't feel like a monster best cajoled lest he rip her in half. The deflating of his ego was a small price to pay for that reassurance. Because of his impressive physique, no one, much less women, ever dared provoke him and Wolf found that he needed to be challenged to feel alive. He relished the thought that he had to fight to earn his pleasure. In that regard, the fiery Saxon was the best person he could have met. And as if that wasn't enough, she made him laugh—as well as heat his blood.

His determination to win her around flared anew.

"I will endeavor to cut the wood into more suitable chunks from now on," he answered, hiding another smile. Merewen did not seem to realize that her request indicated she was expecting to have to tend to the fire in his hut in the future, but he had not missed it. Slowly, she was coming to accept the idea of them living together... It was a good start, undeniably. "This is very good, by the way. You can certainly cook," he said, taking another bite of his bread.

He was not trying to flatter her. The quality of his meals had markedly improved since she had arrived.

"Cooking broth or bread doesn't require blazing heat, fortunately, so there is nothing extraordinary in the fact that I was able do so." It was brief, but he thought he saw a gleam of satisfaction warm her eyes. Though she would never admit it, she had enjoyed his praise.

Better and better. Time for more teasing. He already knew she responded well to it, or at least, in a way that pleased him.

"With those skills in the kitchen, you shall make a fine wife. And now I cannot help but wonder what skills you possess in bed, as a woman accomplished in the art of lovemaking is guaranteed to please her husband," he purred, barely resisting the urge to wink.

Just as he had predicted, she flared up. The dark eyes flashed in fury, making her appear like an angered goddess about to unleash her ire onto mere mortals. Blood rushed to his groin. She had never looked more beautiful and he almost reached out to her to find out just how skilled she was right here, *right now*. His body, denied for longer than it ever had been before, was at a snapping point.

Usually when he wanted a woman, he did not have to wait days to take them to bed—and he usually didn't want them with such force. This was all unprecedented.

"I'm afraid you will have to keep wondering about that," Merewen said, abandoning the rest of her broth before getting up.

Her appetite had quite deserted her. Wolf's provocative words had inflamed her blood and chilled her to the bone at the same time because the taunt had made her realize that she had no idea how to please a man in bed. For all her wild imaginings, she had no experience whatsoever and little notion of what would be expected of her. In her dreams, the men did everything, but Wolf's lewd comment had made her see that perhaps a woman was supposed to do more than just lie there and be pleasured.

It was a sobering, frightening realization because she had no idea what that might be and, even supposing she had been bold enough to discuss such a thing and ask questions, she had no one to turn to.

Biting her lip to hide her distress, she ostensibly went to the river to wash her bowl and spoon. Heavy clouds had gathered on the darkening horizon, bringing a distinctive chill along with them, a chill that seeped into her body and reached all the way to her soul.

What was she to do now?

Making a decision about a possible union with Wolf had just been made even more difficult. Until now, she'd thought she would be the only one regretting her decision. But now she understood she had been unforgivably naïve—again.

Wolf was bound to be disappointed with her lack of experience. He'd just admitted to being eager to discover the skills she possessed. What would he do when he saw that the little innocent did not live up to his expectations? Would he turn from her and choose a more accomplished woman to warm his bed? Would he take lovers to compensate for her inability to please him? The mere idea was enough to make her retch. To finally have a man at her disposal and then having to watch him leave her because he found her lacking would be unbearable, a hundred times worse than being on her own.

If they were to marry, then she wanted to have a true marriage, not just a cold arrangement where Wolf would not think himself accountable for his actions or feel free to bed all the women who took his fancy.

At the moment, he was the one pushing for this union because he wanted her in his bed, but how long would it be before he regretted his decision to buy her for his wife? And if she allowed herself to behave in the way she wanted to when he bedded her, then it wouldn't be much better. Instead of boring her with her lack of initiative, she would horrify him with her wantonness.

A tear threatened to spill onto her cheek. The night of her brother's funeral, she had thought with no small amount of dismay that she might never cry again because she did not have anyone left to cry over. Now it appeared she'd found someone. As consolations went, it was a small one.

"I'm sorry if I offended you. I shouldn't have said what I said. It was crude of me."

The voice was soft, the tone sincere. Merewen did not turn around. Night had fallen, but Wolf would still be able to see that her eyes were too shiny.

"It was." She could not pretend she had not been hurt.

"I'm sorry." A warm hand landed on her shoulder. She froze, not knowing what to do. She had not expected Wolf to apologize to her, or even notice he had offended her. And now he was touching her, again.

And she was melting, again.

When Merewen stiffened, Wolf tensed up in turn. Could she be afraid of him after all? Up until now she had behaved with such brazenness that he had not thought he frightened her. But after all, why would he not? He towered over her and could have snapped her in half in the blink of an eye. She had no reason to believe he would only touch her to give pleasure and considering how intimidating he looked, a certain reluctance on her part was justified.

He should not have teased her about how eager he was to take her to bed, it only made him appear as if he did not really care if she agreed to marry him or not, when he really did.

He took his hand away from her shoulder.

"Take your time deciding what you want to do. You need not rush into a decision. I will not throw you out, even if you do not accept my offer of marriage straight away," he said in a low voice. He could not make himself smaller, but he could certainly try to act less menacingly. "But please stay here with me in the meantime. I cannot bear the idea of you leaving and trying your luck alone when you're in danger. You are not without protection anymore. I'm here. I can, and I *will*, keep you safe."

He would do that if it was the last thing he did. Perhaps that was why he had bought her, he realized suddenly, because deep down he needed to protect someone who mattered to him for a change, instead of villagers who could have turned to anyone for help.

Wolf was looking for redemption, for a chance to atone for his past mistake. He needed to know he had not failed yet another woman who relied on him for her well-being and security. Perhaps if he succeeded in keeping Merewen safe it would lessen the guilt of not having been able to protect Solveig.

This marriage would be mutually beneficial. She might need the protection of his body, but he needed the peace of mind she would grant him.

Helping the villagers for two years had been a step in the right direction, but it had not been enough to give him absolution because they were nothing to him. Only a second wife would help him get over the trauma.

There was no choice, anyway, because if he didn't protect Merewen, no one else would come forward. No father, nor brother, no elusive youth too clumsy to know where to dip his wick.

"So you will feed me, keep me safe and warm, provide for me in every way while you wait patiently for me to accept your offer of marriage, is that what you are saying? You will not try to seduce, coerce or threaten me into an agreement?" Merewen asked, turning to face him, at last.

He smiled. She wouldn't be asking that question if she did not intend to give his offer at least some consideration. But just like before, with the logs, she didn't seem to realize the importance of what she had said.

"I promise I won't do any of that, even if I cannot recall promising to be patient," he told with an effort at honesty.

"I don't know what is more commendable," she mumbled. "Your selflessness or your ability to lie."

Something inside Wolf melted. The attempt at tartness was endearing and the scowl made her appear even more adorable, quite a feat considering how beautiful she already was. How could he not feel drawn to the woman?

One day, as a child, he had got lost in a snowstorm while gathering wood for the fire. After what had felt like days of aimless wandering he had finally found his way back to the safety of his house. The warmth surrounding him after being exposed to the elements for so long had been the most wonderful sensation, something he still recalled in his bones to this day. Being with Merewen gave him the same feeling of well-being and he already knew he would fight tooth and nail to keep it.

"I will leave you to decide which is my most enviable trait. And now it is my turn to ask a question. Are you saying that if I wait long enough you will accept my offer of marriage?" he asked slowly, hope building inside him in spite of all reason.

"No, I'm not saying that," she answered, shaking her head slightly. Of course, she wasn't. Why had he expected her to surrender so easily?

"Because of Æthelred?"

"Who?"

He cocked his head, pleased with her answer. "Your husband?" he drawled, taking a step forward.

She flushed a vivid scarlet. As he had suspected, she had forgotten all about her supposed husband. "I..."

"Should I start worrying? How long before the lad comes knocking on my door to demand I hand you back? Will I find him one morning when I wake up, sword in hand, ready to cut me into shreds for daring to steal his beloved wife? I assume the pup does love you?" he added with mock concern. "Do not tell me this is a dispiriting union where the groom doesn't appreciate how lucky he is?"

"Like ours would be, you mean?" Merewen whispered, doing her best to calm the fluttering of her heart. Could a marriage begun under such inauspicious circumstances be anything other than unsatisfactory? Suddenly she dearly hoped it could.

"Oh, no," Wolf purred, his voice taking on the consistency of honey. "Our marriage would be nothing like that. Believe me, I am fully conscious of the gem I have found in you. A rare gem, indeed."

A gem.

A sob almost escaped Merewen's lips.

Leofric had told her many times that she should give herself a chance to live her own life instead of making his more comfortable, that she should find a man who would look after her, for a change. She was spending too much time at his bedside, watching over him, he'd chided. She needed to think about herself as well, or he would never forgive himself for having robbed her of her youth.

"You need someone to take care of you, sister, and see you for the gem you are," he'd said, holding her hand tightly, fighting the pain gripping his guts. "Promise me if you ever meet such a man you will marry him."

It had been one of the last things he had told her, and to appease him she had promised to do so, knowing it was unlikely she would ever meet such a man.

Yet less than a fortnight later, she was standing in front of Wolf, a man who wanted to make her his wife, a man she desired like she had not desired anyone else and who had just called her a gem.

It was time to make her mind up. Leave before her feelings got into a veritable tangle—or stay and marry him.

CHAPTER SEVEN

Staring at the log at his feet, Wolf shook his head. He was really acting like a lovesick fool eager to please the woman of his choice. Merewen had only had to complain about the size of the logs for him to go running and rectify something he had never before seen as inadequate and him doing her bidding? Was that what marriage between them would be like? Her ordering him about without even raising her voice or issuing direct instructions? Had he not idealized what having a spirited wife would actually be like? It might well turn out to be a nightmare.

Or it might well be everything he had ever wanted.

Shrugging the thought away before he got too hopeful, he split the first log in half with a swing of his axe. Perhaps she had a point. This particular one *had* been enormous.

Once he had reduced half the pile of wood to little more than twigs, Merewen walked up to him, worrying her bottom lip with her small, white teeth. He rested the axe on a tall log and waited, guessing she would not be able to keep silent for long.

"I do have a question," she said eventually.

His mouth quivered. "I thought you might." One—or two hundred by the looks of things.

"Why did you need to buy a wife?" she asked, releasing her lip at last. Blood rushed to his groin when he saw how red and shiny it was now. It would feel amazing against his, all plump and soft. "Could you not have seduced someone the normal way if you wanted to get married? Is there something wrong with you?"

He gave a short, incredulous laugh. Really, the woman was unlike anyone he had ever met. He could not recall anyone ever having the guts to question his abilities in any way, leastwise in bed. But it was yet another encouraging sign. If she wondered about his ability to perform as a man, it meant that she was thinking about accepting his offer but wanted to make sure she would not end up with an impotent lover unable to give her what she needed.

The male inside him roared.

He would give her what she wanted, and more.

"There is nothing wrong with me," he assured her in a low rumble. "I told you. I like women and believe me, I am perfectly capable of satisfying them, unlike your poor husband. I know what to do with a woman in my arms."

Merewen found herself blushing furiously.

Indeed. That Wolf had what it took to make her body erupt could not be in doubt. He had the physique, the confidence, the strength required to make the perfect lover. She, who had spent night after night obsessing about lovemaking, should know. He was made to pleasure women. It made it all the more extraordinary that he would have to resort to such extreme methods as buying a woman to acquire a bride. She needed to understand why a man his age was not yet married if, as his determination to have her seemed to indicate, he desperately wanted to be.

"Y-you know what I mean," she stammered, feeling some of her bravado melt away. How could the wretched man unsettle her so easily? It had taken her all her inner strength to ask him the question, and he had destroyed her confidence in just a few words.

"I do. You want to make sure I will be able to bed you if you decide to marry me."

"Well, I..." Merewen cleared her throat. Actually, she had never doubted that, but all the same, she needed to have it confirmed.

Wolf placed his axe back against the wall of the hut, and it was only then that she realized she should perhaps have waited until he was unarmed before she started questioning his virility. Not many men she knew would have allowed her to get away with such a thing. Why was she feeling immune to danger? Hadn't she seen the size of him? Even without an axe in hand, he should have scared the life out of her.

"You need not worry about my skill as a lover, Merewen," he said, making her name sound like the most exotic word she had ever heard. "I will do more than bed you like a chore. I will give you pleasure."

Oh, Lord. Pleasure. What she had craved all this time. It was the most enticing promise he could have made. But was it enough to sway her? No, of course, not!

"Then why did you—" He stopped her with a light tap on the nose, an oddly endearing move coming from such a beast of a man.

"Let us go back inside," he said, his grave face at odds with the playful gesture. "This is going to be a long story and I'm thirsty."

More curious than ever, Merewen followed Wolf back into the hut. He went to the stool and sat down, then poured himself a cup of ale which he emptied in one gulp. She wondered why the sight of his throat moving as he swallowed the liquid fascinated her so much but found that she could not avert her eyes.

Finally, he returned the cup to the table and planted his clear stare into hers.

"I'm here because I've been sent to exile."

Exile. Cold invaded Merewen at the word. What awful deed had the man committed to be handed out such an extreme punishment? Though he was still sitting down and looked in no way about to pounce, she took a step back. The sight of him, axe in hand, had failed to impress her, but hearing about the sentence chilled her to the bone.

"Why?"

"I was accused of murder."

All the blood left her veins. Had she not felt the table against her hip in support, she might have fallen in a heap on the floor.

Murder.

"I said I had been accused of murdering someone, not that I had actually done it," Wolf said slowly, not missing her reaction.

"So... you're innocent?" She could barely get the words out.

"Of course."

Heart in her throat, Merewen waited for the explanation to come. Was that why he was not married? Because women were afraid of him and what he had done? It was more than possible. What woman wanted to hear they were married to a murderer?

When Wolf finally opened his mouth to explain himself, the door of the hut burst open.

A man entered, shaking his rain-soaked cloak. So lost had she been in their conversation that she had not even noticed it had started raining.

Wolf watched Sigurd walk in with a mixture of pleasure and annoyance. Although his friend could not have guessed he was interrupting an important conversation, he could not help but resent him for having chosen this particular moment for coming to see him. Oblivious to the tension in the room, Sigurd started talking in rapid Norse, complaining about the unpredictable weather.

Then he turned and stopped dead when he saw they weren't alone.

"This is Merewen." Wolf answered the silent question in his eyes, reverting pointedly to English. Merewen would guess that they were talking about her and he wanted her to know what they were saying.

His friend arched a brow. He'd been told about the woman he'd bought from the slave trader but had yet to meet her.

"So you're actually living with the woman... Well, this I didn't see coming, I must admit! What next, hey, marriage?" Sigurd laughed then checked himself when Wolf scowled. "Welcome to the village," he said, turning to Merewen, who had turned bright red at the mention of marriage. "I'm Sigurd."

"Pleased to meet you," she mumbled.

"I will come back later," he said with a broad smile. "Apologies, I had no idea I was interrupting anything."

Wolf groaned. His friend thought Merewen was embarrassed because they had been about to tumble into bed... Nothing could be further from the truth but if it served to get him out of there then he could think what he wanted. The only problem was, thinking about tumbling her into bed had made him as hard as the handle of his axe.

Again.

"Did you tell your friend we were to be married?" Merewen asked once they were alone.

"No," was his emphatic answer. "I would never go behind your back thus. You heard him. He found it hard enough to believe I was living with a woman." And no wonder. Sigurd knew all about his past.

"He seems convinced we will be married soon," she insisted.

"Yes, well, so am I. Maybe not convinced so much as hopeful, now that you know there is nothing wrong with my ability to please a woman in bed," Wolf said, deciding it was best to try and lighten the mood. It did not quite work.

"And once again, I should just believe your word unconditionally?"

He almost laughed out loud. Was the minx trying to provoke him into a kiss? It certainly seemed as if she was. No man worth his salt could have resisted such a taunt, no man could have heard the question and not instantly caught the vexing woman into his arms and shown her what he was capable of.

"No, you should not believe everything you hear," he told her with a faint smile. "But fortunately, I can make true on my word."

With those words, he grabbed her by the waist and drew her to him in a flamboyant gesture. A groan escaped his lips. It felt so good to have her pressed against him, with her breasts crushed against his chest and her breath hot at his neck!

It would be even better to feel her lips under his, her tongue darting into his mouth. In a moment he might, because he could feel her trembling. She was just as affected as he was.

He gave a growl low in his throat. Finally, he was about to taste her.

Merewen could have kicked herself for giving Wolf the excuse to do what he had clearly been itching to do. With their bodies pressed so tight against one another she could feel every muscle, every inch of his amazing body and the contact sent flames coursing down her veins. The contrast between them was so complete it aroused her beyond all comprehension. Where she was delicate he was strong, where she was soft he was hard. He supported, she melted. He was unyielding steel and she liquid wax. They worked as two halves of a whole, one melting around the other until it felt as if nothing could separate them.

This was too delicious, too dangerous.

She had to put an end to it because in spite of everything, she could feel herself surrendering and she had decided only the evening before that she could not base her decision on lust. Not only that but she had just been told he'd been accused of murder and sent away on exile. She had better use her head, not follow her urges.

"Stop this," she said crossly, pushing at his chest. To her relief and surprise, he let her go when he could have restrained her one-handed. "You promised you would not seduce me into an agreement. You had better cease trying because it will not work."

The expression on his face made it clear he did not believe that anymore than she did.

"I said I would give you time to reach your own decision and I mean it. That doesn't mean I cannot do what I can to ensure that this decision is the right one," he purred, sending her a lethal look.

"The one you want, you mean!"

"Same thing."

This answer was so outrageously arrogant that Merewen actually laughed. The man certainly did not lack self-confidence! It was oddly appealing, she had to admit, to have someone want her so much he was prepared, not only to fight, but to fight dirty to have her.

No one had wanted her that badly before, or at all, for that matter.

And now her resolve was hanging by a thread because not only would Wolf be capable of giving her what she had always wanted—pleasure and the enjoyment of a man's body—but it now seemed he was also willing to give her what she had never thought to have, what she had never dreamed of needing. Protection and someone who would look after her.

It would be a welcome novelty. As far back as she could remember, she had always been the carer. If she married this man, she could be cared for, for a change, just like Leofric had wanted. With Wolf as a husband she would also laugh and be allowed to challenge him without fear of being hurt. She had seen enough of him to be convinced that the worst he would hit her with was a stringent retort.

It was tempting, undeniably.

So why was she hesitating? Because he'd bought her instead of wooing her? So what? He seemed to have fallen under her charm, anyway. There was no mistaking the way he looked at her. Because she didn't know him? As husband and wife they would have a lifetime to get to know one another. Because he'd been accused of murder? He'd said he was innocent, and oddly, she believed him. Surely, if he was guilty, he would not have mentioned it. Because she was afraid he would be both horrified by her wanton nature and dismayed by her lack of skill in bed? Yes, that was a concern. But she could not be sure what his reaction would be. Perhaps instead of being appalled, he would enjoy teaching her all he knew?

Wasn't it worth taking a gamble?

One look at him was enough to answer the question.

Yes, yes, it was.

CHAPTER EIGHT

A shout, then a thud, followed by another shout and a grunt. Abandoning the pot she had just placed over the fire to boil, Merewen ran outside and came to a skidding halt when she saw Wolf throw a man over his shoulder with a supple twist of his body. The man landed on his back with sickening force and did not even try to get up.

Her heart started to beat wildly. What was happening? Was the village under attack?

No. With her mind calmer, she recognized the red-haired man groaning on the floor as one of the villagers she had seen milling around before. This was not an attack, but a private disagreement, nothing more.

Wolf snarled something to the man and turned his back to him, evidently considering that the matter was closed. Merewen watched him walk toward her with smoldering intent. Without knowing quite why, she had the feeling that the fight had been over her. She was therefore not surprised when Wolf ordered her back inside the hut, as if to get her out of sight.

What neither of them anticipated was that a second man would want to avenge his friend's honor.

As he reached Merewen, Wolf saw a movement in the corner of his eye. He turned his head just in time to see someone coming at him armed with, of all things, a plank of wood. There was no time to think. By now he was so close to Merewen that the fool might well hit her as well as him when he wielded his makeshift weapon. He placed himself in front of her, offering his back to the man, shielding her with his body.

The pain exploding in his shoulder blade was like nothing he had ever experienced. It was a slap and a burn all at once, and he felt dozens of tiny and not so tiny splinters embed themselves in his flesh, their bite as sharp as if they had been made of iron.

Not giving the man time to swing his weapon again, he sent him reeling with a kick that shattered the plank into a thousand shards, then floored him with a neat blow to the chin.

There, that should do it.

"If you both go back home now we will hear no more of this," he barked in Norse, standing over the two men lying at his feet. "And if you even *look* at her, then you will have me to contend with, and I will certainly not arm myself with a plank of wood. Am I making myself clear?"

A nod was all the answer he got.

"Let's go back in," he growled, taking Merewen by the arm.

For once, she followed without a word of protest.

"What was that all about?" she asked once the door was closed.

Wolf shook his head and took a moment to quell his towering rage. He would not tell Merewen why he had lunged at Rolf. Overhearing the two men discuss what they would like to do to such a fine woman had sent him blind with fury. Still, he might have left it at that if the fools had not then added that it would not be long before he tired of her and then they would take their turn with her.

He'd burst in on them before he could even draw a breath, wishing he was already married to her. No one in their right mind would dare touch a woman he had claimed for himself. With each passing day it was becoming more and more imperative that they marry. It would be the only way to protect her from all sorts of dangers.

"'Tis nothing, just drunken idiots boasting to each other and looking for trouble," he grumbled. "Rolf had it coming. He cannot hold his tongue."

He rolled his shoulder. The whole right side of his body ached, testimony to the force of the blow he had received.

"You will need to remove those shards," Merewen told him, frowning.

"How? I can't see and I can barely reach," he growled, pain making him even angrier.

"No, but I can."

He stared at her in incredulity. "You would offer to do that?"

"I wouldn't offer, I *am* offering it," she answered roundly. "I cannot help but feel that the fight had something to do with me and after all, if you had not stepped in front of me those same shards might well have ended up on my face. It's only fair I should help you remove them."

Wolf was surprised by her willingness to help him and her insight. How had she guessed that she had been the cause of the fight? He had made a point of talking in his language so she didn't understand. And why was she not appalled by his inability to handle the disagreement with Rolf without resorting to his fists? She had just seen him fight him like a man possessed. Wouldn't she think him unforgivably violent? He hoped not.

When he reached out to stroke her cheek, he could tell that

the tenderness of the gesture disconcerted her but at least she didn't pull away.

"Yes, the fool might well have hit you," he said in a low voice. "So I cannot regret taking the blow."

"I..." She seemed at a loss for words for once.

"You can thank me for defending you, you know," he told her slowly. "It is allowed."

"I know," she answered just as slowly.

Wolf bared his teeth when she stayed silent. Evidently the stubborn little minx would not stoop so low as to thank the man who had bought her for any reason... "Never mind. You can show your gratitude by removing these wretched shards out of me."

Heart in her throat, Merewen watched Wolf take off both his tunic and undershirt in one fluid motion. She knew he was a big man but nothing had prepared her for seeing him bare-chested. The only other man she had seen thus was her brother, and Leofric had been a sickly youth, barely on the cusp manhood, not a warrior in his prime. This man was nothing short of breathtaking. Short blond hairs shone like a dusting of gold on stone, covering a chest that was rippling with muscles and sculpted to perfection.

This was a chest meant to be admired, stroked and kissed.

And she wanted to be the one doing it, *could* be the one doing it, if she agreed to his offer.

With one last tug he freed himself of his undershirt and winced when the movement drew most of the pieces of wood out with it.

"Careful!" she cried out, shaken out of her awe-struck contemplation by the sight in front of her.

In contrast to his perfect chest, his back was stained with blood and splinters were sticking out of his flesh. Merewen shivered. Had Wolf not shielded her from the blow the man might well have caught her with the plank and she would never have been able to withstand such a blow. Not only would the wood have ripped her cheek open but she would probably have fallen to the floor and injured herself.

Wolf had not hesitated, not given his own safety any thought, he had stepped between her and the man in the blink of an eye, enveloping her so completely that she hadn't had time to be afraid or feel a thing.

"You don't want to leave some splinters inside when you remove the shards!" she said in a breath as he threw his clothes to the floor.

"I told you. I cannot see!" he growled, glancing over his shoulder— and making her all but gasp when the movement caused the muscles on his taut stomach to twist and stretch. Her insides rippled, mirroring the movement.

Oh, Lord... Why couldn't the man have struck him on the leg instead? She could not imagine being half as affected by the sight of his calf than she was by the honey-colored chest. She shook her head. What was she thinking! If he had been hurt on the leg then he would have had to remove his braies and that would be even worse!

She would just have to take a deep breath and do what she had just volunteered to do.

"Well, I can see where the splinters are," she said firmly, focusing on the task at hand. "So let me take them out."

"Are you not going to swoon?" he asked with a wry smile.

"Swoon? No. It is not as if I had to sew a bleeding, jagged wound!"

"I was not talking about my injuries," he clarified, before glancing down at his naked torso. "Only, you seemed quite over-whelmed for a moment."

Oh, the wretched man! He had seen her reaction to his nakedness and he was enjoying teasing her!

Without a word, she went to the basket by the window and turned to face him, pliers in hand. They could be used to prize the finer shards of wood from his flesh.

"Sit while I put these in boiling water," she ordered crossly. He would not be allowed to amuse himself at her expense for a moment longer. "And once I start working, do not move a muscle or I might hurt you. Unintentionally, you understand."

"Of course," he agreed, sitting down on the stool. "Completely unintentionally."

Well. Wolf allowed himself a smile. His first impression of the Saxon girl had been proven right a hundred times over.

She truly was impossible.

Impossibly intriguing. With each passing moment he was discovering something else he liked about her. She was not only brave, passionate, and clever, but she was willing to help and she had a ready sense of humor.

He would be looking a long time to find a more suitable wife, or one who would appeal to his senses more.

"I'm all yours," he drawled, knowing she would understand the double entendre.

She did, as her next comment proved. "You really are determined to have me accept your offer, aren't you?"

"Yes. Nothing, even your outrageous claim that you are married, will stop me. Doesn't that tell you I can be determined?"

She sighed. "Mayhap your friends should start calling you Bull instead of Wolf."

"Mayhap. It's a thought..." Wolf stroked his chin pensively.

"Why me?" Merewen sounded slightly breathless but she couldn't help it, not when his bicep bulged and the muscles on his forearm twisted so. "Why would you want to marry me, a stranger you bought and who refuses you when surely you can have all the women you want?"

"Ah, don't let poor Sigurd hear you. You will break his heart!"

To Merewen's surprise—and utter delight, Wolf started to laugh. His was a sunny laugh that somehow did not match his fearsome appearance. One expected a man of his stature to growl, roar, or bark, not laugh with such mirth. So far she had only seen him laugh with her, and she liked that. It was as if only she could coax certain emotions from him, ranging from amusement to desire.

Rather than show how his laugh affected her, she waved the pliers in her hand.

"Don't you start reminding me what you like about women," she warned, eyes narrowing. "I am armed, remember?"

"I wouldn't dream of it." He tried to look duly chastened. Failed. The man would never look anything other than commanding and self-assured. "Do your worst."

Merewen took a deep breath and placed a palm on Wolf's shoulder. As soon as her fingers touched the taut, smooth skin she knew her ability to keep a steady hand would be tested to the very limit. How could a man feel so soft, smell so good, be so strong? She already knew Wolf was the most handsome man she had ever set eyes upon but now she was forced to admit that he was also the most compelling.

What a dramatic turn her life had taken in just a few days!

After years of seemingly never-ending boredom, here she was, tending to a man who could, if she allowed it, be her husband before the afternoon was over. In just over a week she had been kidnapped, sold—and bought—as a slave, taken to a place she didn't know, and offered marriage by a stranger. Quite a change from her normal routine.

It was not all bad, though. There had been some interesting new developments. Not only had her dreams finally allowed her to experience the release she had craved all these years, but she had now seen a naked man in the flesh instead of in her imagination and she had been a hair's breadth away from being kissed.

As if that was not enough, she could be bedded before the day was out, and by a man capable of making her scream in pleasure.

Out of the blue, Wolf's comment about being forced to endure flooding after years of complaining about the lack of rain came back to her. This was so appropriate an image for how she felt right now that she knew without a doubt he had been referring to the contrast between his life before they met and now. But did he mean it as a good thing? She could not be sure.

"You're going to have a mighty bruise," she whispered, contemplating the scratched flesh. The whole shoulder blade was red.

"I can already feel it forming," Wolf grumbled under his breath. "A plank... Who would have thought of using such a weapon? What next, I wonder? A ladle?"

"There wasn't much else lying around and it inflicted enough damage," Merewen pointed out, removing another splinter. "I would say it wasn't such a bad idea, if not very noble."

"Yes, well, when there aren't weapons around a warrior uses his fists, not whatever is 'lying around,' as you say. That is the reaction of a coward."

She smiled to herself, amused by this side of him she had not seen before. Wolf sounded rather like a petulant child, but she thought it prudent not to mention it. A warrior probably wouldn't like that any more than he liked to fight with kitchen implements.

One by one the shards were removed. Finally Merewen smoothed her fingers over the round shoulder and hard shoulder blade, telling herself that she needed to feel for any hair-sized splinters she might have missed. Perforce, she had to keep her touch light so as to feel the slightest disruption on his skin and it only added to the intimacy of the moment.

She started. Intimacy? What was she thinking about! This was not an intimate, loving act. She was only removing splinters. It only affected her because the man she was tending to was so impossibly attractive and it was the first time she had touched anyone thus, she told herself sternly. To him it would feel perfunctory, a way of ensuring she had completed her task successfully, nothing more.

She had to stop being such a fool.

Wolf gritted his teeth.

Thankfully Merewen could not see his face from where she was for she would have taken fright. He was sure his eyes had gone ablaze with the desire raging in his body and, of course, lower down, she would see something else, something altogether frightening for a virgin. He was hard enough to hammer nails, and little wonder!

She was caressing him all over, and her breath was coming in short, ragged bursts in his ear, an impossibly evocative sound.

Her touch was so careful he could tell she was not trying to provoke him in any way and yet nothing had ever felt so unbearably, so deliciously arousing. He would not be able to withstand much more of the sensual torture. It had been bad enough when she had extracted the shards with her soft, small hand gripping at his shoulder but now that she was feeling her way around for stray ones, it was pure torment.

It had to stop or he would turn around, march her to the pallet and show her just how unbearable it was to have someone trace their fingers over your bare skin. He would not stop until she begged him to put an end to the torture, which he would do with unforgivable roughness.

"Enough!" he growled.

"Wait, I think there's still—"

"No, that's enough!" he repeated, standing up so abruptly that the stool he had been sitting upon was overturned.

Merewen stood in front of him, eyes wide, mouth open. Heat flooded his veins. By the gods! Was it because he was half-naked or because he'd reared up like a stallion catching scent of a female that she appeared smaller, more delicate than usual? Whatever it was, it made her even more irresistible, her petiteness the perfect match to his strength.

"I need to wash off the—"

He cut her off with a raised hand. "You don't. I can do that myself."

He took the cloth she had prepared, dipped it in the luke-warm water and started to wash himself with brusque gestures, almost relishing the thousand stings piercing his flesh when the rough fabric hit the places where a splinter had been removed. Anything to steer his mind away from temptation and blood from his aching groin.

"Thank you."

He swiveled around slowly. Merewen was standing in the middle of the room, looking at her feet. Had he heard right? Had she just thanked him unprompted?

"What did you say?"

She wrung her hands together, clearly thinking he was making her repeat the words to make her pay for not having thanked him earlier. He was not, only he had been so lost in his own, lewd thoughts he wanted to be sure he had not imagined the words.

"I thanked you for protecting me. It will have hurt."

"You don't need to thank me," he said slowly, putting the bloodied cloth back in the water. "Anyone would have done the same."

"No, they would not, and you know it," she murmured, still

refusing to meet his eye. "Not after... everything that happened, or rather, didn't happen."

Perhaps she was right. Most men he knew would not have wanted to protect a woman who had refused their offer of marriage and pushed them away when they'd wanted to kiss her. They might well have enjoyed seeing her receive punishment for the humiliation.

But he was not most men.

"I hope you don't think I could stand by idly while you were in danger of being hurt?"

"No. And I am thanking you for more than that. It would have been unbearable for me to be bought by someone else at the market. You saved me from a dire fate. No doubt the other men present that day would have made me understand just what being a slave meant. But you... didn't. You never mistreated me."

Heat flared inside his chest. "I would never do that."

"Yes, I know that now. But I can still thank you for it."

Wolf looked at Merewen from under heavy-lidded eyes. He would never have imagined hearing such a heartfelt apology from the proud, self-assured Saxon. Did it mean what he thought it meant? Could he dare hope she was considering accepting his offer? He took a step toward her, then another, and saw her swallow hard. His groin instantly responded, wrenching a frustrated groan out of him.

He cursed under his breath. He'd only just managed to regain mastery over his heated senses and here he was again, hard as granite!

"You don't need to thank me for not hurting you or for protecting you from blows never intended for you," he said, taking her hand in his. "Or, even worse, for not using you as a slave or for not raping you. It was never my intention to do so.

You know what my intentions are with regards to you. They haven't changed."

And they would never change. He meant to marry her, and even if he could not make her his wife he still would not let her go. He would sprout wings and a beak before he gave this woman up. Slowly, he lifted her hand and kissed the inside of her palm, inhaling the delicious smell of flowers that seemed to follow her everywhere.

No, he would never be able to forget her, she was already too ingrained in his life. Too many things would remind him of her now. Every time he smelled flowers, cut wood, ate bread, walked into the hut, he would smell her, hear her, taste her, see her.

Crave her.

"And now it's my turn to thank you," he said slowly.

"It's nothing," she answered in a hoarse voice that sent shards of longing through his spine. She was definitely not indifferent to him as a man, whatever she felt about him as a potential husband. Another encouraging sign... "As you said, you could not have reached over to your shoulder blade."

He shook his head. "I am not thanking you for removing the splinters, even if it was a great help. I am thanking you because I think... I think that despite the way you came into my life, despite what I told you about my exile, you are considering giving me a chance."

Before she could answer, he kissed her fingers one by one, lingering over the gesture, watching her fighting the urge to moan out loud. Hope swelled within him.

"What made you think I was?" she mewled, eyes fluttering under the caress.

"Because after what happened today, you've realized that you could trust me to look after you. And then... I think you want me like a woman wants a man."

Unable to resist, he took her little finger between his teeth. So small, so soft! He groaned and sucked it deep into his eager mouth.

"Oh!"

Merewen sagged against him and he had to catch her by the waist before she collapsed like an empty sack of grain. No, definitely not indifferent, but positively melting. Oh, this was good. Things could be so good between them!

"Let me prove that I do not think of you as an animal or a possession but as a beautiful woman I want to hold in my arms."

"I-I never really thought you saw me as a possession," Merewen stammered, nestling into Wolf's arms. She could not remember why she had ever thought that, even if she knew she had.

"Then let me show you how good it could be between us."

Quick as a flash, he moved, and before she could take a breath, he kissed her with all the hunger she had hoped to provoke in a man.

The heat of his lips seared hers, and she would have gasped if she had been able to utter a sound. Wolf infused all his passion into his kiss. The same passion, wild and uncontrollable, made her raise her hands and weave her fingers through his hair to bring him even closer to her. Desire spread through her veins, reaching all the way to the tip of her toes and the most innermost recesses of her body, filling her with warmth and energy.

He groaned, the sound so filled with masculine need that she instinctively opened her mouth, allowing him to deepen the kiss further, to stroke his tongue against hers in a sensual, carnal dance. His lips were soft but demanding, the hold around her firm but gentle.

Despite her very high expectations, this first kiss did not disappoint. In fact, it quite overwhelmed her and she realized quite quickly that they had crossed the line from mere kissing into something else, something more akin to lovemaking. Odd, what the contact of two mouths could do... Usually what happened to one part of your body did not affect the others parts. When you bit your tongue it did not make your belly spasm in pain, neither did it set your toes to curling.

But her insides had definitely gone liquid and it was not just her stomach and toes but every part of her that was writhing in heated pleasure right now.

Just when she thought he was about to tumble her into the bed, Wolf drew back. Eyes ablaze, body taut, he was a picture of desperate need.

"Say you will marry me," he rasped, speaking against her lips.

Once again, an order, not a proposal.

Should she accept? Perhaps... Yes, perhaps she should accept his offer of marriage, odd though it was, frightening though it was. He had proven he would not abandon her to fend for herself alone. What he had just done made it clear. If he was prepared to come to her aid when she was nothing more than a vexing woman he had bought and who was refusing his hand, then he would not turn his back on her once she was his wife.

Merewen swallowed hard. Though she was well past the age of matrimony, no one had asked for her hand before. Of course, Wolf had not exactly proposed, he had told her he had bought her to be his wife, which was not quite the same thing but still, if she accepted him they could married within the day and spend the rest of their lives together.

She took another glance at him, struck anew by his strength and beauty. She only had to say the word and this man would be her husband. The thought was dizzying, undeniably tempting.

Never more so than now that he had kissed any lingering doubts away and ignited a fire in her belly only he would be able to douse.

"I do not think you set off to buy yourself a wife that day," she said, wanting to be sure his proposal had at least in some part been motivated by who she was, and not because any other woman would have done. "You said that you only passed the market by accident, not on purpose. I think you bought me for a reason I cannot fathom and *then* decided that since you had bought me you might as well marry me."

Wolf gave a slanted smile. He was still holding her tight against his body. "Why are you asking me this? Would it set your mind at ease to know I never meant to purchase myself a wife?"

Merewen was startled to see that he had read her mind so accurately.

"Yes, it would help me."

"Well, then, you're right. I had no idea I would propose to you when I carried you away from that pole," he whispered. "In truth, it was the furthest thing from my mind. There, are you satisfied? Am I less of a monster in your eyes?" he asked slowly. "Less of a... predatory *wolf*, shall we say?"

"Taming a wolf doesn't change the fact that he is a wild animal," she pointed out, feeling weaker than ever. "He remains just as lethal, just as unpredictable."

"Does he? Why don't you try and see for yourself, try and tame this wolf?" he suggested. "I think you lack neither the courage nor the boldness to try."

Wolf bared perfect white teeth that made the resemblance between him and the animal even more glaring. Then she paused. No. She was being unfair. His smile was not predatory, more a warning to people who did not know how to handle him that dangerous things lurked under its smooth surface. But he had just hinted that she was not one of these people.

So did she dare take up the challenge? Did she *want* to tame him?

Yes.

The answer tore through her mind with the force of a clap of thunder. The idea of this beast of a man doing her bidding excited her beyond all reason.

"You want me. You have from the start, just like I have wanted you," he purred in her ear, suddenly more cat than wolf. "So let's go and get married, Merewen. You can have me then."

CHAPTER NINE

I f someone had told Merewen that she would be marrying a strapping warrior only a fortnight ago she would have laughed in disbelief. If that person had added that she would not understand a word of her wedding ceremony she would have laughed some more.

She did not feel like laughing now. The man standing next to her made her body hum with need, his voice made her insides melt and the intent in his eyes made her heart beat like a drum.

Lord, what had she got herself into? Everything had happened so fast.

One moment she and Wolf were kissing with abandon, the next they were in front of a... She did not even know how to call the man, she only knew that he was nothing like the priest she had imagined would marry her as a child. Indeed nothing during the ceremony had looked remotely familiar. The man had tied her right hand to Wolf's left with a strip of cloth and then Wolf—her husband, she should perhaps say— had laced his fingers through hers. She had the odd impression that this was not part of the ritual, and more something he had done on impulse, to reassure her. From then on the man could have switched to her language, and she still would not have under-stood a word. Blood had roared in her ears and the heat of the strong hand wrapped around hers had traveled all the way to her heart.

In that moment, Merewen had truly felt special. Cherished.

Not long after that, the man left, and she concluded that it was done. She was a married woman.

And now she was going to be bedded.

Her throat uncomfortably tight, she followed Wolf back to the hut. Suddenly, the familiar interior was impossibly small. Once the door was closed, he turned to face her with eyes dark-ened by need. The lead ball lodged in her throat dropped to her stomach.

How was she going to survive this? The kiss they had shared earlier had sent her to the verge of madness. If a mere kiss could affect her so, she wasn't sure she had the strength to face Wolf's lovemaking. She was now certain she had bitten off more than she could chew in wishing for a wild, passionate lover. She would not be able to handle him, his intensity might well make her pass out.

Perhaps she should get used to dealing with his fiery kisses before experiencing the blistering heat of his possession. That way she might not get burnt.

"Are you all right, Merewen?"

Wolf tilted her head and she realized she had been staring at him in silence for a long moment, worrying her lip. Her insides twisted. She was not all right and she had to speak now. If she did not it would be too late.

"Could we... Do you think we could wait until we..."

He gave a growl and her voice died out. Evidently, he had other plans and was ready to take her now. How would he react to being asked to wait? He'd not pressed his advances on her before but now they were married, he had no reason to rein in his desire for her. As her husband, if he wanted to take her, he was entitled to, whether she was willing or not. The reality of her predicament hit her hard. Had she not exchanged a bad situation for an even worst one?

Not that she did not *want* him to take her, only that what she had been dreaming about suddenly seemed impossibly daunting.

"Are you afraid of losing your maidenhead, is that what it is?" he asked more gently than she had expected.

She wasn't, well, not of the pain anyway, as he seemed to suppose. But being married had done nothing to allay her fears of revealing her wanton nature to him, and driving him away. A groom might not wish for a bride who refused him access to her bed but neither did men want to marry women who dreamed of opening their legs to men at night and were desperate to discover pleasure. In the same way she wanted to get accustomed to his masculine intensity before they made love, it was better if he discovered gradually what kind of lover she really was, with increasingly hot kisses and whispered confidences. Then he might not be so shocked when she started to act wildly.

All in all, it was easier to play the part of the timid virgin for now, something that wouldn't raise his suspicion or bruise his ego, but still guarantee her the respite she needed.

"Yes, I am wary. And I'm afraid I don't really feel married to you. I did not understand a word of what the man said, that ceremony was unlike any I have ever witnessed and everything was decided so quickly... I think I need time to feel comfortable before we..."

Wolf clenched his jaw but nothing in his demeanor betrayed any anger. He was frustrated, understandably, but he seemed ready to give her the time she needed. She allowed herself to breathe. Perhaps it would be all right.

"I understand," he said with a nod. "All this has been most unusual, even for me. I never thought to remarry."

"Thank y— Wait, did you say *remarry*?" Merewen exclaimed, recoiling in shock. He'd been married before? And he was choosing this moment to tell her as much? She could scarce credit it. "You never thought to inform me of the fact that I was not to be your first wife?"

A pause. "I started to tell you about my marriage the other day and then we were interrupted by Sigurd," Wolf said slowly.

She frowned. The only discussion Sigurd had interrupted had been the one about him being exiled for murder. Ice seized in her veins. No. It couldn't be. "Who is it you are accused of having killed exactly?" she asked in a breath.

A shadow passed in Wolf's eyes. Annoyance? Hesitation? Guilt?

"My wife," he said slowly, never taking his eyes from her.

Merewen's legs instantly turned to water. This was the last thing she had expected—*wanted*—him to say. Moments after having married the man, she was told that he had killed his first wife! Before she could think, she flew to the other side of the hut. Up until now she hadn't been afraid of him. Impressed, yes, but not really afraid. Now...

Now everything was different.

And everything made sense. Hadn't she thought it odd that he should need to buy a woman in order to get married? Well, now she understood why! Because the women of the village knew about his bloody past and were afraid of him. They would never have accepted his proposal. He'd had to find a naïve stranger who could not see past his handsome features, a desperate woman in need of protection who would have no choice but to accept his offer, an inexperienced virgin he could dazzle with his skill at kissing and his promises of pleasure in bed.

In other words, a woman like her.

How pathetic! She had never thought their union was a love match but this! This was worse than she could possibly have imagined.

"You have nothing to fear," Wolf growled, making no move to come closer. "If you remember, I told you I had been wrongly accused."

Oh, she did remember, but this reassurance failed to impress her, as she suspected every man who had been accused of murder had claimed the same thing at one point or another. "Why should I believe you when I don't know you? The people who accused you and the ones who condemned you to exile evidently didn't!"

"The people who accused me did so for a reason I am ignorant of, and the ones who exiled me are gullible fools, or were paid to cover the real murderer's tracks." Though he was still talking calmly, the light in his eyes had become stormy.

"And I am supposed to swallow it all without question," she said in a breath, wondering where she was finding the courage—or the folly—to provoke him. "How convenient!"

He did move then. In three quick strides he was in front of her.

When he grabbed her shoulders and flattened her against the wall Merewen could not stop a squeak from escaping her lips. Was he finally going to make her pay for her defiance? What a fool she had been to believe his promise that he would not hurt her! But, of course, that was before she'd been told he had killed his wife!

"It is not *convenient*," he growled, the resemblance between him and the animal he was named after suddenly glaring. "It is the truth. I did not kill Solveig. However, I see that nothing I tell you will convince you. You seem to have already made your mind up on the matter even though, as you are quick to claim, you do not know me or weren't there when it happened."

With those words, Wolf left the hut before he could frighten Merewen further. He had seen fear in her eyes when she had looked at him, making them appear even darker than usual, and he could not bear the idea that she was scared of him.

But how could she not be? He had snarled at her and all but crushed her against the wall moments after revealing he had been accused of killing his wife! What a beast he really was! He should be able to control himself better than that. It was little wonder if she had taken fright. In that moment he would have appeared like the blood-crazed murderer he was trying so hard to convince her he wasn't.

He ran a hand through his hair in disgust at his behavior. For a brief moment, Merewen had looked at him in the way Solveig often had, with unmistakable fear. It had been like a knife to the heart, every time.

He had once loved his wife, but he had not been blind to her faults. She had been a timid, malleable creature who had never managed to get past her awe of him. He didn't doubt her love for him but no matter how gentle he had been with her she had never been able to shake the diffidence people felt upon first meeting him. No matter how many times he had tried to tell her that she had the right to speak her mind and stand up to him, she had always stayed meekly in the shadows.

Little by little this attitude had started to grate on him and he had begun to wonder why he had been so entranced by her. He had probably been too young to see past the desire she created in his young, virile body, too flattered by the way she looked up to him to question the true nature of his feelings when they had met. Everyone had told him he was in love with her and he had been, in a manner of speaking, but with a bit more experience he would have seen that she could never be the woman for him. He needed someone stronger, more spirited, some fire that would have added a much needed spark to their everyday life and intensity to their lovemaking. Wolves do not mate with tamed dogs. They need to be with their equals.

But as shy as Solveig had been, as passive she had been in bed, she had not deserved to die.

Guilt gnawed at his insides. If only he had not lost his temper that night, she would still be alive...

Wolf grabbed the axe resting against the wall and started to hack at the pieces of wood he had not touched the other day, reducing them to kindling in the blink of an eye.

He would never know if he had lost or one two people that day. He had come to suspect that Solveig might be with child, in fact that had been the cause of the argument. Excited at the prospect of becoming a father, he had asked her about it. In typical fashion, she had refused to answer clearly, murmuring that she could not yet be certain and did not want him to be disappointed if she was not.

"I am your husband, not just a passerby!" he had roared. "I have the right to know if you think you may be carrying my child or not. I can cope with the disillusion if you're not, I understand that sometimes women can make mistakes about such matters. Are you so afraid of what I would do if you gave me false hope? Are you so afraid of me, the man you married, that you never speak your mind?"

Fueled by the need to hear he was indeed going to be a father, Wolf had turned on Solveig in an unprecedented outpouring of recriminations. All the pent-up frustration of the last few months had come bursting out of him, along with some criticism she probably didn't deserve.

The people in the street had surrounded them, not trying to hide their curiosity. His wife had recoiled, both in fright and the shame of having such a private argument in the middle of the village. The sight of her discomfort had brought some sense back into him. What had been wrong with him? He'd ordered her not to be afraid of him while acting like a maniac. No wonder she'd cowered, for once she'd had every reason to!

After leaving her at the door of their hut, Wolf had gone into the forest, intent on sleeping off his anger and frustration alone. Once he had gone back to the village, he had calmed down and was ready to apologize to Solveig for his unwarranted outburst.

But he had never been able to make amends.

Solveig had died because of him, because he had not been able to control his temper, there was no point pretending other-wise. The fact that he had lost his head in such public a place had allowed his unknown enemy to strike. After such a shocking display, no one had even blinked at the suggestion that he had strangled her in a fit of anger and he had been sentenced to exile.

He sat on the bench and placed his head in his hands.

Solveig's death was a burden he would carry until his dying day. And now he had frightened yet another woman he cared about, a woman he had just married, a woman who would surely turn away from him after today. Hadn't Merewen already threatened to leave? What if, in the light of what had just happened, she decided to put her threat into action? He could not very well tie her to the hook by the door to stop her from coming and going, could he?

She was his wife, not his slave!

"Wolf! They have finally found Magnus!" someone called from the other side of the hut. "He's in a bad way. You have to come!"

He swore under his breath. Not now! For once he would have liked someone else to attend to the villagers' needs. He would have liked to stay and mend whatever had been broken between him and Merewen before it was cracked beyond repair. But perhaps it would do him good to walk away and calm down before he faced her again. When he came back he would be calmer and he would be able to explain to her what had happened without snarling or pinning her to the wall.

He found her at the fire pit, stirring a pot of broth. Even if she did not look up at his entrance, the sight reassured him. She would not be thinking of cooking if she was paralyzed with fear.

"The villagers need me. I will be back shortly," he said, hoping that this would be the case.

Merewen nodded, looking at the spoon in her hand instead of him.

"Perhaps it's for the best," she said slowly. "I need to think. I need time to come to terms with everything you told me, everything that happened this week."

Yes. She probably did. Still, he was loath to leave her on her own in such a moment. He needed to reassure her, not give her the opportunity to get her thoughts into a tangle or mull over how violent his reaction had been. It would lead to nothing good.

She turned her back to him, ostensibly to start cleaning the leeks. He knew she was just avoiding him. There was no use insisting.

Wolf left, unable to shake the feeling he was doing the wrong thing.

When he came back after dusk, having been detained for far longer than he wanted by a rambling Magnus, who had managed to find himself embroiled in a befuddling series of adventures, the hut was empty. Where was Merewen? Night had fallen a while ago. She should be safe inside, not wandering outside alone in the dark! Wolf slammed the door with such violence that the axe hung on the wall fell to the floor with a thud.

He should have trusted his instinct and stayed with her! He should have guessed that she would try something foolish! She'd said she wanted to think. Well, as far as he knew, thinking didn't require a person to vanish into the night! It could be done anywhere. So, had she lied, and instead left him, unable to bear the idea that she was married to a violent murderer? He'd wanted to protect her and instead he had driven her away, thereby exposing herself to danger. Did he have to make the wrong decisions all the time?

And then he saw the note.

I need time alone.

She had used a piece of coal from the fire to write the four words onto one of his tunics, for want of something better.

She needed time alone! Away from him, she meant, away from the monster who scared and killed his wives! And now that she was gone, he would never persuade her to come back, even supposing he knew where she was!

Wolf fell onto the pallet and roared. His temper had cost him a second wife, and this one had not even been married to him a day! What was wrong with him? Merewen was on her own, which was to say, in danger, and it was through his fault.

For the first time since he had been forced to leave his village, he felt as if he would never find peace ever again.

CHAPTER TEN

One look was enough for Merewen to establish that the two men were none other than Rolf and his excitable friend. She muttered a curse under her breath and tugged at her hood.

It was just her luck to find herself face to face with the two of them when she'd thought herself far enough away from the village not to be recognized. After a grueling walk, she'd slept most of the morning, hidden in the forest, and reached the town some time before dusk. Then a night in a ditch had almost put paid to her resolve to try and reach her home, for she had woken up barely able to move from the cold. Only the jeers of a group of men approaching had managed to shake her into action. It would not do to be found out alone and unprotected. She was also famished and rethinking her impulsive reaction.

For a moment, shocked by Wolf's revelation she had fled without thinking that it would take her days to reach her house, as first she'd had to establish where she was. Now she knew that she was a fair distance from it, because she'd had to retrace her steps, having unfortunately set off in the wrong direction after leaving the hut.

Alone and with no money, it would be a miracle if she arrived anywhere unscathed.

She missed, not Wolf himself, as she kept telling herself sternly, but the comfort of his home, the protection of his body, and the warmth...

The warmth of his embrace, the fire in his eyes, the heat of his kisses.

But how could she think of him without shuddering at the idea of what he may have done to his first wife? Worse, in the light of what he had revealed, she was reassessing everything he had ever said or done.

How could she believe any of it? He'd said he had not killed his wife but he had no proof of his innocence. He'd claimed not to be able to return to Iceland but for all she knew, he was about to leave and abandon her. He'd told her they were married but she had not understood a word of the ceremony performed. The man could have been saying anything and there had been no guests, no witnesses. So were they really husband and wife or had it all been just a ploy to get her into bed?

No. If Wolf had really wanted to bed her that desperately he would have gone a different way about it. There would have been no need to go through the whole charade of a fake marriage. He could simply have drawn her into his arms and kissed her doubts away. It would not have taken long for her to surrender. But he had not tried to force her hand or balked when she had asked him to wait. So this marriage might well be the genuine thing.

Still, too many things remained in the shadows and too many uncertainties played in her mind. What if he left the village which was not his own and got rid of her once he'd realized she was not the wife he had hoped for? After what had happened to her, she was prepared to believe the worst of people.

So she had to establish a few things before she could return to him, and decide if she wanted to give their marriage a chance.

First, she would have to find someone who could describe to her what a Norse wedding ceremony looked like. Was the fact that the man—she still didn't know how to call him— had tied their wrists together enough to make the marriage legal?

She also needed to put her affairs in order. She had vanished into thin air a week ago, and if she was to live in the village as Wolf's wife she needed to make provisions for her house and lands, reassure the few friends she had that she was alive and well, explain what had happened to her.

And finally, she would have to inquire about Wolf's past and assure herself he was indeed innocent. She could not remain married to a murderer. That, without a doubt, would be the most difficult of the tasks and she had no idea how she would go about establishing what had happened. But she would have to worry about that later. For now, she had to get out of sight from Rolf and his friend.

They were haggling with a merchant about a piece of cloth not far from her. She had to move for fear they would spot her. She was still convinced the argument with Wolf had been about her and she did not trust the way they looked at her every time they crossed paths.

Her nerves, already strained by all that had happened to her, abandoned her, causing her to trip and almost fall flat on her face. This was not good, she was only drawing attention to herself. The men would not fail to notice her if she walked like a drunkard. A change of plan was needed. Too weakened by the cold and the lack of food to escape, she would have to hide.

She sharply turned around and hurried into a small alley, hoping it would be enough to vanish from view. Hidden in the shadows, she watched the entrance anxiously. Had the two friends followed her? A moment later, she saw them walk past.

Lost in conversation, they carried on without even glancing her way or slowing down.

She hadn't been seen or recognized.

Her sigh of relief was cut short when an arm wrapped around her waist. Her first thought was that Wolf had come after her. That hope was shattered when a foul smell reached her nose.

Wolf smelled of leather and wood, not manure.

"Let me go," she instantly cried out. Although panic lent her some strength, it wasn't enough to disentangle herself from the man's hold. "I have to—"

"What's the hurry, my beauty?" the man wheezed in her ear. "Why don't you stay a while, keep me warm?"

A moment later, she was flung to the floor.

"Wolf, your wife."

For the first time in his life, Wolf felt like the animal he had been nicknamed after. As he rushed to Sigurd or, more precisely to the woman he was holding in his arms, he barely repressed the need to howl in fury.

White-hot rage flooding his every pore, he took a limp Merewen from his friend's arms.

"What happened? Where did you find her? Was she..."

He deposited her gently onto the pallet. One look at her was enough to make his heart stop. Her clothes were torn, her cheek was bruised, her lip was cut.

"I think not," Sigurd said slowly, answering his most pressing question first. "As I walked into town, I chanced upon her. Her screams alerted me. I ran to her aid and only recognized her afterward." Though they were alone, he lowered his voice. "The man on top of her seemed more enraged than anything else. I suspect she fought him all the way. He was bleeding even before I got to him."

"Yes, she would have fought him. She is a feisty little thing, but no match for a bastard determined to have her." Wolf's chest constricted at the thought of the dangers she would have faced on her own. "Why is she unconscious?"

"By the time I had prized the man off her she had fallen into a swoon. I guess that once she realized she was not alone, it all became too much for her to deal with and her body just collapsed. She probably has no idea who came to her aid."

"It should have been me." Wolf gently brushed away a strand of hair from Merewen's brow. The sight of her bruised face made him clench his jaw so hard he feared he would crack his teeth. "Did you get a good look at the bastard? I will need to find him."

Sigurd gave a sigh. "He was not someone I know, and he took advantage of the fact that I was attending to her to escape. I'm sorry."

"Don't be sorry. You did well. Your priority was making sure Merewen was all right. I will never be able to repay you for finding her."

He stroked her cheek, wishing he could erase the traces of her ordeal. For the first time, he understood the reaction of the young men whose beloveds had been assaulted. He had helped many such women in the past two years and it had always seemed to him that the men's gratitude toward him was excessive. After all, he had done nothing any man of honor would not do by rescuing the poor women. But now he knew how it felt like to owe to someone else the return of what you held most precious on earth and, indeed, nothing he could do would ever convey his gratitude toward Sigurd.

"Do you know..." he heard his friend say behind him. "When you told me you'd married her the other day, for some reason I had difficulty believing you. I didn't think you would ever remarry after Solveig."

Wolf didn't take his eyes away from Merewen.

"No. Neither did I."

And it was clear he shouldn't have. He didn't deserve a wife if he was unable to defend her from assault. Some protector he made, not there to pummel the bastards to the ground, not even knowing where she was! Wolf gritted his teeth. To know that Merewen had placed herself in danger just to escape him was unbearable, yet another burden he would have to bear. Would he forever be responsible for his wives' misfortunes? He could defend anyone, come to everyone's help, and yet all he could do with the people he had vowed to protect was to stand by and watch them get hurt.

Merewen had been attacked. She could have been raped, mayhap killed, and all because she had preferred to take her chances in the unknown than stay with him.

It was sobering a thought. Had their marriage been a mistake? Had he overreached himself?

Silence stretched in the room.

"Well, I suppose once you meet the perfect woman, all your resolutions fly out of the window," Sigurd commented.

"The perfect woman!" Wolf scoffed, shaking his head. "She is pricklier than a hedgehog and more contrary than a mule!"

His friend was not in the least impressed. "Takes one to know one is all I'm going to say. And you wouldn't want her if she were any different, so stop making it sound as if it were a problem."

"It's not a problem," he agreed ruefully, a smile curling the edge of his lip. Indeed he liked her just the way she was. "You will never guess what she had the gall to tell me the day after we arrived in the village."

Sigurd grinned back. "Whatever it was, you clearly enjoyed hearing it. I know that look."

"Oh, I did enjoy it, but you might not." Wolf gave a small laugh. "She said that I was not married yet because I preferred to bed men and you, my friend, were suggested as one of my lovers."

A grunt answered him. "Well. I hope you denied that most forcefully!"

"Calm down, she knows full well we never shared a bed. She was only trying to rile me."

"And apparently she failed."

"Spectacularly. It only made me more determined to have her."

Just as he said the words, Merewen gave a groan, as if she was waking up. Wolf cupped her cheek, relief flooding through him. She gave a little sigh and rubbed into his palm, soft and trusting as a kitten. He wanted to wrap her in his arms.

"Wolf?" she murmured.

His heart tripped. In her torment she was calling out to him. Perhaps all was not lost, perhaps during her time alone, she had concluded she wanted to give this marriage a try?

"I'm here, it's all right," he murmured so low that only she could hear him. "I won't let anyone else touch you."

"How did you find me?"

She didn't sound as bewildered as she might have to be back at the hut, as if she had known all along he would come to her. He wasn't quite sure what to make of this proof of trust he knew he did not deserve.

"I did not find you. My friend Sigurd did," he said, feeling more dejected than ever. He was her husband. He should have been the one helping her, the one protecting her. He had promised to do so and she had accepted to marry him precisely for that reason.

And then, less than two days later he had failed her!

"Mmm," she said, and for the first time since they had met, he had no idea what she meant.

"I will leave you two alone now she's awake," he heard Sigurd say.

Wolf nodded, not taking his eyes from Merewen. "Thanks again, my friend."

"No problem. Take care of your little wife."

IN THE NIGHT, Merewen woke up and found Wolf by her side, looking at her, his eyes two glowing gems in the moonlight. Not knowing what to say or how to act, she pretended she had not seen him and closed her eyes again. A moment later, his warm hand stroked her cheek and neck. She almost groaned out loud at the pleasure the contact gave her. Either he had seen she was awake and he wanted to reassure her or he could not stop himself from touching her. It mattered not. She allowed the comfort of his caresses to lull her back to sleep.

When she next woke up, it was still dark, and Wolf had not moved. She had no idea how much time had elapsed. Keeping her eyes on the door, she spoke slowly.

"I was not fleeing you, you know, not exactly." It seemed important to let him know that. "I only... I needed time to think."

"Yes." He sounded uncharacteristically tense. "You needed time away from me because you could not bear being my wife after what you found out, after the way I pounced on you. It was unforgivable. You are afraid of me now, and although I understand why, it gores me."

"I'm not afraid of you," she breathed, then bit her lip when he glared at her. She had scuttled away to the far end of the hut and then he had jumped on her. It would be hard to make him believe she had not been afraid of him *then,* at least. And perhaps for a fleeting moment, she had been. But she regretted it now. "I'll admit I reacted badly when you told me about your wife, but I was more confused than anything else."

"I pinned you to the wall and snarled at you," he reminded her, as if he would not have her exonerate him of all blame when he knew himself to be in the wrong. "It must have scared you."

"It was not just you," she said in a small voice. "But everything had spiraled out of control. First I lost my brother, the person I loved most in the world. I had spent years attending to him and after the death of my father we clung to each other. He was the only family I had. Before I had time to absorb the pain and shock of his death I was abducted, sold like an animal by an enemy I didn't even know I had, bought and brought to a place I don't know. Then I was married to a man I don't really know and was told he had been accused of killing his wife."

Wolf had never felt more like an executioner.

"I know... I'm sorry. I hadn't realized how hard all this would have been on you." To his shame, he had forgotten about the death of her brother. But indeed, being abducted in the middle of a loved one's funeral to be sold at a slave market would unsettle the most steadfast of people. "I only knew that you were safe with me, that I could be a good husband to you but of course you have no reason to believe me, or even if you do," he added quickly when he saw she was about to protest, "it doesn't mean that you want to be married to me. And then I frightened you. I would say you had every reason to flee."

He sighed and ran a hand through his hair. What a mess he had made of things!

"I did not flee," she repeated. "I always intended to come back."

Well. That was something, he supposed. As to whether he deserved this generosity, he wasn't sure. And before they could put all this behind them, he still had the unpleasant task of telling her what had happened to Solveig. Would he manage to convince her of his innocence, or would he turn her irremediably against him by talking about it? In any case, he had no choice. If he did not address the problem, she would never be able to trust him.

"Before we can move on, you need to hear what happened to my wife," he said with a sigh.

Merewen hesitated then nodded. "Yes, I do."

She wanted to believe that Wolf was innocent, might already believe it deep down. He had admitted to being accused of killing his wife when he could have made up an excuse for his presence in East Anglia... This fact alone pleaded in his favor. Honesty and courage were not qualities she associated with murderers. But he was right, she did need to hear the whole story.

He looked straight at her before he started to talk.

"I was married to Solveig for two years. We were happy enough, which did not mean there weren't issues, mainly on my side. One day we had a heated argument. I was so furious she would not confirm that she might be with child that I forgot where we were and upbraided her in front of everyone. When I realized we were in the middle of the village I took her back to our hut then left to spend the night in the forest to cool down," he explained, his voice terse, his eyes aglow. "In the morning I found Solveig dead. She had been strangled and..."

"And everyone just assumed that you had been the one to do it," she finished when he remained silent. How could it be any different? She had been found in their home, he had told no one he would be sleeping in the forest, and they had just had an argument. He would have appeared like the perfect culprit.

Wolf nodded, confirming her assumption.

"After the scene on the street it was all too easy to make it appear as if I had strangled her in a fit of rage. Having a physique like mine makes people prone to believe the worst of me, or at least imagine I have a violent nature. I don't think it will surprise you to hear it." He shook his head like a man who'd had to hear the same nonsense all his life but could not bear for her to adhere to it. "When Ingólfur clamored that I had to be judged for the crime, half the village testified that they had seen me shout at Solveig the very night of the murder. It did not appear good."

"Had you manhandled her?"

Wolf's eyes flashed and this alone answered her question. That she thought him capable of such an act seemed to send him in a flurry of rage and besides, her every instinct told her that this man would never pose any threat to a woman. Had he not reined in his temper with her the other day when he had pressed her against the wall, preferring to leave before he could snap and truly hurt her?

"No, I did not manhandle her, that day or ever. I might have grabbed her elbow to hurry her along, eager to bring the argument to an end. I don't know. But I would never have done more than that, hit her or even simply pretend to. I am not a violent man." He lifted eyes dark with anguish to her. "I realize that you have no reason to believe me, but I am truly not. I would never hit a woman, and Solveig was my wife. I loved her. I would have hurt her even less. For all that, I am not completely innocent. My loss of control did cost her her life. That is something I will have to live with for the rest or my days."

They stared at each other a long moment. Merewen could hardly believe she had ever entertained the notion that he might have actually done what he was accused of.

"I believe you," she said eventually. "If you were a violent man I would have found myself at the receiving end of your blows more than once, never more so than the other day, when I all but accused you of murdering your wife."

"I'm truly sorry about the way I pounced on you but I could not bear for you to—"

"I understand."

To Wolf's surprise, Merewen gave him a tentative smile and he understood that not only did she believe his story but she had forgiven him for his outburst. The tightness in his chest eased. Perhaps she would stay and give him a chance, perhaps during her time alone she had decided to accept their union.

He was humbled that she would even want to try after all that had happened.

"You truly are a remarkable woman."

"I don't know about that," she murmured, flushing a delicious pink.

"Well, I do."

When he stood up, he had the pleasure of not seeing her recoil. He towered over her and he found himself wishing he was not so tall and imposing, not such of a menace despite himself. Then Merewen flushed further and he understood that, far from frightening her, his power appealed to her. She didn't even seem fully conscious of it, her response was the instinctive response of a woman in front of a man she desired; it had nothing to with reason. It was purely physical, but it was yet another step in the right direction, yet another encouraging sign indicating they might be able to get along fine as husband and wife.

Once he'd bedded her and shown her how good it could be between them, she would surely see him in an even more favorable light.

The only problem was, it might take her a long moment to welcome him in bed.

"I'm sorry for Solveig and for you. Neither of you deserved what you got," she said slowly. "How long do you have to remain in exile?"

He could tell she had an ulterior motive for asking the question. She wanted to know if he intended to take her away to a remote, icy land. His little wife did not like the cold, he'd already had the chance to see. Or she might fear he would abandon her here if he left. He could reassure her on both accounts.

"I might be able to go back one day but only when my name is cleared. If I go back before that, then my life will be forfeit. Everyone will have the right to kill me and they will not face retribution for it."

"Kill you?" She shivered. "But how would they even know who you were? Perhaps in another part of the country you could rebuild a new life, away from the people who wish you harm?"

He gave a slanted smile. "Perhaps, but I'm sure you'll understand if I tell you I'd rather not risk it. My country is not so big and I am not exactly the most inconspicuous of men. Besides, I am not ashamed of who I am. Why should I hide when I know I haven't done anything wrong?"

"No, of course..." She seemed impressed by this argument and in that moment he understood that she truly believed him. "You don't want to behave like a criminal because you're not one. I understand. I'm sorry I even entertained the possibility."

"But you still have questions," he said slowly, picking up on her hesitation.

She nodded slowly. "You never said why you chose me to be your wife. I need to understand."

Wolf sighed again. This was fair, but how could he explain something he did not understand himself? He felt in his bones that Merewen was the woman for him, but he could not pretend to know why.

Still, he owed it to her to at least try to make her understand why she was the first woman to make him feel as if a future were possible, to make him even consider the idea of another marriage when he had been so convinced he never wanted to be married again.

The problem was, all his reasons would seem shallow, odd, or downright insulting.

He could not admit that he liked her defiance because it would protect him against boredom. She would surely not know what to make of that comment. He could not tell her that he burned with desire for her. No woman wanted to hear that she was nothing more than a way to slake a man's lust. He could not lie and say he loved her, for he knew that wasn't the case. People did not fall in love in so short a time.

So what could he say?

"It is hard to explain. All I know is that with you I felt I could reconciliate myself with the idea of having a wife."

She frowned. "But why would you need to do that? You are not some great lord obliged to carry on the family line. Your life is your own. If you cannot reconcile yourself with the idea of marrying again then you don't have to. It is not such a problem. Many people remain unmarried."

"I know. But I do need a wife, because... I want children," he answered in a low voice. It was the first time he had admitted as much to anyone, and it felt odd, but liberating at the same time. He only hoped it did not sound as if he was trying to pressure her into agreeing to fulfill her marital duty. "Children I can acknowledge and raise, who will live under my roof, who will know and love me as their father. A woman can become a mother without marrying, if she wishes, but a man cannot."

Merewen's heart almost stopped at the emotion in Wolf's voice. In the end it was such a simple explanation.

He wanted to be a father.

It was both the most touching reason he could have given her and the worst, because, if it explained why he needed a wife, it did not tell her why he wanted *her* to be that wife.

If children were all he wanted, then one fertile woman was much the same as another.

"I see," she said, unable to quite hide her disappointment. She was in no way special. He wanted her for the children she could carry, nothing more. Well, what had she expected? That he would fall to his knees and declare his undying love for her?

Her heart plummeted.

Yes, she had hoped he would do something like that, which made her a fool three times over.

"I know what you're thinking," he said softly.

Oh, no. Merewen groaned inwardly. Could this get any worse?

"What is that?" she managed to say. Please let him be wrong, please let him be ignorant of the depth of her feelings toward him, of how much she wanted this marriage to be a true marriage...

"You are thinking I haven't answered your question. You did not ask me why I wanted to marry, but why I wanted to marry *you*."

Well, yes, she had, and she dearly wanted to know the answer to that question, now more than ever. Silence stretched in the hut, then the fire gave a loud pop, bursting through the tension.

"So what is your answer?" Merewen asked, unable to wait another moment.

Wolf rubbed his chin. "If all I wanted were legitimate children then I would have proposed to the first healthy woman I met," he said, boring a hole in her skull with the intensity of his gaze. "But I did not. I do want children but my need to find a woman I actually want to live with outweighs my desire to become a father. I want a family, but not at the cost of my sanity. With you I feel I could have both. Children to love and a wife to cherish. "

A tear rolled down her cheek before Merewen even realized that she was crying. This was not quite the declaration of love she had dreamed of, but certainly more than she could have hoped for in the circumstances, and probably more than many a woman trapped in a marriage of convenience had heard.

She stared at Wolf with undisguised longing and gratitude. The darkness helped, shrouding everything in shadows, softening the intensity of his gaze and hiding the color on her cheeks. She wasn't sure she would have been brave enough to have such an intimate conversation in broad daylight.

Silence descended once more into the hut. Through the window, the sky had gone a shade paler. Dawn was not far, and Merewen suddenly realized that she needed to relieve herself.

"I-I'm afraid I need a moment alone," she said, blushing. What a pathetic thing to say after the moment they had shared!

Wolf never even blinked. "Of course. Let me help you up."

She accepted the hand he was holding out and winced when all the muscles in her body protested as one. It felt as if she had been trampled on by a wild horse during the night.

Wolf barely restrained a growl when he saw the state of Merewen's gown. The front had been ripped open by her attacker and the back torn to shreds by the stony floor where he had pinned her. It was caked in dried mud and traces of blood darkened the russet wool. If the dress was damaged thus, he did not want to imagine what her body would look like underneath.

"I will need to wash your back," he told her once she came back into the hut. "I let you sleep yesterday because you needed rest but we cannot delay any longer." The last thing he wanted was for infection to set in.

"I don't..." She hesitated.

"Fret not. I won't see anything you don't want me to see," he swore. "You once checked my back for splinters. I will check yours for gravel and dirt, that is all. I will go outside while you get undressed. Then lie on your stomach, cover yourself up and call me when you're ready."

He left before she could agree or disagree, trusting her to reach the right decision. Merewen was not stupid. It wouldn't take her long to see that it would be silly to refuse his help. Indeed, a moment later, he heard her call out.

"I'm ready."

He walked in.

CHAPTER ELEVEN

Wolf found Merewen almost buried under the covers.

Clenching his jaw, he went to put a pot of water to boil. He did not fear being overwhelmed by desire for her when attending to the injuries she had sustained during an attack, even if she was all but naked, but seeing the proof of the viciousness of the man was sure to send him into a blinding rage and he did not want to frighten her or add to her distress by glowering like a madman. Mercifully, as she had her back to him she would not see the traces on his fury on his face.

"Can I start now?" he asked once the water had reached a pleasant temperature.

"Yes." He took a clean piece of cloth, the pliers she had used on him the other day and placed them next to the pallet, feeling oddly intimidated. Though he had touched her much more intimately once before, it felt different, much more significant. She had been little more than a stranger back then, if a very alluring one. Now she was Merewen, the woman he had married and toward whom he had come to feel... He shook his head.

What had he come to feel toward her exactly? He had just

told her that in her he hoped to find a wife to cherish but that still did not mean much.

It was not the moment to start pondering on such important questions, however, right now she was waiting for him to tend to her injuries.

"Can I uncover you?"

His voice was hoarse, his hands trembled like those of an untried youth about to see his first conquest naked. He could not remember being half as nervous then or even since, with any of the women he had bedded. He had to master himself before Merewen started to wonder what was wrong with him.

When she nodded her agreement, he peeled the covers to reveal her back. Just as he had feared, it was streaked with blood, peppered with small pebbles embedded into her skin. Anger blazed through him and he let out a small grunt.

"Is it that bad?" she asked in a voice that tugged at his heart. He hadn't meant to worry her.

"I will clean it," he said instead of answering. Yes, it was that bad, to him at least. A single scratch, a single drop of blood would have been one too many for him to accept. No woman deserved to be treated thus, and a woman under his protection should have been safe from harm.

Dipping the cloth in the warm water, he started to wash the dirt and blood away so he could see just how many stones he would have to extract from her flesh. He forced himself to ignore how shapely her body was, with its narrow waist and flaring hips ready for a man's hand, how smooth and creamy her skin appeared to be under the grime but he could not quite do it. It was as impossible as finding oneself outside at dawn and not marveling at the beauty of the rising sun.

Despite his best intentions, Wolf's groin tightened further with each passing moment. Never had he seen anything as sensual as the curve of Merewen's spine. As to the beauty spot on the swell of her right buttock, it had undoubtedly been placed there by the gods with the express purpose of sending him mad with longing. The thought crossed his mind that he might well be the first man to see it, or even the first person. He was not sure Merewen herself knew she was graced with such an erotic mark.

What would he not give to be allowed to kiss it night after night as they lay in bed, naked and sated from passionate lovemaking...

Well, so much for not getting aroused, he thought ruefully.

Slowly, he brushed the cloth over her back, careful not to catch the biggest scratches as he did so. Little by little all the blood was wiped away.

Merewen lay still as a statue while Wolf washed her, remembering how arousing she had found it to tend to his injuries the other day. Dare she hope that he was finding it as arousing as she had found it to see and touch her naked back? But, of course, he would not. Her skin was not burnished bronze like his, there were no muscles under it making it ripple and after her ordeal she probably smelled worse than a farm animal.

Still, he was stroking her so gently that she could almost forget about it all and feel precious.

"It's clean now. Was it not too painful?" he asked slowly.

"No." Merewen could tell how careful he was being and she relished his caresses. If only she could remain here forever, being tended to by a man who treated her as if she was the most beautiful thing he had ever seen!

"I'm afraid you will end up being just as bruised as I am," he murmured, his voice hoarse.

"It's all right," she answered. "I can live with a few bruises."

But I'm not sure how I can handle the memory of a man forcing himself on me.

A knock on the door prevented her from saying this out loud. Through the wood came a sentence, spoken in Norse.

"Can I let Sigurd in?" Wolf asked, covering her back. "He has brought you a potion from old Helga, the village healer. I asked her to prepare it for you, to help with the pain."

Though in truth, she was not in any real pain, Merewen nodded, touched that he would have gone to so much trouble for her. "Let him in."

A moment later, Sigurd walked in, carrying a vial. He avoided looking at her, she noticed, as if he didn't want to make her uncomfortable while she was in bed. Wolf took the potion from his friend and poured some of it into a cup he handed out to her.

"Thank you," she said, accepting it.

While she sipped the drink, the two men started talking together in hushed tones. Merewen assumed they were discussing the attack and she was grateful for their discretion because she did not wish to hear anything about the man who had pounced on her. After a moment she stopped trying to hear her name and just closed her eyes, feeling both refreshed by Wolf's cleaning and soothed by the woman's potion. The raspy, slightly rugged sounds of the foreign language washed over her, lulling her into sleep.

As he talked, Wolf looked at Merewen. She had gone utterly still. Had she fallen asleep? Her hair was fanned over her shoulders in a river of flaming copper. He ached to sink his fingers into it, and feel it flow like water under his touch. He could not detach his eyes from her, imagining the shapely back, the sensual hips and that damn beauty spot! Could Sigurd tell she was naked under the furs? Probably. One of her shoulders was peeking from under the covers, clear proof that she was not wearing anything.

"Thank you for the potion," he told his friend, as an unexpected pang of jealousy invaded him. He didn't want anyone to see or even imagine his wife naked. She was his, and his alone. "You can leave now."

Sigurd cocked his head at the sharp command but left without a word. Once he was gone, Wolf leaned in to speak into Merewen's ear.

"Sleep, little one," he murmured, not knowing whether she was awake or not.

"Am I so little?" was her somewhat slurred answer.

"You are to me."

"That's only because you are such a big brute of a man."

"Is that so?" A smile threatened to break through.

"Yes. A big, hulking brute. Don't tell me you hadn't noticed!"

He understood that old Helga would have put some herbs in the drink to calm Merewen's anxiety as well as her pain and send her to sleep. Would she have called him a big hulking brute otherwise? Mayhap. His wife was not exactly the shy sort, after all. The smile he had been fighting bloomed on his lips.

She had never sounded so calm and happy before, so at ease with him. It was wonderful.

"What else am I? Please tell me." He was not going to let this opportunity pass.

She sighed. "Many things. Too many things, and not all of them bad, unfortunately."

This time Wolf chuckled outright. "You can't know how flattered I am to hear this."

"And I like the way you laugh. You sound like a little boy."

"A little boy? You just told me I was a big brute."

"Well... Maybe not so big, and definitely not a brute," she mumbled. "I feel sleepy."

"Then go to sleep, there is nothing better for you to do," he answered, before doing what he had been itching to do all along.

He buried his fingers into her glorious hair and heard her sigh of contentment when he started to massage her scalp. So soft... "Sleep, little one," he repeated, enjoying the intimacy of having a special name for her and being allowed to murmur into her ear while stroking her hair. "I'm here. You're safe."

As he watched her sleep, something swelled within him. Once again he was kneeling down next to her while she was barely conscious, like that night in the pig sty. What if she started to stroke herself in her sleep? Would he resist the temptation of taking her?

Then she placed a balled fist next to her face and he had his answer. Yes, he would be able to resist, because everything had changed between them.

That night, lust had blazed through him.

But now he was overcome by something else, something altogether deeper, something he was afraid to identify. So many things had changed since that night. They were married and he was desperate to make Merewen see they could have a satisfying marriage. He needed to earn her trust, now more than ever. He had promised to wait until he bedded her and he would keep his word, however much it cost him.

The only thing he would do if she started to pleasure herself was make sure she got as much satisfaction as she could get before wrapping her into his arms and watching her sleep.

CHAPTER TWELVE

"Wait right here, I'll go and get Wolf," Sigurd said, opening the door to allow a woman into the hut. He nodded toward Merewen as if he trusted her to look after the guest. Before she could ask him anything, the door closed again.

After a long, restorative sleep, she had woken up alone, and wondered for a moment if she had not dreamt the whole intimate scene. Had Wolf really all but declared his feelings for her and then tended to her injuries as tenderly as a mother would? Had he really lingered over the cleaning as sensually as a lover would? Had he really called her 'little one'—and had she accused him of being a big brute?

Yes...

It had all been too real. All too wonderful.

She forced herself to come back to the present and her mysterious guest.

"I'm sorry for intruding..." the girl started, nodding toward the pot of water and piece of cloth on the table, evidently thinking she had interrupted her wash. Wolf had provided her with everything she needed for when she woke up and even replaced the ruined dress with a new one. Without checking, Merewen knew it would smell as fresh as a meadow, nothing like the one he had found for her the day he had bought her.

"You are not intruding," she answered, going crimson. That all seemed such a long time ago now...

Not quite knowing what to say, the two women looked at each other in mutual curiosity. The girl was small and blond, with a delicate heart-shaped face, and lovely brown eyes. At the moment she appeared ill at ease but it seemed to Merewen that in normal circumstances she would be more prone to smiling than scowling. What was making her so nervous?

"No need to ask you why you're here," the girl said in a low whisper.

With a pang of dismay, Merewen understood why the girl was so uncomfortable. She thought herself in the presence of a fellow Saxon who had been purchased like an animal and used as a slave, and didn't know how to act. In her grimy, disheveled state, with her lip cut and her face bruised, Merewen knew she would be the very image of the oppressed, ill-treated female.

In other words, the exact opposite of what she was.

"I-I am not Wolf's slave, rather his..." she stammered, not quite able to introduce herself as his wife, even to a stranger .

"Oh, you don't need to tell me you are not his slave!" the girl answered as if the mere idea of Wolf owning a slave was too ridiculous to even entertain. "And whoever did that to you, you can be sure that he will make them pay for it. He... did the same for me."

She lowered her eyes and wrung her hands. Merewen's heart constricted when she finally understood the cause of the girl's nervousness. She too had been attacked and was finding it hard to have people know it.

"But I thought..." She frowned. The woman looked and

sounded distinctively Saxon. "I had assumed he only helped his kinsmen. You are a Saxon, are you not?"

"It makes no difference what I am. He helps whoever needs him. He walked in on one of the men from the village forcing himself on me. Although the man was someone he knew and perhaps even liked, he didn't hesitate and beat him to a pulp for what he did to me." She shook her head as if to chase the dreadful memory away. "I came here today to thank him again and tell him... that is... He'd asked me to inform him whether I had fallen with child so I came to tell him that thankfully no, I had not. My courses have returned, you see, and... well, I—"

Merewen cut the girl's embarrassed explanations short by taking her hand. "I understand," she said, giving it a squeeze.

So Wolf had taken a Saxon's defense against one of his people. He had sided with an unknown woman rather than with a man who might have called himself his friend... He had even bothered to enquire about her future when she knew how adverse men were to discussing women's troubles. This kind, thoughtful, protective man who wanted a family and a wife to cherish was married to her.

And as soon as he had made her his wife, she had left, making him think he scared her and she wouldn't come back.

Something snapped inside of Merewen. She had fought the notion that Wolf was a man she wanted for so long that something had to give.

She broke down into a sob.

The girl instantly wrapped her arms around her. "It's all right," she soothed. "It's over. You are safe now."

She nodded, unable to talk. Yes, she was safe. And it was time she stopped hiding from what she felt, accepted the situation she was in and started to ask herself the right questions instead of living her life according to other people's dictates and her own unrealistic expectations.

So what if Wolf had bought her and not met her in a meadow on a sunny spring day? It did not change the fact that he wanted her. What if he had not wooed her before asking to marry her? It did not mean he would not be a good husband to her, attentive and thoughtful. What if she harbored unholy, carnal feelings toward him? It did not make her appreciate his other qualities less, or unworthy of his respect.

She would never find another man who appealed to her more, who accepted her with her faults so easily, who could make her happier than she had ever hoped to be.

Merewen mentally kicked herself in the backside. Yes. It was high time she stopped dreaming of a perfect life and started living the one she had instead.

Moments later, she watched as the girl threw herself into Wolf's arms. He rubbed her back gently, the gesture comforting, almost paternal, as he told her his relief that she would not have to give birth to her aggressor's child.

Wishing to give them some privacy, she exited the hut quietly, taking the new dress with her. She would go to the river and bathe, a thorough cleansing to clear her mind and rid her body from the last traces of the man's smell.

Once she had rubbed her skin until it hurt, Merewen sat on a log and thought hard.

"I'm cold. I'm frightened."

Swallowing her pride and doubts, Merewen crept to Wolf's pallet on the other side of the hut. She had woken up in the middle of the night, and after all the rest she'd had in the last two days, had found it impossible to go back to sleep. For a while she had lain there, shivering and reliving the nightmare she had endured at the man's hands.

And so she had gone to the one man who could make her feel warm and safe.

Her husband.

In the darkness she could not make out his reaction but before she had time to wonder what he would make of her plea, an arm wrapped around her waist and he drew her to his side.

"Come here, then. You'll be warm with me, and safe."

She nestled against his body and gave a sigh of contentment.

"Are you never cold?" she marveled, feeling his chest warm under a simple tunic.

A low chuckle answered her question. "Of course, I am, but not when there isn't even enough ice to freeze the mud in puddles."

"I suppose it gets colder in Iceland," she mused.

"Far colder," he agreed in a hoarse voice.

It did not take Merewen long to wonder whether she had made the right decision by going to Wolf's pallet. True, she wasn't cold or afraid anymore, but she was getting increasingly, unbearably aroused in his arms. Her imagination started to run in all sorts of licentious directions. She wanted him, and she had concluded earlier that it was time she accepted that fact and consummated their marriage, even if it meant risking revealing her true nature to him. Could she do it now?

Only a few days ago she had told him she was afraid of being bedded and would rather wait until they knew each other better. What would he make of her sudden change of heart?

She was already in his arms, pressed hard against him. Could she start to stroke him? Mayhap if she did he would understand what she wanted without her actually having to speak the shameful words?

No.

She guessed that Wolf would never touch her while she was recovering from an attack and, as he still thought she was afraid of being taken, he would never make the first move. It would be down to her to initiate their lovemaking. But before she did that she would have to clarify a few things. Tell him that she wasn't afraid, even if she was a virgin, assure him that she had not been raped and make him understand she didn't want him just for his body, even if she did harbor shameful, lustful desires.

She balled her hands into fists to resist temptation and willed herself to be calm. He was probably half asleep already. Making love would have to wait.

Wolf wondered how long he would be able to resist until he rolled Merewen under him and positioned himself between her thighs to beg for her agreement to finally make love to her. Every muscle in his body was taut as a bow string and his manhood was so hard he knew it would never soften of its own accord. Either he did what he ached to do, plunge inside Merewen's softness, or he would have to bring about his own release once she was safely asleep. He knew which one he preferred to do and only the knowledge that her back was raw gave him the strength to stay still.

He stared at the ceiling, doing his best to convince himself that waiting was the most sensible course of action.

Merewen had come to him in search of warmth and comfort, nothing more. She didn't want or need him to start acting like a lust-filled beast. She had been brutally assaulted only two days ago. Sigurd had told him the man had not had time to actually possess her but he could not be sure it was the case, and even if it had not, she had been frightened enough to swoon. Right now lovemaking was probably the furthest thing from her mind. There was nothing for it, he would have to wait.

Little by little, he felt her body relax against him, while his remained as hard as wood.

CHAPTER THIRTEEN

The bed was empty and Wolf was nowhere to be seen.

Merewen stretched. To her surprise, she had fallen asleep mere moments after joining him on the pallet last night. In the end, comfort had won over desire. It had felt so good to be in his arms, to be so warm, to know no one could get to her.

She looked around. The sun was already high in the sky and she could hear the villagers going about their business outside. It would be mid-morning at least. No wonder Wolf was already gone. On the table she saw three reasonably-sized logs and smiled. As usual he had seen to her needs.

Just as she was throwing the wood into the fire, the door opened. Without turning around Merewen knew it wasn't Wolf and her body immediately tensed.

"I'm glad to see you up and about," a voice said, cutting through the tension. Relieved, she turned to face a smiling Sigurd. He was limping slightly, she noticed. Had he been hurt during his fight with her attacker? She didn't dare ask.

"Thank you. So am I."

She purposefully allowed a strand of hair to fall over her

temple and cheek, hoping to hide her bruises from view. Something passed in Sigurd's blue eyes, something she had seen in Wolf's eyes, too. He did not seem to think any less of her for not having been able to defend herself, or even to pity her. Rather, he seemed full of admiration for her fortitude. Comforted, she lifted her chin and met his gaze square on. After all, she had nothing to be ashamed of.

"I never got the chance to thank you for coming to my rescue the other day."

"Please. What else did you want me to do?" Sigurd shook his head. "I only wish I had not let the bastard escape."

"It matters not. You stopped him before he had time to..." Her voice wavered. "It's the important thing."

"Mm." The grunt made it clear Sigurd didn't agree with her but he did not comment. For all his smiles, he seemed more intense than Wolf.

"I was in that alley because Wolf and I had an argument on the day of our wedding and I left," she blurted out, surprised by the urge to confide in him.

The expression on his face was unreadable. Then he gave a sigh. "I know all about the circumstances of your meeting and can easily guess what your argument was about. You must resent me for bringing you back here, if you were attempting to flee this marriage, but I thought I was acting for the best." He made a grimace.

She hastily corrected his mistake. He'd done exactly what she would have asked him to do had she been conscious at the time.

"No, I'm grateful you did." She touched her lip gingerly. It was still tender and all of a sudden she felt absurdly close to tears. If Sigurd hadn't gone to town that day, if he had not heard her, if he had been less strong and honorable, she would have been raped, perhaps even killed afterwards. And all because, for a moment, she had doubted Wolf. "I wasn't fleeing my marriage... In any case, I was punished for my folly. If I had not—"

"No." The word was said with implacable certainty. "That man had no right to attack you, regardless of who you were or the reasons for your presence in town. Do not even think of blaming yourself for what happened. I will not hear of it. Do you think Frigyth is to blame in any way for what happened to her?"

Frigyth. The Saxon Wolf had rescued. "No, of course not!" she cried out.

"Well, then, neither are you. The only one who deserved what he got is that bastard Olaf. I'm not sure he will ever be able to walk properly after the pounding he received from Wolf, but I still think he got away too lightly." A flash of fury made his eyes glint. Yes. Definitely more intense than Wolf. Was Olaf his personal enemy, she wondered? "I only wish I had done the same for the man in the alley. I repeat, you did nothing wrong."

The words were spoken with such feeling that Merewen suddenly went limp, as if a weight had been lifted off her shoulders.

"Thank you." How had Sigurd guessed she needed to hear that?

Silence stretched between them. Then he came to face her.

"I have never seen Wolf behave as he did when I brought you in," he told her softly. "Of course, I have only known him for two years but in that length of time I have never seen him react half as strongly to anything. He was beside himself with worry and guilt. Perhaps... perhaps it is something worth thinking about."

Merewen watched Sigurd limp away pensively.

Yes. It was definitely worth thinking about...

When Wolf came back later, her whole body expanded at

the sight of him, so strong, so dependable, so willing to protect her without expecting anything in return.

"I'm sorry I took so long, but one of the men in the village is in a frenzy," he told her, taking his cloak off. "His son has been accused of molesting a Saxon girl a few nights ago. The father and his friends are now demanding retribution. It is a common problem I'm afraid." He gave a sigh. "It might even be that the girl was not attacked and the men are looking for an excuse to stir up trouble with us Norsemen. After all, why would the father wait so long to confront his daughter's supposed aggressor?"

"That's terrible!" Merewen was appalled.

"You don't know the half of it. As you can imagine, many people in East Anglia are not too happy to be living so near a Norse settlement. I had to go and see the Saxons, assure them the boy could not have committed the crime he is accused of for he was with me drinking that night."

"Why would you lie and expose yourself to danger thus?"

Wolf smiled wryly. "I'm not. In this instance I am telling the truth, though I have on occasion provided someone I trusted with an alibi. I cannot stand to have anyone accused of something they didn't do."

Of course... Merewen nodded. It wasn't hard to guess that the need to help and defend people stemmed from the accusation he had suffered from. Now she knew why he never turned anyone down, why he always responded to the many solicitations from the villagers, even when it was obvious he would rather have been doing something else. He was trying to repair the wrong caused to him by ensuring no one suffered from the same injustice. It was a noble endeavor, but she couldn't help but wonder, who took care of him?

It wasn't fair that he should be forever helping people and

have no one to value him for himself, and not for the comfort and protection he gave.

Merewen realized that she wanted to be that person. Would he let her look after him? She was his wife now. She should be the one to do it.

"What's wrong?" Wolf asked when he saw her eyes fill with tears. He was at her side instantly, his face creased in concern. "Did something happen to you while I was gone?"

"Nothing. I'm fine," she assured him. Evidently he thought she had been attacked again in his absence. This further proof of his regard warmed her to the bottom of her soul. How wonderful to be cherished, if nothing more. When Leofric had died she had feared so much never to feel she mattered to someone again!

Her whole body sagged when a wave of emotion over-whelmed her and, had two strong arms not encircled her, she might have collapsed to the floor.

"You're lying to me, little one. Something happened to you today," Wolf cried out, appalled and frightened all at once. Merewen had gone limp and pale. His heart almost stopped. Had she been attacked again? Why had he left her alone? Couldn't he have stayed with her? Nothing or no one should have taken precedence over her!

"No, nothing happened," she murmured, her voice thick with unshed tears. "I was thinking of my brother, that's all. He was the only person who loved me, who wanted me to be happy."

He placed a hand on her hair, barely resisting the impulse to stroke her. She had washed and changed into the fresh gown he had found her and, but for the purplish bruise on her cheek, was the most flawless beauty he had ever seen. He wanted to scoop her into his arms and cradle her.

"Your brother would have been proud of you for being so

strong," he whispered in her ear. "As am I. And I want you to be happy."

She burrowed further into his chest. Then she spoke, her mouth against his pectoral, causing shivers of need to course all over him.

"Can I sleep with you tonight again?"

The quiet, tentative voice, the very intimate question made his heart go faster. Pressed as she was next to him she probably felt it but he cared not. Let her know how much her proximity affected him. He was not ashamed of his feelings.

"I fear that you will have no other choice," he answered softly. "If you do not come to me, I will come to you."

Wolf smiled faintly. Why was he putting himself in such an impossible situation? Too fired up by the unexpected intimacy, he had hardly slept the previous night. Because he hadn't been sure whether she was awake or not, he had not dared stroke himself to relieve the desire boiling in his veins and simply waited, hard as a poker, with his arms wrapped tight around her.

In the end, he had collapsed out of sheer exhaustion when dawn had started to gray the horizon.

In all likelihood, it would be the same tonight. Yet if it was a choice between staying awake because Merewen's body against his was making him mad with desire or not sleeping because he ached to join her in bed, he knew which one he would choose.

"Come to me whenever you need me. I'll be there."

Could he dare to hope that once she was in his arms she would overcome her fears of lovemaking? Last night he'd briefly thought she was responding to the intimacy of their embrace. But she had fallen asleep before he could be sure.

Merewen lifted her head to him and in that moment Wolf knew she wanted to kiss him. Her tongue darted out to moisten the corner of her lips and his reaction was so strong that he could have sworn she had just licked the tip of his throbbing shaft.

A low groan of male satisfaction rumbled in his chest and his hands tightened around her waist. Surely even if she was wary of lovemaking she would not refuse to be given pleasure? He was desperate to taste her honey and at least that way he could guarantee she was not hurt. Could he offer to do that for her? Was she aware that such a thing was done? Would she not be too shocked? The last thing he wanted was upset her.

He drew away, desperate to do the right thing. "We will sleep together tonight, little one," he said, his mouth at her temple.

And he privately vowed she would not leave his pallet without having experienced the pleasure he wanted to lavish on her.

But when he released her she didn't move away. Instead she started squirming against him, letting out small sighs and moans that tested his endurance almost past what he was capable of enduring. If she carried on like this there would be no helping it, he *would* tumble her onto the furs.

"What's the matter?" he asked through clenched teeth. Did she have no idea what she was doing to him, rubbing her soft stomach against his throbbing manhood? "Are you in pain?"

It almost sounded like it.

He held her out at arms' length so he could look into her face. In the late afternoon light, she looked flustered, unsettled, almost... guilty. His heart started racing.

"What is it? he repeated, alarm replacing desire.

"It's nothing," she said, shaking her head, refusing to meet his eye.

"Don't lie. You're different all of a sudden."

Oh, if only that was the case, Merewen thought, if only her

unwomanly cravings were a new phenomenon, and not the bane of her life! But Wolf was mistaken. She wasn't different. She was being her usual wanton, sensual self. As if it weren't bad enough to dream day and night about such forbidden things, every month between her courses her craving for a man's touch grew even worse.

From the way her body had heated at his proximity, she guessed that she was now in this most propitious period and if Wolf were to touch her intimately, he would feel it.

She squeezed her thighs together, mortified.

It had been a constant struggle to hide this side of her she couldn't control from the world. Today it was a hundred times worse because she was in the arms of a man of flesh and blood, a man she craved and who craved her. Up until now her dark desires had not centered around anyone in particular. They had just been a way of escaping her dreary life and compensate for the lack of excitement in it. All that had changed from the moment she had met Wolf. Now her lustful thoughts most definitely revolved around one man, the man holding her tight against his hard body, the man who had married her and was waiting for her agreement before taking her to bed, thinking her afraid of lovemaking.

Suddenly she couldn't lie anymore, she needed to admit out loud who she was, to free herself of the burden she had been carrying for so long. Perhaps Wolf's reaction would bring some sense into her. Perhaps if he recoiled in horror it would give her the shock she needed to put it all behind her.

And if he did not shrink away, then she might finally start to accept this side of her, accept these shameful feelings, and stop living in dread of Wolf knowing the truth about the kind of woman he had married.

Right now she was positively on fire, desperate for his touch, so there would never be a better time to open up.

"There's something wrong with me," she whimpered, hoping she was not making a fatal mistake.

He stared at her, worry in his eyes. "I knew it. You were more hurt than you led me to believe the other day!"

"No, it's nothing like that." She hid her face in the crook of his neck, inhaling his delicious smell of cut wood. "But I have these desires... This need deep inside of me... They have plagued me for years."

It had been all part of the guilt she had carried. Her brother had been a sickly child from birth, whereas she had always enjoyed a robust health and a voracious appetite, in all senses of the word.

While Leofric lay on his sick bed for days on end, she roamed the land from morn till dusk, while he nibbled at his food, she devoured entire pies and gorged on desserts, while he had never even looked at any girl with interest, she was constantly allowing her eye to wander over the male guests their father received. After his death, it had all become worse. Unable to keep up with her active lifestyle, constantly at Leofric's bedside, starved of visitors, she had taken refuge in her imagination.

And it had all become too much to handle because now she wasn't content with dreaming about making love to a man anymore, she wanted to experience the real thing.

"I cannot bear it."

"Why? There's nothing wrong with having desires and needs," Wolf answered gently. Far from being horrified, he sounded almost... amused. "Look at me, Merewen," he said, lifting her chin when she wanted to disappear into the ground. "I have the same desires, the same needs. And since I met you it's been a hundred times worse. I'm hard for you, have been for days. Yet I never thought for one moment that there was anything wrong with me," he purred. "You're a beautiful woman. It is normal I should respond to you."

She wasn't appeased by this reassurance. "I suspect it is different for men. It is accepted that they would be lusty, but women are not supposed to..." She shook her head.

"Mayhap it is not discussed or even acknowledged because, unlike with men, there is not obvious physical manifestation of their inner desire, but I doubt you are the first or only woman to experience such needs. Believe me, there is nothing wrong with you. There's nothing more normal than what you are experiencing. You need a man, that's all. You want pleasure." He gave a growl that resonated all the way to her core. "Let me be that man, let me give you that pleasure. I want nothing more. If it helps to assuage your guilt, remember that we are married. No one will judge you for bedding your husband, least of all me. I'm bursting with the need to finally make you mine."

Her insides became liquid with longing. He wanted her still, he wasn't disgusted, he was even begging her to make love to him! And she had thought he would be horrified, appalled at her wantonness! She couldn't have been more wrong. Relief washed through her.

Her husband desired her.

Desperately.

"You are... bursting?" she whispered. "For me?"

"I am." He frowned, as if worried his answer would frighten her. It did not. It was the most wonderful thing she had ever heard. "But I will be gentle, I swear. I won't hurt you."

"No, I know that." Even unintentionally, even in anger, he had never caused her any pain. And now he wanted to pleasure her... That's what he'd said. He had made it sound as if this would all be for her benefit. "I am not afraid being taken, rather, I'm desperate for it."

There. It could not be clearer.

"Then please, Merewen, let me fill your body, let me be the one to give you what you crave," he murmured in her ear. "Let me make you my wife in deed as well as in name. At least allow me to convince you I can bring you the pleasure you deserve."

"Yes."

In the blink of an eye, she was on her back on the pallet, with the bodice of her dress open.

Without warning, Wolf dipped his head and bit at her nipple though the fabric of her shift. Her body gave an almighty jerk at the incredible sensation. He tugged again, and she moaned, unable to resist. Her hands came to cradle his head to keep him close.

She inhaled sharply, delirious with anticipation. This was it. Finally.

While he suckled her, Wolf closed his hand on Merewen's other breast, growling at the indescribable softness of her. Finally he was about to do what he had been aching to do for days. Seeing that she wasn't protesting, quite the opposite, he brought his hand between her legs. She gave a cry and immediately started to squirm against him. By the gods, but the woman was so responsive, so hot, so wild!

Contrary to what he'd thought, she was not afraid of being deflowered. She had merely been ashamed to reveal what she considered a shamefully wanton disposition. As if he would take issue with that! Didn't she know what it would do to a man to know that the woman in his arms was desperate to discover pleasure and eager to bed him? It was the greatest gift he had ever received.

What he had he done to deserve to be married to such a woman?

When he stole his hand under the hem of her skirts, Merewen let out a moan charged with such longing that flames started to course down his veins and he knew he wouldn't stop until he had convinced her to surrender to him, until she had allowed him to give her what she needed, what they both needed. But mercifully, she seemed to have at last realized that denial was futile.

She wanted him and she was begging for more. Her actions made that clear, even if she had not uttered a single plea. He lowered the shift and placed his mouth on her bared nipple, sucking it deep into his mouth, savoring the feel of it hardening under his tongue, the taste of her soft skin. He could have come just from the heavenly sensation, from the knowledge that he was just moments away from having her, of finally giving her what she had been craving all this time.

"Ah, you're so wet," he growled, brushing her inner thigh.

"I know," she whimpered, averting her eyes. "I'm sorry."

He forced her to meet his gaze. "Don't be sorry, sweet. I will not have you any other way, because this proves you want me and your body is ready for me. It makes me feel like one of the gods. Now let me show you pleasure."

It would be better that way. Even if he knew she wasn't afraid of being possessed, he owed it to her to make this first time memorable and he feared he would not last long once he slipped inside her heated flesh. Better to ensure she was satisfied first.

When Wolf pressed hot fingers to her throbbing core, Merewen knew that she had lost, or rather won. Her husband would make love to her, show her what she had been hankering for all this time. She would finally know what pleasure felt like in real life, with a real man, not just in a dream.

Soon, she lost the ability to think coherently and simply let the heat of Wolf's touch warm her all over. His tongue slid over her breast, rolled around her nipple, teased it into a hard point, made her squirm and buck. When the sensation became too much, he sucked her nipple deep into his mouth, easing the burn, and then finally bit the tormented bud with exquisite delicacy. At the same time, his thumb came to circle the nub at the apex of her thighs.

During her nightly explorations, Merewen had come to understand that this was the place that could bring her the most pleasure and when Wolf started to rub at it she realized she had been right in her assumption. But the sensations he provoked in her were nothing like the pleasant waves she had created with her caresses... He brought on a storm over her senses, stealing her breath, making her body arch in supplication and every single nerve ending ignite in turn until finally thunder exploded in her skull and lightning flashed under her closed eyelids.

The world disappeared in a whirl of darkness, then slowly came back into focus.

Lying panting, she opened her eyes and looked at Wolf as if she were seeing him for the first time.

"It was you," she said simply. That night at the pig sty had not been just a dream, it really had been him poised over her. He had been the one giving her the blinding pleasure she had been obsessing about for days. "You caressed me."

She was sure of herself, for she had never been able to coax such heavenly sensations from her body, still had not idea how he had done it. She had tried to reach pleasure enough times to know that her own caresses were nothing compared to his assured touch.

"Yes," he said, his voice deeper than usual. "I woke up to your moans. I saw what you were doing and I couldn't resist. Forgive me."

"F-forgive you?" she stammered. "What for? For giving me pleasure? Twice? For making me experience what I only suspected could happen?"

He smiled. "If you put it like that I guess it doesn't sound so bad."

"No, not so bad," she breathed. Wolf ran his fingers through her hair, massaging her scalp, murmuring soothing words in his language. Before long she started to squirm again, an involuntary reaction that took her by surprise. It was as if her body had taken control and was forcing her to acknowledge what it needed.

"I want more," she said slowly when she understood what was happening, hoping he would not take offence and think he had not satisfied her. "I need something... something else."

"I know. You need a man inside you. Have me. I'm ready for you."

Oh, he made it sound so tempting, so simple. No guilt, no explanations... And she'd thought he would be appalled!

"Yes," she answered in a heartbeat.

Indeed. So simple. Without hesitating, Merewen removed her clothes and was pleased to see Wolf undress in turn. She would never have dared ask him to bare himself but she was desperate to see him, all of him.

"I would like to touch you," she whispered, awed by his beauty.

A grunt answered her. "As would I, but please... Not now. I am near to spilling already. I don't think I could bear it if you touched me and then you would have to wait to have what you need."

Though she did not quite understand what he meant, Merewen was only too happy to surrender to his superior knowledge. Deciding that they were well past the point of modesty, she opened her legs and he immediately came to position himself over her. Having such a large man covering her was overwhelming but she barely registered his weight. Evidently he was careful of not crushing her and this proof of his thoughtfulness made her melt. Only a considerate man would act thus.

"I... I'm afraid I don't know what to do with a man, or how

to please you," she murmured, embarrassed. She might as well reveal the whole painful truth and rid herself of all her doubts. He'd been so understanding with regard to her unwomanly desires, perhaps he would not mind her lack of expertise. "I know you wanted to see what skills I possessed in bed but I have none."

"Oh, little one." Wolf let out something between a grunt and a chuckle. "Don't you worry about that. You are doing exactly what's needed to send me mad with need."

"How?" She hadn't done anything!

"By being here, under me, naked and willing, by allowing me to touch you and melting under my caresses. You are so beautiful," he murmured, letting his gaze wander over her. "Do you know how satisfying it is for a man to see a woman come undone?" A warm hand closed over her breast, englobing it completely. "You gave me your pleasure and you are going to give me your innocence. I can think of nothing better."

Merewen could not have answered. Her mouth had gone dry with emotion. Was this fearsome beast of a man talking to her gently, touching her as carefully as if she might shatter, calling her beautiful and looking at her as if she meant the world to him?

The thought made her dizzy.

"Let me kiss you," he begged, his lips coming to within a hair's breadth from hers. How was she supposed to say no? He was naked, he was over her, he was stroking her breast and she... She would burst if he stopped now.

Instead of answering, she lifted her head and wrapped her arms around his neck to draw him into the kiss they were both desperate for.

After a heady, spine-tingling kiss, Wolf tore himself from Merewen, the effort making him grunt. He was ready to plunge inside her and ride her hard and fast, bring about the release he could feel boiling in his spine. But he could not, not yet, not like that.

This would be her first time, he could not forget it and allow his urges to take over. The last thing he wanted was to hurt or frighten her.

"Merewen... Before I lose my mind, I need to be sure," he said in a rasp, holding himself very still. "You are a virgin? You haven't known any man?"

Although he had felt the evidence of it himself, he didn't want to admit as much. Besides, hearing that she was untouched might help cool his ardor.

She nodded, keeping her eyes on him. "You know I was never married and mercifully the other day Sigurd arrived before..." Her voice trailed and he placed his forehead against hers in encouragement. "So yes, I am untouched," she said after a while.

His whole body sagged in relief. He had not been able to shake the feeling that she had hidden the true extent of the man's assault from him. But now he knew she had indeed not been raped. His manhood twitched.

"When I take you I will breach your maidenhead. It might be uncomfortable at first but I swear it will be better afterwards. I am here to give you pleasure, not pain," he said, placing a kiss on her temple then another on her lips. He closed his eyes. The woman's mouth was softer than silk. "Just remember that, remember what you felt before."

"Yes," Merewen gasped. "I will never forget that as long as I live."

"Your back is not too sore?" Concern and guilt colored his voice. Perhaps he should make her sit on him or lie on her side but he wasn't sure she knew about all the ways a man could take a woman and he didn't want to shock her by asking her to position herself in a way she would find degrading.

"Not at all," she assured him. "In truth, I'd completely forgotten about my injuries."

"Good."

After that there were no more questions.

Merewen mewled when Wolf started stroking her body, leaving no place untouched. The heat of his hands, the velvet of his mouth, the brush of his lips were everywhere, building her need to an almost unbearable point.

"Wolf, please," she croaked, not caring if she sounded desperate.

"I'm going to take you now," he grunted, sounding on the verge of control himself. "Are you sure you want this?"

"Yes."

Merewen did not hesitate. She was burning, so ready for him that she spread her legs wider to welcome him. Needing no other invitation, he surged inside her with a growl. The sudden flash of pain was as unwelcome as a stab in the gut would have been, and almost as painful. A cry escaped her lips. She had not expected anything as painful as that and before she could think, she pushed at his chest, protesting against the shocking invasion.

Surely this was not normal, surely he'd made a mistake! If he had not been pinning her in place she would have doubled up in pain.

"Wait! Stop!" The words were out of her lips before she could think.

Wolf froze when he realized how spectacularly he had misjudged her sensitivity. Because he had taken the time to prepare Merewen, because she had felt pleasure once already and her body was slick with arousal, he had thought it best to break through her barrier in one thrust, trusting in his ability to make her forget the initial discomfort.

But it was now obvious that he had been too forceful and what she had experienced was real pain, not just a pinch, which was hardly surprising because breaching her maidenhead had felt different from what he had expected. There had definitely been resistance there, nothing like what he had felt on his wedding night.

He gritted his teeth.

Solveig was the only other virgin he had bedded and he had thought, evidently incorrectly, that it would be the same for all women. When he had entered her, he had not felt anything tearing, and she had not complained or flinched, never uttered a single whimper of protest. He had always assumed that this was because being taken for the first time only brought a minimal amount of discomfort to a woman if she was ready for it but judging from Merewen's reaction he was forced to reassess this first, hopeful opinion. He was now wondering if his wife had not in fact hidden the fact that she was in pain from him.

It would be in keeping with her character to keep silent when she was in agony, to spare him from the real extent of her suffering so as not to inconvenience him. The thought brought a twinge of guilt crashing through him, as well as anger.

He would have liked to be told something as important as the fact that he was hurting his wife! Didn't a man deserve to know what the woman he was making love to was feeling? He had told Merewen it might be uncomfortable when he surged inside of her but it looked as if painful was a more accurate description of what she had experienced. If he had known the reality of it, he would never have behaved in such a manner.

But as unwelcome as the realization that Merewen was in pain was, at least it meant that he had stopped. Had she not shown her pain he would have carried on, too fired up to think of stopping, too lost to his pleasure to ask if she was all right.

"Merewen, look at me. I'm sorry, I didn't know it would be like that. Please, I—"

"It's all right," she panted, sounding mercifully less panicked. "Only I... It was not what—"

"I know, you didn't expect this. Neither did I. I'm so sorry." He gave her cheek a stroke. "But the worst is over now, at least I'm sure of that. Let me show you the pleasure I promised you. Will you let me do that?"

She took in a shaky breath and nodded.

He withdrew an inch, then slowly pushed back in. Going so slow would be the death of him but there was no other way. He refused to hurt her again. "Better?" he asked, teeth clenched against the urge to start pumping into her.

"Yes."

"Wolf, Harald is here to see y—"

The man walking into the hut stopped in his tracks when he saw the two people in front of him naked and locked in the most intimate of embraces.

"No!" Merewen cried out, reaching out to her shift, the fur covers, anything to cover her nudity. Then she turned her face to the wall and screwed her eyes shut. Wolf cursed at length, withdrew from her and heard her hiss when the move caused her more pain. There was no time to apologize or ask if she was all right. Hugo spoke again, hesitantly, like a man torn between his duty and common decency.

"I'm sorry but it's important. What shall I—?"

"Leave!" he barked at the youth, doing his best to shield Merewen with his body. He could feel her trembling against him, though whether it was because of the pain he had caused her or the shame of being seen in such a compromising position, he could not tell.

Probably both.

To add to his dismay, he guessed that Hugo would have heard her cry of pain. The lad would be thinking that he used his wife to slake his most brutal urges and ignored her protests.

The thought sat ill with him, even if he knew it had been nothing like that.

By the gods! Was the world conspiring against them? This was not what he had envisaged for their first lovemaking! To be interrupted after his first thrust was the worst thing that could have happened, for him and most especially for Merewen. It had been her first time and it had not gone as she had expected. Right now he needed to be with her, reassure her, and make good on his promise to give her pleasure, not pain. She was mortified, hurt and bewildered by what had happened. The last thing he should do was leave her.

But how could he refuse to go? Harald had told him the day before that his wife had disappeared. He suspected her of having fallen victim to the mysterious attacker who had struck the village lately. A number of women had been assaulted, and a few had even disappeared. The affair was too grave to ignore. A woman's life might be at stake.

"Forgive me." He shook his head. "Hugo said it was important, I should—"

"Go," Merewen cut through his fumbled explanation. "I know the role you play in the community. I know your life is not your own."

He winced. Indeed, it wasn't, but in this instant he dearly wished it was. "I cannot leave you, not now." He looked around in indecision. How could this have happened to him? He was still lying between her spread legs, ready to resume their lovemaking.

"I'll be fine," she assured him.

Wolf rewarded her generous answer with a swift kiss to the temple. Then as he stood up, her gaze fell on his manhood, still hard and tainted with blood.

Her blood.

He saw her bite her bottom lip and felt himself grow pale at the same time. Could this get any worse? As if Merewen had not been traumatized enough, now she had seen him fully aroused and bloodied by the loss of her innocence. Seeing the blood would only remind her of the pain he had caused her. That was another difference with his wedding night. Solveig had not bled at all. Perhaps she had not lied after all and her deflowering had not been anywhere near as painful... Small consolation, because he had definitely hurt Merewen.

And now he had shocked her.

What was wrong with him? Could he not have covered himself before standing up? Or at least keep his erect member out of view? He reached out for his clothes, cursing his ill luck. Only a moment ago he had discarded them in anticipation of the most satisfying lovemaking in his life and now he was towering over Merewen's prone form, feeling like an executioner looking at the butchered remains of his victim.

Once he was dressed, he knelt beside the pallet. "Merewen, I'm so sorry."

"I know. It's fine. Just go."

She did not avert her eyes and to his relief, she did not appear frightened or resentful. Perhaps she did not hate him.

After one last caress on her cheek, he stood up and walked out the door.

How many times had she imagined that moment, Merewen asked herself, imagined having a man inside her, finally giving her what she needed? Yet what had just happened had not resembled anything she had ever envisaged.

The first surprise came from her lover himself.

Handsome as an angel, chiseled and incredibly strong, yet gentle and careful, Wolf was a man the likes of which she had never thought could exist, nothing like the faceless men who populated her dreams, who never seemed to have any real substance or personality, only bodies with which to take her.

And somewhat disconcertingly, he had pleasured her *before* making love to her, which had been a pleasant surprise, but not during, which had come as a shock.

His possession had not brought her any of the pleasure she had anticipated. Instead, it had hurt, a lot more than she had thought it would. Whether that was because she was very naïve, because he was abnormally large or she particularly tight, she wasn't sure, but one thing was certain. The pain had shocked her.

It had never happened that way in her dreams.

And as if that wasn't enough, they had been interrupted before they were able to get past the awkward moment. Wolf had deflowered her but he had left before he could actually make love to her.

No, this was not at all what she had imagined when she finally lay with a man and became a woman.

Cold without the heat of Wolf's kisses warming her skin, she stood up and got dressed, wondering how odd life was sometimes, forcing you to accept a situation you had thought abhorrent at first and then showing you that what you had always dreamed of having was nothing like what you had imagined.

CHAPTER FOURTEEN

The door opened on a mussed Merewen.

To Wolf's relief, she seemed composed enough. She did not appear to have been crying and she was walking normally. No one could suspect that only a moment ago she had been crying out in pain. The guilt in his chest eased somewhat. They would be able to recover from this, the simple fact that she had come out of the hut to meet Harald proved it.

She nodded when she saw him surrounded by the man, his wife, and their three children, two of them were barely able to walk.

He knew she would guess what had happened to Ingrid. Not that it was hard, one glance at her made it painfully obvious. Her face was bruised and her eyes were lowered in shame. Indeed, as soon as she saw her, Merewen blanched and touched her own cheek. Wolf almost ran up to her to sweep her into his arms. But before he could say or do anything to comfort her, the children started wailing.

To his utter shock, Merewen knelt in front of them and ruffled their hair in an affectionate gesture. He knew in that instant she would be the mother he had hoped to find for his children. Something in him shifted.

"I bet you're as hungry as I am. I am so famished I could cry too," she told them with a smile. "Would you come inside and have a glass of goat milk and some oatcakes with me?"

When the children looked at their parents expectantly, he saw her face fall. Evidently she thought they only spoke Norse and hadn't understood what she had told them. He stooped toward them because he knew they did understand her language. They were merely waiting for permission before accepting the offer.

"You can go with my wife. She will look after you." Pride swelled in his chest at being able to introduce her as his wife. "But make sure you leave a cake or two for me," he added with mock severity.

"Yes, Wolf!"

While the three little ones bounded into the hut Merewen exchanged a look with Wolf and saw gratefulness in his eye. Indeed, the children were best out of the way while their mother told him all about her ordeal.

Though her heart bled at the thought of what the woman had endured, she could not help but smile at the sight of the children devouring the cakes and telling her all about their new puppy.

A moment later, the door opened on Wolf and Harald. She noticed how the Dane did not look at her face, as if he could not bear to think about why she was bruised in much the same way as his wife.

"Come," he said, extending his hand toward his children. "It's getting dark. Thank the lady for the cakes and milk and let's go home to see Badger."

"That's the puppy's name," the eldest boy told her excitedly.

"I chose it," the youngest added.

"That's a lovely name!" Merewen laughed. "Well, make sure to give Badger a hug from me."

A moment later, she was alone with Wolf. She had thought the moment would be awkward, but meeting Harald and his children, seeing the proof of his wife's ordeal had wiped everything from her mind. What had happened to her was nothing in comparison. She had merely lost her maidenhead to the man she was married to, to the lover she desired above all others. And even if it had hurt her a lot more than she had anticipated, it was of little import. Wolf would make sure that the next time he took, her she burst into flames.

Now that her maidenhead was breached, being taken would never hurt again.

"How is she?"

Wolf gave a sigh, as if he'd feared having to face her reproach after what had happened and was relieved to see that she was not blaming him. "Not too well. But I suspect she will be better now that she has been reunited with her family. Harald swore to get his revenge on the bastard who raped her. I know he will put his threat to execution, and I do not blame him for wanting to avenge his wife, but I convinced him to wait until he could do it without getting caught, for what would happen to Ingrid and the children if he was killed?"

"Yes." Merewen breathed. Indeed. The satisfaction of knowing that her aggressor had been punished would mean nothing to the woman if her husband was killed and never got to see their children grow.

"Thank you for looking after the boys while we talked," Wolf told her, taking a step toward her. "It was better they never got to hear what we discussed even if they know something is wrong."

"Of course. Poor woman."

He stared at the bruise on her cheek, his meaning clear. He

was thinking that she had almost been subjected to the same fate.

"We think we know who was behind the crime," he said, talking to himself as he started to pace around the room. "A Saxon who seems to have a particular taste for our women. It is as if he considers the Norse settlement his personal hunting ground. It started when King Knútr died a few months ago. Evidently, he hoped that in the confusion over the succession, the climate would turn against Norsemen and he would not be held accountable for any wrongdoing against them. I have tried to catch him many times but the man is more slippery than an eel and I only ever glimpsed him once. We were unable to find out his identity."

"Has he attacked many women?" Merewen asked.

"Yes. Women, and even very young girls." Wolf grimaced in disgust. "Virgins mostly. It is always the same. They are taken away while they are alone out in the forest and vulnerable. It took us a while to link all the disappearances to the same man, as the few women who came back were either too shocked to remember anything, too frightened to speak out or had been assaulted with their faces covered to prevent identification. More often than not, they simply vanish. Ingrid was luckier than most."

A chill descended down Merewen's spine, for Wolf calling a raped woman lucky could only mean one thing. The others had been killed once the man had slaked his lust with them.

"The girl who came to see you yesterday... Frigyth. She said you had taken her defense when she was attacked," she said slowly. "But if I understand, this man was not to blame. It was a man from the village who had assaulted her. Does that mean that you side with Saxons if need be?"

"I side with the victims, always, whoever they are."

Merewen swallowed hard, unable to move. Wolf loomed

over her, his eyes burning with intent and she knew what he would tell her next.

"Will you forgive me for leaving you at such an inopportune moment earlier?"

"Of course."

"And for—"

"As to that," she cut in. "There is nothing to forgive. You did nothing wrong. The fact that it hurt had nothing to do with you, and all to do with the fact that I was untouched. Next time it won't be like that."

She flushed so violently she had to avert her gaze. She had just admitted out loud she was already thinking about their next lovemaking.

Gratefulness flooded through Wolf. Merewen had forgiven him everything, and she was already thinking about the next time he would make love to her. She didn't think him a monster. She was ready to give him another chance. The relief was dizzying.

"Yes, next time will be better, I swear it." He crushed her into his arms. He would give her pleasure beyond her wildest imaginings, be the lover she had been waiting for. She deserved no less.

"Could it be..." The tentative voice came from somewhere below his chin. "Now?"

That one word had blood rushing to his groin so fast he inhaled sharply for fear he might collapse. The idea that he could be inside her with his next heartbeat was enough to bring him to his knees.

He forced himself to reason.

"No, little one. I want to make sure your body recovers first. I can't bear to hurt you again, even unintentionally." He was so hard, so much bigger, stronger than her and so desperate that he needed to calm the tempest in his body before he claimed her.

Never did he want to hear her protests or see her grimace with the pain he had caused her.

Merewen pressed herself against him, not in the least impressed—or afraid—and placed her hand on his straining member.

"But I... I think you want me."

"I always want you," he said in a low rumble. "It doesn't mean a thing. I'm not a green boy anymore. I can control myself."

The minx gave him a stroke. "Can you?"

He let out a feral growl that caused her lip to curl. Oh, so she was enjoying torturing him?

"Stop that. You are not getting anything tonight." He took hold of her wrist to stop her from sending him over the edge. He'd just claimed not to be a green, excitable youth! Now was not the time to act like one and spill in his braies!

"Very well, we'll wait," she purred. "But I'm warning you, there will be no stopping me tomorrow night. I will have you inside me, I will have the pleasure you promised me. And then we will start our married life in earnest."

———

MEREWEN WOKE up with a smile on her face. She was no longer a virgin, she had experienced mind-blowing pleasure at her husband's hands and tonight she would know what it was to have a man surge inside her. Wolf would give her what she had craved all this time—and more, if the heat flaring between them when they touched was any indication.

She stretched, pleased to feel she had recovered from her ordeal in town.

Last night, before wrapping his arms around her in bed, Wolf had made her swear she would not try to seduce him and she had promised, seeing the strain on his face and loving him for his restraint. He was determined to forget his own needs to make sure she was not hurt. Such thoughtfulness deserved an effort on her part. She was certain it would not hurt her the next time she welcomed him inside her body but perhaps it was better to err on the side of caution. Experience had shown that there was a vast difference between what she imagined and what actually happened. The last thing she wanted was to cause him more distress so perhaps he was right, and it was wiser to wait until her body had recovered because she could not guarantee there would be no discomfort so soon after her deflowering and she did not want to worry Wolf. A little delay would not hurt.

She could wait, now that she knew she loved him.

A bolt of thunder seared Merewen's insides when the thought burst through her mind. Was she in love with Wolf? Surely not! But then again... It would explain a lot of things that did not make sense otherwise. Anxiety was not responsible for the fluttering in her heart every time she looked at him, lust alone could not account for the heat pooling in her loins every time they touched, gratefulness did not explain the way she yearned to be with him constantly. But love...

Love *would* make her heart flutter, her loins boil, her soul ache and everything in between.

She stole a glance at the empty pallet next to her and took a deep breath. Perhaps it was for the best that Wolf was not here right now, as she needed time to absorb the momentous discovery on her own. How would he react when she told him of her feelings for him? Certainly he would be stunned to hear she had fallen for the stranger who had bought her. But would he be pleased? Suspicious? Uncomfortable because he did not return her feelings? She shook her head, refusing to put thoughts in his head or get carried away. She had twisted herself into knots over his reaction to her wanton nature and look what had happened! He had been delighted. So she would do him the honor of believing he would be sensible about her revelation, even if he did not love her back. Hadn't he proven enough he could do the right thing?

In just a few days, Wolf had gone from being a blond giant who had frightened her to a husband she had fallen in love with.

And so it was decided.

Tonight, while he was making love to her, she would tell him she was in love with him.

CHAPTER FIFTEEN

A nother fish was thrown into the basket. Wolf shook his head in disbelief. He could not recall ever being so successful before. His hands and feet had gone numb with cold but it mattered not. He could get out of the river now because in no time at all he'd caught four trout, more than he and Merewen needed for their supper. The fish had swam straight into his waiting hands, an unprecedented event which only served to highlight how well things were going for him at the moment.

He was married, and his wife was the most entrancing woman he'd ever met.

She was also the first person who had ever crawled under his skin in this inexplicable manner. Now that she had burst into his life with the force of a torrent, he realized that timid Solveig had only barely scratched the surface. The fiercer Merewen had hacked her way past all the barriers he had erected to burrow where no one else had gone before, so deep he wasn't sure he would ever be able to root her out. Not that he would need to, because after an all too understandable moment of panic when told about his past, she now seemed determined to stay and give their marriage a chance.

Tonight she would welcome him into her arms, and cause his body to erupt in ecstasy. And in a few months' time, she might announce she was with child and make his heart burst with joy.

All in all, it was a dream come true.

He frowned. What if it *was* just that, a dream? An illusion? Surely he did not deserve such luck and something was about to go wrong? He'd been convinced for so long that he could not remarry that he found it difficult to accept he had found a wife, and was on the verge of having everything he had ever wanted. A new, exciting chapter of his life was about to start.

Tonight.

The prospect of Merewen's heat closing around him chased the cold from his limbs. The little Saxon was as fearless and bold in bed as she was in life. This lovemaking was going to be explosive. What had he done to deserve such a woman?

Nothing.

Had she got as good a bargain as he'd had?

Unfortunately, no.

He knew Merewen had had difficulty accepting her situation at first, and had only agreed to marry the man who'd bought her for want of a better alternative. Then the day she had resigned herself to marry him, she'd found out he was accused of having killed his wife. She had hoped to have found a protector, but she'd been attacked the day after her wedding. She'd expected company, but she had to wait for him at the hut day after day while he saw to the villagers' needs. She'd craved a lover who could show her the pleasure she was after, but instead she had been hurt.

In the circumstances, he would understand if she felt cheated. He would have to make it all up to her. Tonight, he would be the lover she deserved, from then on he would be the protector she needed, and in time, the companion she desired. He would enjoy his marriage before... The niggling feeling was back, sending prickles along his spine.

Before something went wrong.

Wolf shook his head. No matter how much he tried to tell himself he was just being silly, he could not shake the conviction that he did not deserve such happiness and that sooner or later everything would come crumbling around him like a sand tower, exactly like it had two years ago.

A fish idly swam by, and came within catching distance. Wolf could not resist and he closed his hands, deftly spearing his fingers into the gills. Too easy! With a snort he threw it into the basket but, in his overconfidence, he misjudged it. The trout landed slightly to the side, unbalancing the basket. It overturned and all the fish were instantly released into the river. Before he could blink, they had all swam away, leaving the basket completely empty.

He stared at it in disbelief. He had been too presumptuous. He had tried to get more than he was entitled to—and here was the result. He'd ruined everything. Another shiver of foreboding scuttled along his spine. Was this a warning, a sign that he should not ask for more than he deserved, that he should count himself lucky to have had a fortnight with Merewen and leave it at that before he destroyed everything?

It was then that he heard the voice calling in the distance. "Wolf!"

He turned to see Magnus the blacksmith running toward him. "What is it?"

Instead of answering, his friend asked, "Where is your wife?"

This time the ice closing around his heart had nothing to do with the temperature of the river. Wolf hastened back to the bank. "Why are you asking?" Wasn't she at the hut where he'd left her? "Has anything happened?"

"No, not yet, but you'll want to keep an eye on her. I over-heard a group of Saxon men at the market in the next village talk about you this morning," Magnus explained, looking ill at ease. "They were unhappy, saying you had prevented their friend from exacting his revenge on a bastard who had raped his daughter. I found that hard to believe so I told them you would never do anything like that but they wouldn't listen to me. They asked..." A pause.

"What?" Wolf barked, shoving his ice-cold feet into his boots.

"They asked me how you would like it if a woman you care about got hurt."

His heart stopped beating for just a moment. There was only one woman who fitted the description. The woman he'd married, the woman he'd fooled himself he could protect.

The woman who was alone at the hut.

Horror rooted him to the spot. There. There was the cata-strophe he had feared only moments ago! What had he been thinking? Of course, he wouldn't be allowed to have a peaceful life next to his wife, of course he would not be able to raise chil-dren with her and have a happy marriage!

What had he done bringing Merewen into his life? His complicated, dangerous life, his life that was not his own, to echo her words. He'd known all along it was a bad idea to remarry, so why had he not listened to his instinct? Why had he not let reason guide his actions instead of his hopes and desires? How could he have been so selfish! He was not free to take a wife, there was no place for a woman in his life!

His various commitments toward the community took him away from her night and day, often at the worst moments—their first lovemaking came to mind—and worse, they had now made her a point of pressure over him, a weakness his enemies would be able to exploit. By defending the community, he had not only put himself in danger, but also made the people he cared for potential targets. Three weeks ago, that wouldn't have mattered, because he'd been alone.

But now it did, because now he most definitely cared for someone.

He had to go find Merewen now. Magnus was right, he could not let her out of his sight for a moment. Solveig had been strangled when she had done nothing wrong, by a man who'd had no quarrel with her but wanted to get to him. She'd been an innocent who'd paid in his stead. He could not let the same thing happen to Merewen.

Leaving everything on the grass, he hurried toward the hut. Where had she gone? He had to find her because the group of disgruntled Saxons was not the only thing he should be worrying about. The man who preyed on the women of the village was still lurking about. Not to mention that there was yet another threat hanging over her. They still didn't know who her enemy was. For all he knew, the man who had sold her into slavery had watched him buy her and would sooner or later come to ensure she disappeared for good.

How had he not thought of that before? He should have insisted she never left the hut. How unforgivably remiss he'd been!

Merewen was three times at risk; for being his wife, for being the slave he'd bought, and for simply being a woman. And he'd gone to fish instead of guarding her. If anything happened, he would never forgive himself.

Just when he was about to enter the village, he saw her.

At the edge of the forest, next to a man who was not a villager. Before his mind could fully form any thought, his legs started to move.

He ran.

"Merewen? Is that you?"

Merewen dropped the mushroom into the basket and turned around. One of her old neighbors was staring at her in disbelief, a man she had last seen on the day of Leofric's funeral, a man who belonged to her former life and she had never thought to see again.

"Alaric," she greeted him. "Yes, it's me."

"But I... Everyone thought you were dead!"

"Yes, I can well imagine you did," she said with a smile. She had disappeared off the face of the earth without a trace. What else were they supposed to think? But she had not died. Instead she had been rescued, in more ways than one.

"We thought you'd killed yourself in grief over your brother's death."

Merewen shook her head. She would never do such a thing after seeing how much Leofric had fought not to die. She owed it to her brother not to give up. What better way of honoring him than living the life he had wanted her to live?

"No, I didn't die, but you wouldn't believe what actually happened to me."

Alaric eyed her speculatively. "I think I can hazard a guess, considering the way you look and where we are."

It wasn't hard to guess what he meant. They were in a village populated by Norsemen and, dressed in a simple gown with her hair loose and a bruise at her temple, she would appear like the ill-treated slave she could have been. Which went to show how appearances could be deceptive, because she was not a slave but a married woman and she had never been happier.

"I am not here against my will," she told him. "And I intend to stay."

Yes, she was ready to start this new, exciting chapter of her life.

Alaric did not appear convinced. "No one is around," he whispered, glancing about. "I could help you escape."

Had he heard what she'd said? She didn't want to escape! Clearly, he wasn't the brightest of individuals—or the best-looking of men. The thought made her smile. That wasn't fair. Wolf was so stunning that he would make most men appear like ugly trolls. Still, undeniably, Alaric was less well-favored than most. The purple stain covering his left cheek didn't help, but even without it, he would never have been called attractive.

"I thank you, but I'm not going anywhere." She was right where she wanted to be.

"If you're sure..."

"I am."

There was a pause.

"You know, it is propitious I met you today," Alaric eventually told her, rubbing a hand over his chin. "Only yesterday, a man came asking for you at the house and I could only tell him that no one knew where you were or even if you were alive."

"A man?" Merewen opened wide eyes. She could not think of a single person who might be asking after her. Her whole family was dead. Who could that visitor be? Her heart almost stopped. The slave trader? Had he found her again? Surely not! "Who was it?" she asked, heart in her throat.

"I had never seen him before. He said he was your father's brother whom he hadn't seen for years. Something about a feud that had kept them apart, and he'd come to regret."

"Oh?" She had never heard of an uncle before! But, of course, if he and her father had fallen out before her birth, she wouldn't have. Hope swelled in her chest. Perhaps she had been wrong, and she did have some family left! "Did he say where he—"

Alaric interrupted her with a small laugh. "Oh, I have no idea. You would have to ask him that yourself! Only... I'm not sure how long he will be around if he thinks you're dead. He and his family might be gone by now."

His family! That man had a wife and children with him? Which meant *she* had a family! Joy burst through her. Could this day be more perfect? Only this morning she'd realized that against all odds she'd fallen in love with her husband, that she could build a family, and now she was told she was not alone anyway.

"I... I need to see them!" She had to get to them before they disappeared. Without a name or any information about her uncle, there would be no finding him again if he left.

Alaric scratched his head. "Well, I'm heading back home now. I suppose I could take you on my horse. He's sturdy enough..."

This offer was unhoped for, and exactly what she needed. On foot it would take her a whole day to reach her home but on horseback she might well make it in time to catch her uncle. Then a thought struck her. In her house, she could find an object to sell to repay Wolf for the sum he had spent on her... How had she not thought of this before? It was perfect! She would finally be free of the debt she was in.

Once she had given Wolf the money back, they would be able to start their marriage on a sounder basis. She would be his wife, nothing more. Not the woman he had bought and then thought to marry to rectify the situation. Now she knew she was in love with him, she needed to feel he was with her for who she was. Surely he would understand this was important to her and allow her to repay him?

Yes, all in all, she needed to get home as soon as possible. There was only one problem.

If he didn't see her at the hut when he came back, Wolf would think she'd left him. She could not have him go through this agony a second time, not after everything they'd shared.

Merewen looked around desperately. It was just her luck that there was no one in sight. Once she had reached home, she would have to send a messenger to the village to tell him why she had gone and assure him she was coming back. They had plans for tonight but perforce they would have to wait. She had to reach her uncle before it was too late. Mayhap it already was.

"Would you take me home?" she asked, turning back to Alaric.

He seemed to hesitate then he nodded. "Let's go."

CHAPTER SIXTEEN

"Let go of her, you bastard! That's my wife!"

The roar of rage was heard all the way through the forest, causing the birds to take flight and the man to stop in the act of helping Merewen up his horse.

Wolf brandished his dagger and pumped his legs faster. She was not going to be taken away now, under his very eyes!

"Get your hands off her! *Now!* Before I cut you to ribbons!"

"Stop, Wolf! It's not what you think!" he heard Merewen cry out. But he was too far gone to pay any heed to her. Fear had seized his guts and fury blinded his vision. He only wanted the man incapacitated before he could hurt her.

In a moment, he would fall on him and pummel him to the ground. Just when he raised his fist Merewen placed herself in front of him. No! What was she doing? He tried to slow down but it was too late, the momentum carried him forward. He only had time to lower his weapon before barreling into her. The impact was impossible for her to absorb and they rolled to the ground together, Wolf doing his best to wrap his body around her to break her fall.

For a moment, they stared at each other in disbelief, panting with the realization that he had almost skewered her with his dagger.

"Ow!" Merewen cried out, pushing at his chest. He instantly slid off her. What was he doing crushing her under his massive body? At least he did not appear to have hurt her. "What was that?"

"That man... He was abducting you!" Another moment and he would have been too late.

"He was doing no such thing!" she hissed, doing her best not to shout so as to keep their disagreement private but Wolf did not care if the man or the whole village heard them. "He's a friend! Well, not a friend exactly but one of my neighbors. We met by chance earlier. He told me..."

Wolf closed his eyes. A neighbor! This was not one of the Saxon bastards who had sworn to make her pay, or the monster who preyed on the villagers... Merewen had not been in any danger, he'd completely misread the situation. By the gods, he'd almost killed an innocent man, he'd almost plunged his blade into her stomach and all because for a moment he had not been able to control his temper! Would he ever learn?

His first wife had died because of him and the guilt had almost killed him. Now he had almost stabbed his second wife. He might not have been Solveig's murderer but he could have been the instrument of Merewen's death. It did not bear thinking about.

"I didn't hurt you, did I?" he asked, cutting through her explanations. What the man had told her mattered not, all that mattered was that he had not been about to abduct her. And more than anything he needed to hear he had not cut her or crushed her or frightened her or done any of the things he'd sworn never to do.

What a brute he really was! He should protect Merewen, not place her into danger, he should make her feel safe, not threatened, he should give her pleasure, not inflict her pain every time he touched her.

He was losing control, fast.

"No, I'm fine," she said with a sigh. "But next time, please, think before you act."

Next time.

The words were like a punch to the stomach.

Yes, there would be a next time, another danger, another attacker, another disaster. He would have to be on constant guard day and night, and there were no guarantees it would even work because he could not forbid her to leave the hut, nor could he jump on every person who approached her. He had allowed himself to be persuaded that he could look after her properly when she had come back battered and bruised from the man's assault. He should not have been so complacent. This man who'd been her neighbor might not have wanted to hurt her but others would, and they did not even try to hide the fact, they had told Magnus as much. They were coming for her.

Sooner or later, she would pay the price of being his wife.

"Alaric was only telling me a man came visiting my old house yesterday. An uncle I never knew I had," Merewen told him, oblivious to his grim musings. Her eyes were sparkling with joy. "Can you believe it? I have a family after all, I'm not alone, contrary to what I thought! I was about to go and see for myself, before they leave. That's why I was climbing on the horse, because time is of the essence. If I'm not there, then they have no reason to linger. I fully intended to send you a message as soon as I could but I cannot miss this opportunity. I hope you understand."

Oh, Wolf did understand. He understood all too well.

"So... You have a family?" he said slowly. It was as if an answer had been given to him. The answer he didn't want to hear but which would be the solution to his dilemma. If Merewen was not on her own after all, but could call on the protection of an uncle, then everything had changed. She didn't need him anymore.

Slowly, he got to his feet then helped her up. As she lifted her head his gaze fell on the bruise on her cheekbone. No more, he swore, she shouldn't have to endure any more violence, least of all in his stead. There was only one way he could ensure that.

He would have to let her go.

It was for the best, the only way to protect her. Away from the menace the mob of Saxons represented, far from the village where a predator lurked on the look out for beautiful women, surrounded by a family who would be overjoyed to have found her again she would be safe, more than she would ever be here with him. He had once bought her to spare her a dire fate, he would now have to let her go to save her from an even worse one.

"Go with your neighbor," he said, feeling all the blood drain away from his veins at the idea that she was about to walk out of his life. They'd only had two weeks together but it would have to suffice. This time he would not be greedy, he would stop before he ruined it all.

"Thank you." Merewen gave his hand a squeeze. "That you understand why I need to go means a lot to me. I know..." She blushed. "I know we had plans for tonight but I will be back as soon as I can, I swear."

The smile she gave him was radiant. That decided him. She had never looked that happy since she had arrived in the village and he wanted her to be happy as much as he wanted her to be safe.

So she had to go.

"No. You misunderstand me. Go back home and don't come back. There is nothing for you here." Every word was a stab to his heart.

"Nothing?" She staggered against him. "But that's not true. There's you..." He took a step backward. If they touched, he would never have the strength to do what he must do. She frowned at his sudden coldness, then her eyes grew wide as cart wheels when she finally understood what was happening. "You're sending me away?"

"Yes." The word was pushed through gritted teeth.

"But we're married, we can't—"

He cut in, eager to make the difficult moment as quick as possible. It was precisely because she was his wife that she was in danger, and he would not stand by and watch while she got hurt. "I can't protect you. You will be better off with your family. They will look after you. It's too dangerous here."

"I don't—"

As much to put an end to a discussion that was excruciating as to feel her one last time, he crushed her into an embrace. All at once, her smell hit him, her softness stole his breath. They felt so good together, entwined thus! How would he bear to be without this woman?

By knowing she was alive, and safe.

It would have to be enough.

Oh, but the cruelty of having to let her go the moment he had realized he was in love with her! Because, unlike what he had thought only a moment ago by the river, he did not simply care for her, he *loved* her. Fool that he was, he had allowed himself to do the one thing he shouldn't have done, and fallen in love. It was the worst thing that could have happened because if it made it even more imperative for him to ensure her safety, it also made it impossible for him to keep the clear head needed to accomplish such a task.

She had to go, before it was too late.

"I love you, wife, but I'd rather see you live without me than die because of me," he murmured in Norse in her ear, safe in the knowledge she would not understand he had just bared his soul to her.

For a long moment, Merewen remained frozen in disbelief. Wolf was sending her away. Her husband did not want her. It was not possible. Only a moment ago she had congratulated herself on being happy, on the fact that they had put the hardship behind them and were finally ready to start on their marriage... And now she was being told she had to leave, she was ordered never to come back. How could things have gone wrong so quickly?

Wolf was still holding her in a tight embrace, as if he cared about her, he was speaking in velvety tones in her ear, like someone trying to seduce her. But if he was sending her away, it was all an illusion! He cared nothing for her, and seducing her was the furthest thing on his mind. It only served to show her everything she was about to lose. Never again would she enjoy the warmth of his body, or hear his voice in her ear, or feel his arms wrapped protectively around her.

How could he be so cruel as to taunt her thus?

Everything within her erupted.

"If you have anything to tell me then I suggest you tell me in a language I understand!" she roared, pushing at his chest. Her fury was such that she actually managed to free herself from his hold. Either that or he was not trying very hard to keep her close. "Even better, stop acting so odd and tell me you..."

Tell me you want me to come back, tell me you want to be the one to protect me if you're worried for my safety. Tell me you care! At least a little.

Her voice wobbled. She'd been so full of hope this morning, so full of happiness only a moment ago. Wolf was sending her away, when she had finally discovered that she loved him, when they had agreed to make love that night, when she had been convinced they could start anew. It was unbearable.

"We have plans... Tonight, we agreed..."

He closed his eyes as if he could not bear to think about those plans. Her stomach plummeted further. He didn't want her as a lover, he *had* been disappointed by her reaction and lack of experience. Her worst dread had been confirmed. Wolf didn't want her. In any way. Not as his wife, not as his lover, not even as his slave.

He just wanted her gone.

He bunched his fists. "I'm sorry. I can't keep you here with me."

"You can. You must! We are married!"

But he just shook his head.

"Merewen. I'm going now. I don't want to be on the road after dark." Alaric said, sounding eager to put an end to the awkward moment. He was standing by his restless horse, ready to mount. "Are you coming or not?"

Should she leave? Or should she stay and fight, at the risk losing everything? Because if she chose to try and convince Wolf to keep her with him, and he refused, then she would miss her uncle, the only person in this world who might want her, and find herself all alone.

"Go with him," Wolf said, clenching his jaw. He looked like a man in pain and she briefly wondered if he wanted to let her go, despite what he was saying. "I can't... Solveig..."

Was that what was eating at him? He thought he would fail her like he had his first wife? Well she did not agree, she knew he was a protector to the core. Wasn't that why he had bought her? To protect her? And what danger did he think she was in anyway?

"I trust you," she started. "I know you can—"

"Well, I don't. I can't protect you!" he snarled. Then something in his eyes changed, as if he'd taken a decision. "I don't want to be the one looking after you anymore. So you'll just have to go."

With those words, he turned and walked away.

"No!" Merewen cried out. But the word got stuck in her throat. How could he just abandon her like this?

A moment later, Wolf was gone.

As soon as he disappeared from view, her insides collapsed and the world dimmed, as if all the light had been taken away along with her bones and blood. Was that how life without him would be? Was this how she was going to feel day after day? An empty husk of a woman with only memories of the few moments spent together and no hope of feeling joy ever again? No. She would not let it happen. She had once needed to think about her marriage, she did not anymore. She was sure she trusted Wolf, and wanted to spend the rest of her life by his side during the day and in his arms at night.

She loved him, and this was worth everything, certainly worth fighting for.

In that instant, Merewen knew she would risk missing her uncle, the only family she might find to try and salvage what she already had with Wolf. He was her husband. He could give her a family, the family he craved himself. She just had to convince him she preferred being with a man she loved with the risks it entailed than being safe without him.

This time *she* would make the decision. And it would be the right one.

Before she could take a step toward the hut, an arm closed around her waist. Alaric. Evidently he thought she was about to fall, which did not surprise her. She probably looked as pale as a corpse.

"Come. It's time to go."

She shook her head, trying to disentangle herself from his grasp. She was *not* about to falter, not now, not when she had something so important to do! "I'm sorry, I can't go with you. I need to go and see my husband, tell him—"

"Your husband? You mean that man who abandoned you?" The hold around her tightened. "It seems to me he doesn't care about you."

"He does!" Merewen protested, willing it to be true.

Surely he did. He wouldn't think of her safety if he did not in some way or other care for her... He was only reacting that way because of Solveig, because he didn't trust himself to keep her safe. She could not have misinterpreted the gleam in his eye. He didn't truly want her gone, he only thought it safer because he didn't want to fail her. Surely that was all it was, and she could convince him he was wrong if she went now...

It was not too late.

"Please tell my uncle if he's still there when you arrive home where to find me and that I'm waiting for him. But I can't go with you."

Alaric laughed and something about that laugh made the hairs at the back of Merewen's neck stand on end. Then he spoke and his voice in her ear had all the warmth of a puddle of ice.

"Oh, Merewen, you little fool. There is no uncle, don't you see? I only made him up to lure you in."

"You—"

"Your dear husband was right all along, I *am* abducting you, but you obligingly convinced him he had nothing to fear from me. A good thing, too, because I do not rate my chances against him. The man's a beast. And now that I've finally caught you, I'm not going to leave without you." The arm around her was like an iron band. "You're on your own. No one cares about you.

The only person who could have stopped me from taking you has washed his hands of you."

A scream built in her throat. But Alaric's hand clamped over her mouth before the sound could escape. A moment she was on the horse, galloping away.

CHAPTER SEVENTEEN

"You must be wondering what you are doing here." Alaric planted himself in front of Merewen, a malevolent glint in his eyes. After a reckless ride he had brought her to his house and inside a spacious hall. Even the fire roaring in the middle of the room failed to chase the chill from her bones. "Let me answer that question. Your lands are really what I'm after."

Relief flooded through her. During the whole journey she had feared he would tumble her into bed as soon as they arrived but it seemed he wanted her lands, not her body. She could live with that. Let him take what he wished. All she wanted was to get back to Wolf. Her life was with him now. Her house, only a few yards away, did not call out to her in the way the hut back at the village did, because it was empty. She didn't want a house when she could have a home. Alaric could have it all. It would even do her a favor.

"There was no need to abduct me. I will gladly sell them to—"

"Sell!" he cut in with a laugh. "I never pay for what I want when I know I can get it for free. Isn't it more satisfying that way?"

"What are you talking about?" How did he imagine he would get her lands if not by buying them from her?

The answer was not long in coming.

"At the death of your father, your brother became his heir. I had hopes he would not survive past childhood. Such a puny, pathetic weakling he was... But against all odds he was still alive two years after your father's passing. Who would have thought it?" A sinister laugh escaped Alaric's lips. "I could not afford to wait any longer. If the boy had lasted until the age of fifteen, there was no telling how much time it would be until his health finally failed him. Who knows, he might even have outlived me. I could not take the risk. It was much easier to slip him a little potion. No one noticed anything, naturally, with him being so obligingly weak."

Bile rose in Merewen's throat as the meaning of the words hit her full in the chest. Her brother had not died of a bloody flux.

He had been murdered.

Leofric might have lived, but because of this monstrous, greedy man, he was dead. And now, as the last surviving member of the family, she stood in his way. Suddenly the fact that he wanted her lands took on a new, terrible meaning.

He was prepared to kill her to have them.

By an odd twist of fate, being kidnapped by the slave trader had allowed her to elude his murdering hand. Momentarily, of course. There would be no second chance, she could feel it in her bones.

"People didn't think I was dead," she whispered. "You told them I was."

"Of course."

"And now you are going to kill me."

"Do you know," Alaric said, twisting his mouth in mock consideration. "I had hoped to avoid this outcome. I am not a cruel man, I only kill when there are no other options. There was no need to kill you, you're only a woman, after all. But you certainly needed to disappear. Being sold to a barbarian should have ensured that no one ever got to hear from you again. Either your new owner would have sailed away with you or he would have treated his slave so appallingly that you would not have lasted a month. Alas, it was not to be."

Realization dawned.

She had not escaped Alaric by being kidnapped. He was the one who had kidnapped her so he could rid himself of her! She would have died but his hands would be clean, no one would have been able to attribute her murder to him. After Leofric's death and her mysterious disappearance, he would have stepped forward and taken over their lands, safe in the belief that no one was here to challenge him. Wolf had been right to say she had an enemy she hadn't known about...

Wolf. The thought of him sliced through her like a knife cutting into butter.

After making her believe that they could have a respectful, even loving marriage, he had sent her away and turned his back on her. The loss of him felt almost like the loss of a limb.

Alaric came to stand in front of her. She willed herself still, not wanting to give him the satisfaction of seeing her flinch.

"Although... It seems a waste to kill such a beautiful woman, in the prime of her life. No, I think I am not going to kill you, after all. I think I would rather marry you. Your lands will end up as mine in that manner."

Marry her! The idea horrified her even more than hearing he wanted to kill her. How could she marry the man who had killed her brother and sold her into slavery? Her insides withered at the thought. This time she did recoil. She did not want to show her fear but she had no problem letting him see her disgust.

"I will never marry you! Even if I wanted to, I could not! I'm already married."

Alaric snorted. "Oh yes, apparently you are. To the man who handed you over to me, a barbarian who bought you as a slave and killed his first wife. Well, I think we both know what to think of that marriage. "

Merewen's shock was such that she did not think of denying the accusation of murder. "You know him?"

"I decided to take in interest in the man when I realized I would have to get rid of him if I want to carry on taking my plea- sure with the women in his village. They are rather to my taste, if you must know."

"You..." Bile rose in her throat. This man was the one who had attacked Ingrid and the others? This was getting worse and worse. What else would she discover about him?

It took all her inner strength not to curl up into a ball and scream.

"I only found out he was the one who bought you the other day, quite by accident. Of course, when I found that out, I had to go and get you back. I had half expected you to have fled your new owner by now, but it seems you are fond of persecutors... I guess it's good news for me." The man actually laughed, a sound that made her flesh crawl. "What's your supposed husband's name again? Bear? Wolf? That's it, Wolf. A barbarian name for a barbarian. How fitting."

He gave a satisfied smile at what he deemed to be superior wit.

"Names are not a reflection of anything. If they were you would not be called Alaric, but viper or pig," Merewen spat.

"Hot for your man, I see? Well, you can stop considering him as yours. I doubt the barbarian will have married you in a ceremony we civilized Saxons recognize as legal. You probably merely held hands in front of a fool blabbering in Norse. What of it? I don't see that as any impediment to a proper union between us."

Merewen's stomach sank further. How had she not thought of that before? Indeed, there was no proof of her marriage, no witness that would testify to it having taken place. It would be her word against Wolf's and he had sent her away without as much as a backward glance. If anyone came to ask him if she was married to him he would find it all too easy to deny it. Hadn't she feared the very thing and resolved to find out the truth when she had left the village? And he had said he didn't want to be the one looking after her. At the time she had wanted to believe it was a lie, but perhaps it was not. Wolf was not prone to lying.

Her heart broke anew.

It had all been an illusion. He had never been hers, and she had only been his because he'd bought her, not because he'd married her. And now he had abandoned her.

Alaric saw her discomfiture and bared his teeth in a grimace. "In my generosity I will give you the night to think on your options and realize that you have none. Tomorrow I will come and find you and you will give me the answer I expect."

"That will never happen."

Even if he were right and she was truly not married to Wolf, even if he didn't care about her, she would never be this man's wife. Merewen already knew she would be gone before the morning. Alaric evidently saw the intent to flee flash in her eyes because he made another grimace.

"I think I will take some precautions against you," he said, coming closer. "You seem foolish enough to attempt an escape."

Before she could move, he hoisted her up onto his shoulder and carried her out of the hall. Although Merewen kicked and screamed all she could, it had no effect on him and no one came to her aid. Evidently, such a scene was all too common. His people would have learnt to ignore women's cries of protest a long time ago.

Once he had kicked the door shut with his heel, Alaric yanked her back onto her feet and started to tear at her clothes even before she had recovered her balance.

"No!" Merewen cried, utterly terrified. Was he about to rape her, then beat her so much that she could not move? Was that his plan?

"Stop this!" Alaric snapped, tightening his hold on her. He was a lot stronger than his lean frame had led her to suppose. "Or I will have to hurt you and I don't want to. Appearances have to be preserved. It would not do for my bride to sport fresh injuries on our wedding day. Officially, you will be marrying me willingly."

"Willingly! Why not add that it is a love match while you're at it!" she roared in powerlessness when he tore the front of her shift in much the same way the slave trader had done. He laughed a horrid laugh.

"No. I won't go that far. But you will be reported to marry me in order to escape your barbarian tormentor, a man who bought you as a slave, and even obliged me by leaving traces of his violence on your face for all to see."

He pointed at the bruise on her cheekbone and smiled. As she was now naked, Merewen covered her breasts with her hands and turned to her side to try and preserve her modesty as best as she could. In doing so she exposed part of her back. Alaric's eyes widened when he saw how scratched and bruised it was.

"My! The man really is a savage." There was a chilling note of respect in his voice, as if he admired the sort of man who treated women thus and got away with it.

"He was not the one to hurt me so!" she protested, unable to let him believe the worst of Wolf when *he* was the monster.

"It matters not who did, as long as it looks as if you were mistreated. This is even better than I could have hoped for." The fiend actually rubbed his hands together in satisfaction.

"Wolf will kill you for this!" she cried out, wishing with all her heart it were true, that Wolf was this moment running to her rescue. Unfortunately, she knew he was not.

"Oh, I doubt it. He doesn't want you, didn't you hear?"

"Well, even if he doesn't, you can't have me!"

Pain caused Merewen to lash out at Alaric. What did she have to lose? He had just said he didn't want people to see her sporting fresh injuries. He would not hurt her now. As stars exploded in her skull she realized that she had been foolishly complacent. He was not above mistreating anyone who crossed him, especially if they were women without protection.

"I will do just what I please," he hissed. "And if the heathen really comes for you then he will be killed like the rabid dog, pardon me, *wolf* that he is. Now, if you'll excuse me I have important matters to attend."

After he was gone, Merewen spent a long time staring at the door.

How could it have all gone so spectacularly wrong? This morning she had woken up in Wolf's bed, she had been looking forward to making love to him, certain that their future as a couple was assured.

And now she was at the mercy of a monster who wanted to marry her and the husband she had realized she loved had forsaken her.

Or... Was he truly her husband?

She wasn't sure of anything anymore. Alaric's poisonous words kept playing at the back of her mind. Try as she may she could not dismiss them because she had wondered the same thing herself. How could she be sure she was married in a manner that would be accepted in this country? And even if she was, what difference did it make if her husband didn't want anything to have to do with her? Was that why Wolf had so readily abandoned her? Because he knew deep down they were not married anyway and he didn't owe her anything? Had he even meant the ceremony to be legally binding? For all she knew it had been only a betrothal or even simply a masquerade meant to get her where he wanted her to be—in his bed and grateful for the attention he was lavishing onto her?

Had he meant from the start to send her away once he had slaked his lust with her? Had she fallen in love with a man who didn't care about her?

Her mind full of painful questions, her body shivering from cold, Merewen fell to the floor. There was no use torturing herself thus; it was all over, anyway.

Tomorrow she would die.

***

THE FLAGON WAS empty and there was a mighty pounding in Wolf's head. Through the window he could see the sun starting to rise. As he stared at the bottom of his cup, the door opened, letting in a ray of light that hurt his eyes. He winced and covered his face. A moment later, a voice pierced the fog in his brain, as jarring as a blow to the temple would have been.

"Where is Merewen? I need to see her."

"No, you don't!" he snarled, before walking out of the hut.

Would that accursed, pig-headed Sigurd never leave him alone! Why did he have to ask about Merewen now, when he was trying to come to terms with the fact that he would never see her again? Was his friend to be the instrument with which the gods had chosen to torture him? The mere idea that his marriage was over made his stomach churn, an unfortunate thing for a man already sick with drink.

Last night he should have been making love to her. Instead, he'd drank himself numb, and yet it hadn't been enough to make him forget what he had done.

He had sent his wife, the person he had fallen deeply, irrevocably in love with, away with no hope of reconciliation. That it was for her benefit did little to ease the pain he was feeling.

Despite his best judgment, every fiber of his body was aching to go to her, to beg her to give him a chance to prove he could protect her, after all. He could not, he would not place her in danger. Hard as it was, he needed to place her needs above his own, because she deserved to be safe, to be happy with a family who wanted her and would protect her more efficiently than he ever could. He destroyed everything he touched. He would not let Merewen be destroyed.

But the internal struggle was pulling him apart, sapping all his energy. And now Sigurd had come to add to his torment. It was not to be borne.

"Where is she?" his friend's voice called from behind him. Predictably, he had not taken the hint and was following him.

"She's not here."

"How come? It's only early."

"I don't want to talk about it!"

"Well, even if I have to pummel you to the ground, you must listen to me. This is important."

"If anyone is going to pummel the other to the ground, it will be me," Wolf warned, turning slowly on his friend, who merely shrugged.

"So be it. I will gladly take a punch or two in aid of the woman."

"Oh, and why is that?" he sneered, trying his best to hide his fury. Was his friend attracted to his wife? It would not be extraordinary if he was... After all, she was the most beautiful woman he'd ever seen but the mere thought made him want to tear him limb from limb. "Are you sweet on her, perhaps?"

Sigurd only ignored the provocation, which reassured him somewhat. "Listen, we are wasting time. I need to speak to Merewen, warn her. She is in danger,"

"Is that all you have to say? I already know she's in danger," Wolf said through gritted teeth. "That's precisely why I sent her away."

"You... *what*? You sent her away when you knew someone was after her?" Sigurd snarled, sounding mightily unimpressed. "Are you mad?"

"She's safer away from me. It's only because she's married to me that she's in danger."

"That's not true, and you know it. She was in danger before, or have you forgotten that she was sold to a slave trader?"

Oh, he remembered, but that man was not the most pressing danger she was facing right now. And hopefully her uncle would take her away, somewhere where she would be safe from her elusive enemy and all the dangers threatening her.

"With people after me, she was risking her life just by being here in the village. So I sent her away for her safety. It was for the best," he repeated. Perhaps if he said it enough he might start to believe it.

Sigurd made an impatient gesture. "I know how mulish you can be when you want to be. Once you have convinced yourself of something you will close your eyes and ears to all arguments. It is not usually a bad thing, as you have an uncanny ability to see to the truth of things but in this instance..."

"What is different in this instance?"

"This time your heart is involved, not just your head, and—"

"Not my heart," Wolf cut in, refusing to admit he had fallen in love with Merewen to anyone. It had been hard enough to admit it to himself and what purpose would it serve to remind himself of the fact now that she was gone? "My lust, perhaps, but nothing more."

"Oh please!" Sigurd actually rolled his eyes. "I've seen the way you are with her! You love the woman, 'tis plain as the nose on your ugly face!"

"Enough! And who are you to talk to me about love when you've been saying you would never get married and allow a woman to lead you by the bollocks!" Wolf roared, goaded beyond endurance. This conversation was plain torture.

"I hadn't met Frigyth back then. Shows what a fool I was for thinking that wanting to be with someone was a sign of weakness."

Wolf arched a brow at his friend's unusual seriousness. "Frigyth? The Saxon woman I helped?" he asked, momentarily distracted. He knew that his friend had met her the day she had come to assure him that she had not fallen with Olaf's child but he had not noticed they had formed a special bond. "You've known her for less than a week!"

"It matters not. When you know, you know."

The scathing comment he intended to throw back got stuck in Wolf's throat for he knew exactly what his infuriating friend meant. He had known the moment he had seen Merewen tied to the post that she was not like the others, and might well be the answer to all his prayers.

He growled. Why was he persisting in thinking of her in those terms? She would not be an answer to anything because she was gone! And it was better that way.

"Frigyth is the most precious thing I have ever seen and she's taught me a thing or two about women. First and foremost, that you must *listen* to them! You might as well believe she is the only reason I haven't flattened that bastard Olaf to the ground yet." Sigurd punched a balled fist into his palm, evidently dreaming of doing just that.

Wolf laughed. "Well, I hope you never regret doing the woman's bidding and wake up one day feeling like a prize fool because all you wanted to do was get between her—"

Sigurd grabbed him by the front of his tunic before he could finish the sentence. "Careful what you say! I have not promised not to beat *you* to the ground," he hissed, his face only an inch from his. "I'm aching to kill him for what he did to her, but she begged me not to, arguing that you already punished him and that she wanted to leave the past behind. So now, fool that I am, I am putting her wishes before my own."

And what to you think I'm doing! Wolf almost shouted. *I'm putting Merewen's safety before my wishes, when I want nothing more than be with her! I know exactly what you mean!*

"My... Such a model for us all you truly are," he sneered, although, in truth, he was impressed by his friend's restraint. The tall Dane was not renowned for his patience.

"Enough of this nonsense. You will listen to me!" Sigurd added, shaking him. Then he sniffed the air between them and made a grimace. "Are you drunk?"

"What if I am? What is it to you?"

"I never thought I would ever be ashamed of you, that's what!"

"You can think what you want," Wolf replied, pushing Sigurd away before he snapped and sent him to the ground. He did not truly want to fight his friend but his control was hanging by a thread.

"That's good because if what you told me is true then I will have to think you a despicable coward. Did you really sent your wife away when you know someone wants her dead?"

"Yes, well, Magnus told me about the Saxons coming after her to get revenge on me. What else was I supposed to do? Wait until the mob hurts her before taking a decision? Didn't you rush here to warn me as well? Didn't you want her safe from them?"

"What mob, what are you talking about? I came to tell Merewen I had found out who had sold her to the slave trader."

Wolf's whole body jerked. Sigurd had not come to warn them about the Saxons?

"Who is that?" he asked in a low growl. The bastard would have to be punished. If he could at least remove one of the threats hanging over her, he might feel better.

"A man called Alaric, who apparently supplied the trader with various women over the last few months. I don't know where he lives but he—"

The rest of the sentence was lost as Wolf tried to clear the fog in his mind. Alaric. Where had he heard that name before? And why had the hairs at the back of his head started to tingle? Oblivious to his sudden stillness, Sigurd carried on talking.

"He got the impression that the women had been sent to him once this Alaric had his way with them. Merewen should be able to identify him easily if it's someone she knows, because he has a purple stain on his left cheek."

And just like that the fog parted.

Alaric. Her neighbor. The man who had tried to take her on his horse.

In other words, the man he had entrusted her to only yesterday, thinking he was protecting her. Oh, what had he done? Heart in his throat, he ran to Demon.

"Wait!" Sigurd called out.

But Wolf could not wait. He was going to get his wife back —if she was still alive.

CHAPTER EIGHTEEN

To Merewen's surprise, in the morning, a woman brought her a fresh set of clothes. Repressing a shudder at the idea that the dress might belong to one of Alaric's victims who was now dead, she put it on. The last thing she wanted was to face him naked.

A moment later, she congratulated herself for the initiative, when Alaric entered the room. Although it was only mid-morning, he looked drunk. Perhaps he had spent the night drinking, celebrating his future victory over her.

"So. Have you changed your mind?" he asked without preamble. "Shall we get married this day?"

"No."

"You know I will have to kill you if you refuse?"

"Am I supposed to prefer being your wife to being dead?" she sneered. "Well, I don't."

"Very well. Kill you it is, then. I don't mind." He came to a halt in front of her and bared his teeth in a parody of a smile. "But why do that before I get the chance to enjoy you?"

All the blood left her veins, and, for a moment, Merewen thought she was going to be sick. "You don't mean—"

"Oh, I do. I usually prefer blond women but you're very beautiful, you know that?"

A finger slid over her cheek, reminding Merewen of a slug slithering over a leaf. Unable to bear the contact, she made to bite his finger, but Alaric was too fast for her. He grabbed her throat in a death-like grip.

"Keep that for later," he snarled, his fingers digging into her neck painfully. "I will give you something to wrap your lips around. But first..." He pushed her against the wall while he fumbled with his braies.

"Kill me," Merewen rasped, closing her eyes. "You need me dead. Kill me now."

"No. Not before I have—"

He never finished the sentence. It took Merewen a moment to realize that the fingers around her neck had slackened their grip, then released her altogether. What had happened to make Alaric change his mind? Had someone come in? She hadn't heard a thing. When she dared risk a look she found herself staring straight into Wolf's blue eyes. His hands were wrapped around Alaric's neck. By the looks of it, as soon as he let go, the man would crumple to the floor in a heap.

"Wolf!" she croaked.

"The man seems to like choking people, so I thought I would show him just how pleasurable it is," he growled. "I think he might be rethinking his previous opinion."

With a disgusted grunt, he released Alaric who fell onto the floor, unconscious.

"Oh!" Merewen sagged against the wall. The relief of knowing she was not going to be raped, or killed, the joy of seeing Wolf... She could scarce believe it. "I didn't think you would come for me."

"Neither did I."

He had arrived in time. He had not left it too late... Wolf

could have howled with the relief of it. How could he ever have considered sending away the woman he loved, his wife, considered trying to live without her?

It had been all he could think about on the way to Alaric's lair, as he urged Demon on over fields and streams.

That he loved her like he had not loved anyone before and that he would not let history repeat itself, not without a fight. He would save Merewen or die in the attempt. He had been overcautious, sending her away before a problem had actually arisen and that had been just as dangerous as keeping her with him, could have proven disastrous. From now on, he would not trust anyone else with her safety, not men he didn't know, not uncles who probably didn't even exist. If he had to fail her, let it be because he was overcome by a mob whilst fighting for her, rather than because he had entrusted her to her tormentor when nothing was threatening her.

"How did you get in here?" she whispered.

He made a dismissive gesture. "Getting in was no issue. But getting out of here with the woman Alaric has no doubt instructed his people to guard should prove much more of a challenge," he added grimly.

In his haste, he had not given the matter much thought. All he had cared about was making sure he could reach Merewen in time but undeniably, getting past the guards would not be easy. Still, now that he had her safe with him he felt invincible. He'd been wrong to doubt himself. Loving her did not make protecting her any easier but it made him ten times as determined.

He took a step toward her but stopped before he could take her into his arms. After the way he had forsaken her, she probably didn't want him to touch her and he did not feel he had the right to even look at her.

"Did he touch you?" he asked, and he almost drew his

dagger out to plunge it into the bastard's heart when he thought back to the way he'd pinned her to the wall.

"No."

His eyes narrowed as they landed on her neck. The imprint of Alaric's fingers was very visible, red blotches on her flawless skin. There was also a new bruise on her cheek. He *had* hurt her, it was plain to see. "You're lying."

"He did not touch me in the way you mean," she amended quickly. "He meant to kill me, not bed me. I think if he hadn't been drunk he would never... He wouldn't have tried..."

Wolf wasn't so sure but he didn't tell her as much. The man wouldn't need to be drunk to want to tumble her into bed. Even dressed in a shapeless gown, with her hair in disarray, she was a vision of beauty such as was rarely seen.

The only thing marring the effect were the bruises on her face. Two men had raised their hand to her in less than a week. The bastard who had assaulted her in town and Alaric. He bunched his fists, swearing no one would hurt her again as long as he lived.

"We need to go. Someone might come. They mustn't find me here."

He placed a hand on the small of her back to lead her toward the door. But Merewen did not make any move to follow him. Instead her eyes filled with tears.

Alarm spiked through him. Was she in too much pain to be able to move? "What is it, little one?"

"Are... Are we truly married?"

He recoiled. "Of course, we are! You were there with me during the ceremony, weren't you?"

"I was but I-I didn't understand a word of what the man said. There was no one with us and then yesterday you told me to go. You turned your back on me as if I didn't matter so I wondered..."

Of course. Wolf's heart plummeted further. She had every reason to doubt him after what he had done. Unable to resist any longer, he wrapped her in his arms. Forget what he had the right to do or not, he had already done all the wrongs things he could have done anyway. One more would not hurt and he needed to touch her.

Against him, she trembled. He guessed that Alaric would have taunted her about the validity of their marriage just to hurt her, and his own unpardonable behavior had made it possible for her to believe every venomous word. Oh, he had so much to atone for! Would a lifetime be enough?

He inhaled her floral smell before speaking with his mouth at her temple.

"You do matter more than life itself. What I did was unforgivable, it is agreed. But you are my wife, and we are truly married. What happened that day bound us as surely as if I had taken you to one of your priests. I'm sorry if that's not what you wanted to hear but I assure you we are husband and wife and that I intend to honor my word to you and fulfil my role to the best of my abilities. I tried to do the right thing by you and ended up making a catastrophic mistake. It won't happen again."

Instead of answering, Merewen closed her eyes and allowed herself to sink into the comfort of Wolf's embrace. He was wrong, he had told her exactly what she wanted to hear. They were legally bound, he had not lied to her, and he wanted her as his wife. It was all that mattered.

"So... You still want me?"

"Oh, I want you, and I need you more than my next breath" he said in a low rumble. "The question is, do *you* want me?"

"More than ever."

"Then as soon as we can I will marry you again, in the

Saxon way if such is your wish. A dozen times if you wish. You will never be able to doubt my sincerity again."

"I don't."

She felt his shoulders sag in relief. Then, as if now that he had heard what he needed to hear, he could focus once more, he straightened up and looked around the room.

"Is there a way out of here other than across the main yard?" he asked, every inch the formidable warrior on a mission.

"Follow me."

"Wait." He removed his tunic and threw it over her head before she could take a single step. "It's cold outside."

Merewen melted. He had remembered how susceptible she was to cold, and was taking care of her. Everything would be all right.

A moment later, they were outside, creeping along the wooden palisade. That way they should be able to reach the gate without attracting anyone's attention until the very last moment. Luck was with them, and the gate was clear but just outside the walls, as if to taunt them, three men were stationed by a dying camp fire, a precaution Alaric must have taken against her escape last night.

Wolf and Merewen came to a skidding halt. Three guards were too few to absolutely rule out an escape, but too many for a single man to overpower. But Wolf was not alone. He could use her.

Merewen turned to him.

"You are going to have to abduct me," she said hurriedly.

"I thought that was what I was doing," he growled.

"I mean you're going to have to make it *look* as if you are. Threaten me, hold me like a hostage. It is the only way we can get out unharmed. The men will let us pass if they think you will kill me. I will tell them Alaric doesn't want me hurt because he means to marry me." It was not even a lie and with luck, the men would have been told about his plans, which would play in their favor. "I will kick and scream as if I was afraid for my life."

"And are you afraid of me, little one?" He sounded appalled at the idea.

"Not in the least," she assured him, before stepping over to him and starting to fumble at his belt. Wolf's eyes widened in shock.

"What in the..." he hissed between his teeth, lowering his head to her. "Are you seriously considering ravishing me here and now, wife?"

"Unfortunately, no."

She smiled to herself when she felt that despite his protests, he had gone rock hard. Unable to resist, she stood on tiptoe and kissed him. It was a kiss in which she put all the desire that had exploded in her body at the feel of his response to her proximity, all the relief she'd felt at seeing he had not abandoned her. For a moment, they forget where they were and just allowed their mouths to worship each other's.

It was delicious, as heady and forbidden as their first kiss, but after a while Merewen forced herself to be reasonable and pull away. They would have their whole lives to kiss, first they had to get out of here. She raised the dagger she had retrieved from the sheath at Wolf's belt and smiled when understanding dawned on his face. Had he really thought she wanted to ravish him? Well, mayhap, and in any other circumstances she might well have done just that.

But all this would have to wait until a more appropriate time.

"Threaten me, you big brute," she said, handing him the weapon. "I trust you."

Wolf made a growl deep in his throat, a growl that resonated all the way to her core. "Then turn around... woman."

My. She could have collapsed then and there.

Clearing her throat, she complied.

Though she knew it was all just pretend, she could not help a yelp when Wolf's hand closed around her neck and the dagger nudged at her ribs.

"Hush, it's all right. I'm not going to hurt you. I'm only doing what you suggested. You're right, it is our best chance." A kiss on the top of her head, a soft groan in her ear made her close her eyes in pleasure. "Ready?"

She nodded, unable to talk.

Wolf marched her forward, stepping out of the gate.

"Move!" he snarled. "Let me pass or I'll gut the woman."

The voice was icy, lethal. Merewen whimpered and screwed her eyes tight, not finding it hard to pretend she was about to faint. Had Wolf been a real attacker she might well have passed out in fright.

Then she heard the men draw out their weapons. No! The men were not supposed to put up a fight!

"Don't provoke him! He will kill me!" she screamed, her voice tinged with a panic she could almost feel. The dagger nudged at her gently. She obeyed the silent command and let out piercing scream. "Let him through, he's hurting me! My future husband will not want me harmed in any way!"

Wolf saw the men hesitate. They were evidently wondering if they could overpower him. Considering he would have to fight the three of them and keep an eye on Merewen at the same time, it was not impossible. A single man could only do so much.

"You heard the woman. Move! Go and stand over there," he ordered before they could work up the courage to try. Faced with the prospect of Alaric's wrath when he found out they had allowed him to escape with the woman he meant to marry, they might well decide that they had nothing to lose. Dying now in a fair fight was probably better than being tortured later on.

"You will never have the nerve to do it," the tallest one

called out to him. "The master is a man to be feared, enough to make anyone think twice about harming his intended bride!"

This Wolf could well believe, but he was not just 'anyone', he was not truly harming Merewen and he would have faced a hundred Alarics for her.

Still, the men needed to be convinced that he was not going to leave the place empty-handed. Inspiration struck. He would impersonate Harald, who had every reason to hate Alaric and nothing to lose either.

"I care not what other men think. I am Harald the Strong and I swear that if you haven't dropped your swords by the time I have finished talking I will slice the bastard's bride open in retaliation for what he did to my wife Ingrid last week," he said, speaking every word with deadly intent. "You know I'm not lying. You will have seen her and what happened to her. I am here to avenge her and nothing will stop me. Now, *move!*"

To his relief, the men took a step back and lowered their weapons.

Immediately, Wolf pushed Merewen forward and felt her stumble as if her legs had turned to water. This was good. After such a performance no one would suspect her of being complicit to the scheme. If they were caught he would be the only one facing reprisal, everyone would swear she had been weak with fright. He half dragged, half carried her around the dying fire and toward the safety of the trees in the distance.

As soon as the shade engulfed them, he sheathed his dagger but kept his arm about her waist in support. Even if she wasn't limp anymore, he could not bear to let her go. He wanted to hold her tight, kiss her again, hold her tighter, grovel at her feet, beg for her forgiveness.

"Are you all right?" he whispered, barely resisting the urge to take her earlobe between his lips. It was so good to have her in his arms again!

"Yes. I'm sorry, I feel—"

"I know. But we need to move before the men alert every-one. We don't have long before they come after us. Do you want me to carry you?"

"No, no." Merewen shook her head. His heart swelled at the sight of her bravery. "I need to pull myself together, that's all."

Just then, shouts were heard in the distance. Now was not the time to dally, soon the men would be after them.

"Let's go, then," Wolf said. "Demon is waiting for us."

They ran to the meadow where the horse was tethered. The stallion snorted softly when his saw his master but, thankfully, made no other sound. Wolf hoisted himself into the saddle then helped Merewen to climb on behind him.

"Hold on tight," he said, wrapping her arms around his waist. "I'm going to go as fast as I can."

A heartbeat later, they were thundering toward the coast. For a long while, they raced across fields, jumping streams and fences in silence. It was a cold, misty morning, as if nature had decided to aid in their flight by making it impos-sible for the pursuers to see more than a few yards ahead. With each passing moment, Merewen could feel her anxiety melt away. Surely they would not be caught now? Once Demon had slowed down to an easy canter, she finally picked up the courage to ask Wolf the question uppermost in her mind.

"Why did you decide to come back for me? I thought you..."

Biting her lip, she stopped. What could she say without revealing the extent of the pain he had caused her?

I thought that you didn't care what happened to me, that, as you knew we were not really husband and wife, you jumped at the chance of ridding yourself of me, that you had been disap-pointed in my performance in bed.

That you did not feel anything for me.

Unable to voice her most secret fears and doubts out loud, she stayed silent.

Why had he come back? Wolf gritted his teeth because the answer to that question did not reflect well on him. Once again, had it not been for Sigurd, Merewen would have died. His friend had done twice what he should have been doing himself. Should he lie, tell her he had come to his senses on his own?

No. He owed her the truth, and he didn't deserve to be spared from whatever accusations and reproach she chose to throw at him.

Before answering, he slowed the horse to a walk. Talking with his back to her would help.

"You thought I'd forsaken you. With good reason, I might add, because I did, most shamefully, and handed you over to the very man who wanted you dead," he said slowly. Never had he been more ashamed of himself. "My only excuse is that I was genuinely trying to ensure that you would be safe. Will you ever forgive me?"

There was a pause, then he felt her cheek against his shoulder blade. Hope surged through him, as potent as one of Helga's potions. Surely she would not do such a thing if she thought him beyond redemption?

"I might forgive you if you actually answered my question," she said in a low voice. "I need to understand."

Of course, she did.

"This morning at dawn, Sigurd came to tell me he'd found out who had sold you to the slave trader. When he said the man in question was called Alaric and had a purple stain on his left cheek I realized it was none other than the neighbor you had disappeared with. I ran, hoping I wouldn't arrive too late."

Wolf shivered. He had almost not made it. Another moment and Alaric would have raped and possibly killed her. He owed his friend so much...

What would happen now? Could he and Merewen pick up where they left off after what he had done? He was not so sure. One thing was certain, he was not going to let her out of his sight ever again. If anyone was going to look after the woman he loved, it would be him and no other. He would warn his friends at the village, tell her all about the dangers she was facing, make sure she was well guarded.

He shook his head. The future was not something he could afford to think about just yet. First he needed to make sure they were not recaptured, and then he would see. Once he had Merewen in a place of safety, he would be able to think about it all, and set about earning her forgiveness. Jaw set, he scanned the horizon, on the lookout for shadows indicating Alaric's men were riding in hot pursuit. When nothing disturbed the mist surrounding them, he allowed his body to relax. Then two words reached his ear.

"Thank you."

He brought Demon to a halt so he could turn around to see Merewen. She looked so beautiful that for a moment he forgot to breathe. Then he saw that she was about to cry and his heart broke in two.

"Oh, little one, don't cry! And don't you dare thank me! Without me, you wouldn't have been in danger!" he groaned, unable to hear her gratitude when he was so ashamed of what he had done.

"But I would," Merewen told him. "You did not force me to go with Alaric, I had already decided to follow him, fool that I am! He lied to me, luring me in with promises of being reunited with long lost family members. I wanted to go because I wanted to see the uncle he'd made up, of course, but also because I thought to take the opportunity of going back home to get money."

He frowned. She had agreed to follow a near stranger for *money*? "What do you mean?"

She blushed. "I wanted to give you back the sum you'd spent on me that day at the market, because I... I didn't want to feel that you had bought me but rather chosen to be with me."

Everything within him roared in protest. "I did choose you! I would never have married you otherwise. As soon as I started to live with you I knew I could never let you go."

"Then why did you—?"

"Send you away?" he finished for her. "Do the one thing that tore my heart in two and put you in the clutches of the bastard who wanted you dead? Because I want you safe, whatever the cost. I need to know I'm doing everything to ensure you are not in danger. I think after Solveig you will understand why." He clenched his teeth, desperate to convince her of his good faith. "I fear I will never be able to protect you as you deserve. The incident in town proved it and then there was the—"

But she did not allow him to finish. "I don't want to be protected if it means being apart from you! Besides, I trust you absolutely with my safety. Didn't you buy me to protect me? Didn't you just save me? Don't you see? I would rather fall prey to someone's scheming than think you don't care about me."

A tear rolled down her cheek. Wolf's whole body lurched at the sight because he was responsible for her misery.

"I'm sorry, I should never have made you think that I did not care for you," he said, wiping the tear tenderly. "Because I do."

I love you. Even though I have no right to.

She recovered quickly. "No one can ever be totally safe, there is no guarantee. But the fear of what might happen should not prevent anyone from being happy." She shook her head. "Anyway. It's all in the past now. I don't want to have to think about it ever again."

"No. Let's go."

Wolf nudged Demon back into a walk. They would soon have to stop and find a place for Merewen to get some rest. After the events of the last two days, she would be exhausted and, in truth, he was feeling weary himself. He had barely had any sleep last night and now that he had her safely in his arms he could feel the tension in his body melt away, leaving an immense fatigue in its wake.

She never wanted to let him go, Merewen mused, as she tightened her hold around Wolf. Her rightful husband. With her arms wrapped about his waist, the heat of his body warming her, the muscles of his back rippling against her breasts, she could have fallen asleep. Too frightened to let her guard down, too wretched and cold to lie still, she had not been able to get more than a few moments of rest in the night.

"What are we to do now?" she asked after a while, trusting him to have come up with a plan.

"Hide for a few days, then go back to the village."

"We cannot go there! Alaric will find you," she cried out, all thoughts of sleep forgotten. "It's the first place he'll look!"

She felt Wolf shake his head. "He won't come for me. He thinks I have forsaken you, remember? And you heard what I told his men. As far as everyone is concerned, a Dane called Harald the Strong abducted you in retaliation for Alaric's attack on his wife. That is what they will report, as they have no reason to doubt what I said. As for Alaric, he never even saw me."

"Of course. How clever. And I thought I'd been quick-witted by having you pretend to abduct me!" Merewen mumbled.

"You were. Without that I might not have had the idea to pose as Harald and we might not have gotten out."

A dark shadow to the right suddenly caught their attention. A farm, set a small distance away from a village nestled in a bend in the river. Perfect. With the promise of some coin the farmer would allow them to sleep the afternoon away in his barn. Wolf steered them in that direction. Once he had brought Demon to a halt, he jumped down from the saddle, then helped her down. When she touched the ground, he kept his hands at her waist a moment and stared deep into her eyes.

Lord, she had forgotten just how massive he was. How hot, how comforting.

How irresistible.

"It's a good thing I happen to look like a bloodthirsty savage. It undoubtedly helped to give credence to the whole abduction thing," he said in a low voice.

"You look nothing like a bloodthirsty savage!" Merewen was indignant.

"No?" Wolf arched a devilish brow. "Is it not the same as a big brute?"

"Absolutely not, the two have nothing in common," she answered, stifling a giggle. Truly in that moment he looked nothing like a savage or a brute, rather like the most splendid savior you could imagine. *Her* savior. It was the second time he had saved her from Alaric's machinations and she knew there would not be a third time. He might not believe in his ability to protect her but she knew no one was better suited to the task.

Besides, she would rather have an uncertain life by his side, than a safe one without him. She'd had a sedate existence before and she had been so lonely she had literally dreamed a way out of it. As Wolf's wife, she would never need to do that, he would provide all the excitement she needed—and more.

"I'm glad to hear my wife doesn't think I look like a blood-thirsty savage," Wolf replied, his voice low and sensual. "Could I ask what I look like then?"

"You could, but I'm not sure I would tell you." She blushed.

If she told him even half of what she thought of him she would die of embarrassment.

"That sounds promising. I will find a way of making you talk, make no mistake about it," he warned.

"I'm all atremble."

"So you should be. I am of a mind to try my luck with a ladle to get a confession out of you."

The laughter Merewen had tried so hard to contain finally escaped her throat. It felt good to be reunited with Wolf at last, and secure in his feelings for her!

"You can try," she said. "But you will find that I am more resilient than you think."

His eyes threw flames. "That, little one, I do not doubt."

CHAPTER NINETEEN

After tying Demon to a tree surrounded by lush grass, they made their way to the farm.

"Stay here. I will go on my own."

"Surely there can be no danger?" Merewen answered, automatically scuttling closer to Wolf. She would prefer not to leave his side, even for a moment.

"I think not, but still it's more prudent. In your disheveled state, you might raise suspicion." She had to agree with him there. After her ordeal, she most probably looked a fright, bruised and exhausted, every inch the abducted female and he looked too much like a formidable Norseman for the Saxon farmer not to want to come to her aid. "And that way the farmer will be able to tell anyone looking for us that he did not see any fleeing couple but merely a lonely traveler if Alaric men's question him."

It made sense. Merewen nodded and remained hidden in the bushes. She would simply have to be brave. But while she waited for Wolf, her anxiety returned. In the mist, every shadow seemed to her like a man about to pounce, every noise was made by an enemy creeping up on her, ready to take her back to

Alaric. At this rate it would not take her long to have her nerves reduced to shreds.

"The man agreed to let me sleep in the hay barn," Wolf announced when he came back a moment later. "Come, he will soon come to bring me food and drink. He thinks I'm alone, so we need to hide you first."

She hurried to the barn and crouched behind the hay while he went outside to meet the farmer who was already on his way with a basket and a bucket of milk. Coins were exchanged and a moment later, Wolf was back inside.

Merewen took a long sip of lukewarm milk while he divided the bread into two equal portions. Now that they were not out in the open, she was oddly intimidated. Glad to have an excuse not to start a conversation or meet his eyes, she started to eat, discovering with the first mouthful that she was starving, which was hardly surprising. She had not been offered anything to eat during her captivity.

As soon as the last of the cheese had been consumed, Wolf turned to her.

She gulped. There would be no avoiding him now.

"Are you very badly hurt?" He cupped her cheek on the place where Alaric had hit her then allowed his fingers to brush against her throat, where she guessed he could see the traces of his fingers.

"I'll be fine."

He grunted, as if not quite believing her, then he moved his hand over to her ribs. "*I* didn't hurt you, did I, when I pressed the blade into you?" he asked, his voice full of anguish.

"No." Merewen could barely talk for the lump in her throat. The heat of his hands on her, the gentleness of his touch felt incredible. This was truly the man she had come to love. He'd come to find her, and she could tell he would never leave again.

"I should have killed the bastard for what he did to you,"

Wolf said slowly, bringing his forehead in contact with hers. "But I could not. Forgive me, I just could not choke him. It—"

"It reminded you of poor Solveig," she finished with a nod. He wouldn't have wanted to do something he had once been accused of doing and that had cost him so much. How terrible for him to have to see Alaric holding her by the throat when his first wife had died in that way. It would have brought home the reality of what the poor woman had endured. "I understand. And I don't want you to become a murderer for me. You had the opportunity to get me out without actually killing anyone and you took it. It was better that way," she assured him.

A growl was all the answer she got. Then he dropped to his knees and the hands at her waist slid down to grab her buttocks in a shocking, proprietary gesture.

"Will you forgive me for abandoning you?" he asked, resting his chin against her stomach.

Merewen's heart almost stopped. "You did not abandon me. You sent me away for my protection. We established that. You couldn't have known Alaric was my enemy. I didn't realize it myself so how could you have? And in the end you saved me. Again. So we will say no more of this." She placed a hand on his cheek. "Please. Stand up, I cannot stand to see you at my feet like a slave."

The blue eyes flashed. "You had better get used to it. I intend to spend a lot of time on my knees in front of you."

Without Wolf's strong hands around her, Merewen might have fallen backward. Did he mean what she thought he meant? Was he about to finally make love to her? Surely she had not mistaken the intent in his eyes? Surely being at her feet, so close to her, with his hands round her buttocks would fire his blood as much as it fired hers? But instead of lifting her skirts as she expected, he got up and took a step back. Something fell to the pit of her stomach.

This man had once been desperate for her, to the point of coming at her in her sleep, and taking her with all the impetuousness of a stallion mounting a mare. Now he was stepping away.

She didn't understand what had changed. Or rather, she understood all too well. He had been put off by her reaction when he'd taken her to bed. Not only hadn't she done anything to please him but she had even recoiled and pushed him away. He would understandably be hurt in his pride.

Unable to bear it, she said in a small voice, "Oh, I've ruined everything, haven't I! You don't desire me anymore."

A storm gathered in his eyes. "Not desire you? Merewen, I want you so much I can hardly breathe. I am dying with the need of you," Wolf said in a growl. Shivers ran along her spine as hope and desire bloomed in her whole body.

"Then what's wrong? Is it because I—?"

Before she could finish the question he had lifted her into his arms. "It's nothing you did. But I don't see why you would ever want me to touch you again. I don't deserve it, any more than I deserve your forgiveness. I have done nothing right so far. I couldn't stop myself from pleasuring you without your consent. I acted shamefully and touched a woman I had just bought, who was afraid of me, who did not know what I was doing."

"Oh, part of me knew *exactly* what you were doing," she said softly. "And believe me, it didn't hurt."

This time his eyes sent sparks. "Maybe it did not that time but..." He gritted his teeth. "When I took you to my bed I promised to give you pleasure and I hurt you instead. Then exposed you to another man's gaze and left you before I could set things right!"

Wolf ran a hand through his hair. How could she trust in his promise that he could give her pleasure after his first pathetic performance? He had caused her pain, abandoned her naked and confused on the pallet and left her to deal with it all on her own.

"It was not your fault the man walked in when he did," Merewen said, placing a hand on his pectoral. "As to the pain, it did take me by surprise, I will admit, but only because, although I had dreamed of this moment so many times, I'd ended up forgetting it would hurt. And I wanted you so much—"

"I did too, and I was too impatient. I truly thought it would be nothing more than a pinch and it would better for you if it was over swiftly." Wolf shook his head. This went to show how much he knew about women, or rather virgins... "I never wanted to hurt you. I also did not think I would be denied the chance to make you forget all about it."

Merewen laughed. "No. Neither of us could have predicted that someone would walk in on us in such a moment. I swear the poor man was more embarrassed than even I was. But please, I never held you accountable for any of it. The pain was not of your doing. It would have been the same with another man, except I doubt they would have taken the time to pleasure me first or stopped when I cried out."

No. Perhaps they would not. And he *had* stopped as soon as he had seen her pain.

Wolf looked at her, hope filling his heart. Could she really mean it? Did she really think he had done nothing wrong? She did not seem to hold any of what had happened against him and he knew he was telling the truth when he claimed he had not meant to hurt her.

Was it enough? Could they just put their disastrous first time behind them and move on?

Did she still want him as a lover?

"Just think of one thing," Merewen murmured, as if in answer to his question. "I'm not a virgin anymore. My body has

had time to heal and it will not hurt ever again to be taken. So...
Will you make love to me?"

"Oh, little one, I want nothing more but—"

"No but," she interrupted, placing a hand over his lips.
"Take me. Now. Show me the pleasure you wanted to show
me that day, the pleasure I have dreamt about all this time. Let
us do what we were prevented from doing, what we promised
to do yesterday evening. Please, Wolf, I need a man. I need
you."

No man could have resisted that plea. With a roar he lifted
her into his arms and marched her to the table by the door. A
heartbeat later Merewen was sat on it with her legs spread wide,
he was on his knees in front of her and the hem of her dress was
bunched around her waist. Blood was pulsing so hard in his
groin he feared he would spill his seed as soon as he saw her
most secret opening.

"Allow me to taste you first," he growled, thinking that it
hardly mattered if he did. His desire for her was so great that he
would be hard again before he had time to blink. "This is something I've been dreaming about since I felt your pleasure on the
tip of my finger that first night. Now I want to feel it on my
tongue."

"On your... *tongue*? Is that something we can do?" Her voice
was full of wonder.

He let out a growl. "One of the many things we can and will
do, if you allow me."

"Do you really think I would stop you from doing something
so enticing?" she croaked. "Taste me, Wolf."

The fingers of one hand came to entangle themselves in his
hair while she uncovered herself with the other, exposing
herself. Apparently the mere idea of baring her sex to him
aroused her so much that it overcame any shame she might have
felt. His fearless, brazen wife! Fascinated, he watched as the

pink petals swelled and grew slick with need under his gaze, and then he could wait no longer.

He dipped his head.

Silk and heat met Wolf's tongue. The smoothness of her had him groan in pure ecstasy. Something like a cat's mewl answered his growl. Merewen sounded so aroused that he knew it would not be long before she found her release. He licked along her folds, teasing her, marveling at how much pleasure he could feel by simply touching her. Closing his eyes, he plunged his tongue inside her, and was rewarded with a raw cry that wrenched another growl out of him. Had anything ever tasted better than this woman he loved?

Wild with need, he pushed her legs further apart and placed his hands under her buttocks to lift her up to his mouth. Once he had her where he wanted, he started to devour her with a hunger that had her whimpering in moments and then exploding in a rush of heat so intense he felt it all the way to his bones.

Everything shattered in an array of light.

Merewen remained panting on the table for a long time, too weak to move a muscle. Never in her wildest dreams had she had a man do such a thing to her. Up until that moment she hadn't even known that it *could* be done. But, oh, she already knew that she would beg Wolf to do it again and again.

And he'd said there were many other things they could try!

Just as she was thinking that he had not given his own pleasure any thought, he took hold of her thighs and positioned himself at her entrance. She felt the skin of his muscular legs bare against her calves. He must have removed his braies while she was recovering from her earth-shattering release, even if he was still wearing his undershirt.

"Merewen?" he asked, the strain in his voice obvious. "Do you want this?"

"Yes." From somewhere she found the strength to give her agreement. He grunted, as if he could not have borne to hear that she was not ready after all. His hardness pressed against her, making her insides convulse in need, luring him in. She closed her eyes.

Finally.

"Take me, Wolf, please!"

"Fire!"

For a moment they looked at each other in wild incomprehension. Who had spoken? Then pandemonium broke outside the barn. People started to run everywhere, shouting at each other.

"What the—?"

Merewen was too dazed to react but Wolf was already restoring order to his braies, cursing under his breath. Not again! He covered her bare legs and helped her off the table, muttering his frustration in his language. Was he going to be forever denied his pleasure, be prevented from giving Merewen what she was desperate to discover?

A moment later, a young man burst into the barn.

"We need your help!" he cried, barely pausing to look at them as he rushed to get the two buckets stowed by the far wall. The farmer must have ordered his son to fetch the strapping visitor in the barn and he was so intent on getting back to the fire that he barely registered the fact that the Norseman was not alone. "Please, we need to put the fire out, over there in the village!"

By the time the fire was contained there wasn't a single inch of Merewen's skin that wasn't covered in soot and she could not breathe without gasping in pain. Every muscle in her body ached and she was more tired than she ever remembered being.

Panting, dazed, she turned to Wolf. Although he was as just black as she was, he appeared relatively unaffected by the afternoon's exertions. The grueling task of running to the river to fill the buckets and then throwing their contents over the fire didn't seem to have drained him of any energy.

"You really are not made of the same stuff as I am," she mumbled when he joined her.

He chuckled. "More's the pity for me. Never have I seen anyone made of lovelier stuff than you."

"You choose your moments to pay compliments," Merewen sighed. "At the moment it feels as if I am made of naught but soot and sweat. Hardly a tempting combination."

"Depends what lies under the soot and sweat. I know for a fact that your skin is whiter than snow and you smell as good as honey—taste of it, too." With another chuckle, he lifted her into his arms as easily as if he had not just spent hours hoisting heavy buckets and clearing rubble. "Come, little one, you need a wash and a drink," he said, taking her back to the barn. "And then you need to sleep."

"Yes," she agreed with a groan. That sounded heavenly. "What about you?"

This time he laughed outright. "What I need will have to wait until you can move, I fear. I need you rested and eager for what I have in mind."

Being so grimy at least had one advantage, Merewen thought as Wolf carried her amongst the assembled villagers. No one would be able to see just how red she had gone.

While he went in search of food she washed, using the bucket of water he'd brought for her. Despite her hunger she barely managed to eat more than a strip of dried meat and a slice of bread before she lay on the hay. All she wanted to do was sleep. The day's activities, coupled with a sleepless night, had utterly exhausted her.

As soon as she closed her eyes, darkness enveloped her.

When she woke up, Merewen wondered if she had slept at all. Her mind was foggy and outside it was still light. Blinking, she turned to stare at Wolf. He was lying next to her, an arm folded under his head, the picture of easy contentment. Evidently he had been braver than her and gone to the river to wash, for his hair was slick and clean, and no trace of soot remained on his face or on his naked chest. He had even shaved the blond stubble that had graced his chin earlier.

He was breathtakingly handsome.

"Is it still not nighttime ?" she asked in a thick voice. Yet it felt as if she had been asleep for days.

"Nighttime has come and gone, little one," he laughed, turning to face her. "It's morning. You slept with the sleep of the dead."

"Oh." She made to go to him, wanting to nestle against his flank and groaned when the move caused her whole body to protest. "What happened to me?" she cried out, worried. Had she been beaten into a pulp?

"You must have carried your weight in water a hundred times over," came the answer in her ear.

"Ah, yes, that I definitely remember." Two arms drew her atop a lean, hard body. "Are you sure no one hit me with a club while I did that?" She sighed, feeling as if she was finally where she needed to be, and draped herself over Wolf.

"Quite sure," he chuckled. "Believe me, I would have taken issue with that."

"Mmm." For a moment she let the warmth of his body seep into her. "You smell of smoke." Although he had washed, the smell would likely take days to vanish.

"So do you. Smoke and spice. Rather a delicious combination. I could eat you alive, like the wolf I am," he growled, nipping at her earlobe and sending delicious shivers all the way down her body. An image of his head cradled between her thighs flashed through her mind and the shivers quickly turned to molten heat.

"No, not this time," she breathed, her voice hoarse. "This time I need you inside of me. I won't be denied a third time."

"We should wait until you feel stronger," he gasped when she ground her hips against his. "You just said you—"

"I feel strong enough for this. And I am not walking away from this barn before I've had you, preferably more than once."

This provocation was more than Wolf could withstand. All morning he had watched Merewen sleep next to him, wishing she would wake up and finally welcome him inside her heat. With a snarl he rolled her onto her back, feeling like a man possessed. Then he came over her, already undoing his braies.

"This will be quick, forgive me," he growled, in between heated kisses. "I want you too much."

"I want you too," Merewen answered, lifting the hem of her shift with equal urgency.

"Wait, let me undress you, at least. I had better—"

"No," she protested. "I could not bear to be interrupted again."

"Very well. But do not think I will not take my time the next time I make love to you." He would make it up to her, he promised himself. "I will savor every inch of your skin and make you desperate for my touch."

"I'm already desperate!"

"Good. So am I." Before Merewen had time to answer, Wolf lifted both her legs and settled her ankles over one broad shoulder. "There," he said with a possessive growl, as he positioned himself at her entrance.

Her insides instantly dissolved in anticipation. As shocking, as primitive as the position was, it reassured her to see that Wolf did not fear to behave as he wanted, that he trusted her to know he was not a lust-crazed maniac who cared nothing for her.

"Take me, Wolf."

In one thrust he plunged inside her silky depths. Merewen cried at the relief of it. Instantly, Wolf stilled.

"Did it hurt again?"

"No," she whimpered. "Please, don't stop."

He did not, and soon he started to move in earnest, sliding into her with ease, withdrawing slowly. The sensation of being filled by a man, the man she loved, the knowledge that Alaric would never get to her now that she was reunited with her husband, the thrill of finally being able to make love to Wolf, everything conspired to make Merewen reach her pleasure with frightening speed and intensity. It took hold of her and she could not stop a series of cries as ecstasy flowed through her in one seemingly never-ending wave of sensations.

Wolf gave a groan of his own and after two final, swift thrusts he stilled, head thrown back, body jerking violently.

After kissing her ankles he slid out of her and fell onto his back.

She immediately joined him and lay against his flank, breathing as hard as if she had been running for her life instead of being shown what being a woman really meant.

"I hope I wasn't too forceful."

Now that the haze of desire had dissipated Wolf realized just how fierce his lovemaking had been. He had driven into Merewen like a man possessed, riding her with frightening intent, positioning her just as he needed, immobilizing her under him, exposing her in a shocking position.

"You were exactly what I needed," she soothed, placing a hand on his pectoral.

He gave her a scorching kiss for this answer and, although it had been moments since he had achieved a bone-shattering release, he felt his manhood stir at the sweet heat meeting his lips. He wanted her. Again.

And again.

"Are you in here?" a tentative voice asked from behind the door. "I have some milk—"

"Do not even *think* about coming in!" Wolf snarled. "Put everything by the door and leave this instant!"

Merewen giggled when they heard the man scuttle away in fear. "There was no need to frighten the poor lad out of his skin," she murmured against his neck. Tingles coursed under his skin at the feel of her lips brushing his skin. "We are finished."

He gave something halfway between a growl and a snort. "We are far from finished, little one. That was far too quick, and if you remember, I promised I would savor every inch of your body."

"Mmm, I do, how could I have forgotten such a promise? But what if *I* wanted to do the same?" she teased.

"I believe I would allow you to," he groaned in response, before stretching onto his back to show her just how ready for more he was. "I'm all yours."

"Wait. There is something I would tell you beforehand." Merewen bit her lip, looking like a woman about to jump off a cliff—and more beautiful than words could express.

His heart melted.

"You need not worry about telling me what you feel," Wolf said, cupping her cheek. "I love you too. I don't mind being the first one to say it."

He would not have minded putting his heart on the line even if she had not returned his feelings. But in this instant he knew with absolute certainty that she did. The bone-deep, inexplicable longing he felt for this woman, the connection between them was love, had been from the start. As it had sprung from an unlikely source, he had not seen it at first, in the same way you do not expect to see a stream surge in the middle of an arid land. How could he have expected to fall in love when he had been convinced he did not want it, and with a woman he had bought, of all people?

As for Merewen, what had happened to her was barely better. He could not blame her for being bewildered by the notion that she had fallen for a man who had been her captor and for not daring to express it out loud, considering how he had treated her.

It had been a complicated journey for both of them. But they had finally arrived.

"Oh, Wolf, I love you too!" she said, her eyes filling with tears.

"Don't cry, little one," he soothed, wiping at her cheek. "'Tis not a bad thing to love someone."

"No," Merewen said in a shaky voice, relieved beyond measure. "Not a bad thing at all."

It was wonderful, and meant that she was not alone, after all, that she would never be abandoned. She had a husband who cherished her, and soon, she might have a family. A child might well have been conceived just then. The thought made her melt. She knew Wolf wanted nothing more and she sensed he would be a wonderful father.

"Tell me you love me in your language. I would like to hear it."

"You already have. The other day in the forest, I whispered it in your ear. I couldn't resist telling you the truth. *Ann ek þér.*"

She froze, because, indeed, she remembered those three words. And she had berated him for talking in a language she didn't understand, thinking he was teasing her! If she had guessed he was in fact opening up about her feelings she would have...

Merewen shook her head. She wasn't sure she knew what she would have done.

"You beast!" she cried out, giving his chest a light tap. "You sent me away moments after telling you loved me? Are you mad?"

Wolf shook his head. "I must be. And I have so many things to atone for. Fortunately, I have my whole life to do it." He looked so dejected that Merewen kissed him, long and hard. He groaned into her mouth, then drew away. "Now, there is something I simply must do before I go mad with the need to do it."

Without waiting for an answer, he rolled her onto her stomach and brought her wrists above her head, pinning them in place with one hand while he tugged at her shift with the other, exposing her buttocks. Merewen's heart started to beat wildly in her chest. This was so unexpected that she did not know what to think.

"What..."

All sorts of ideas flashed through her mind. Was he going to punish her for not having accepted what she felt for him earlier? Use her to slake his basest needs now that he was assured of her love? Surely not?

Mind reeling, she waited. Had anyone else placed her in such a vulnerable position she would have been frantic with fear, and done all she could to escape his hold.

Because it was Wolf, the man she loved, she simply waited.

Wolf felt something primal rise within him. This beautiful, wild woman was his. Although he had bought her and then married her, two things that made her legally his in the eyes of others, he had never felt she belonged to him. Now, at last, he did. They had made love, and just admitted their love for each other. It was what mattered, a lot more significant then a mere monetary transaction or a ceremony conducted in a hurry. And he could not wait another moment to do what he had obsessed about for days.

"That accursed beauty spot has had me almost losing my mind," he said between his teeth, as he bared it to his gaze.

"What beauty spot?" he heard Merewen say, her voice hoarse, confirming what he suspected. She had no idea she possessed the most enticing mark on her luscious body.

"Here," he said, lowering his head until his mouth was a bare inch above the swell of her buttocks. "You have a beauty spot just next to the dimple gracing the small of your back. The sight is almost enough to undo me."

He licked the little spot then swirled his tongue around it, barely resisting the urge to nip at her flesh. Merewen moaned and fire started to course through his veins. He straightened back up. If she carried on making these maddening noises he would not be able to indulge her wish to explore his body and he was very curious to see his bold lover in action.

"Now that I've done what I needed to do, I'm wondering. What are you going to do to me, little one?" he whispered in her ear before catching the lobe between his teeth. "I've seen you spit, bite, and kick at men... Should I be worried?"

"You should," she answered, slightly breathless. "That was nothing I haven't done a dozen times before. But there is something I have never done to anyone that I ache to do to you."

He growled. "That sounds just like the sort of thing I would like to hear."

"You will do more than hear it," she promised. "But you will have to release me first. I feel quite powerless under you like this."

"Mmm... I imagine you do but rest assured you could bring me to my knees with nothing more than a glance. I'm telling you, this wolf has been well and truly tamed." In one effortless move, he rolled onto his back, taking her with him, then turned her around so that she was sitting astride him. A finger came to tease the hard nipple poking under her shift. "I have just one request. Whatever it is you intend on doing, I insist you be naked for it."

"That can be arranged."

With a smile, the temptress lifted her shift above her head when another woman would have demurred or at least pretended to be uncomfortable. Not his brazen wife. She bared herself to him as easily as if her body had been his to gaze upon. Wolf stared at her, utterly transfixed. She was perfection, her beauty heightened by the wild glint in her eyes and the defiant posture. Never had he seen anything so alluring as his wife sitting on top of him, ready to pleasure him.

His throat went dry, and though he wanted to tell her how beautiful she was, the words got stuck.

"What is it? Has my pet wolf lost his tongue? I hope not, I rather like what he can do with it." The minx had the gall to tease him when he was on the verge of explosion! He narrowed his eyes but she merely smiled. "Now, it's my turn."

Her turn... Surely she did not mean...

Before he could said anything, she started to lower the waistband of his braies. Wolf sucked in a breath. What was the woman thinking? He would never last when the liquid heat of her mouth engulfed him, not when he was about to burst already! He opened his mouth to beg her to stop, closed it, opened it again, screwed his eyes shut, clenched his teeth and, with a groan, surrendered to his fate.

If she wanted to pleasure him then he would just have to bear it like a man.

Merewen licked her lips. Wolf was bare-chested, but he was still wearing his braies and that would not do at all. Not only did she want to see him in his full naked glory but she needed access to every inch of his body for what she had in mind.

A gasp escaped her lips when he sprang free, hard and heavy in her hand. She'd not had the chance to see his member so clearly yet and the sight was as daunting as it was enticing. Once again she wondered if she had not bitten off more than she could... accommodate.

"Now who's lost their tongue, I wonder?" he smirked, bringing his arms up to cradle the back of his head, the position making his biceps bulge, his pectorals contract, his stomach tense up.

Oh. He was perfection. And he was hers to use at will.

Unable to wait a moment longer, she lowered her head.

"No, I haven't lost my tongue," she purred. "As you're about to see."

Smooth and hot, hard and pulsating, he slipped between her lips. Merewen could not help moaning and wondered if Wolf had felt half as much pleasure from tasting her intimately as she was feeling right now, worshiping him with her mouth. For a long time she teased, licked and sucked, exploring the length of him, taking her time savoring him, sending him—and her—mad with the need for more.

Then she heard him say something in his language, something that sounded like a rough command or a curse. His manhood quivered under her tongue and a heartbeat later she found herself being lifted by two steely arms.

"Enough."

"It's not fair," she protested when he brought her back to sit on his lap. "You're too strong for me. I wanted to pleasure you!"

"You have," he growled. "You pleasured me almost to the point of madness. And now once more I find I cannot control myself." Grabbing her by the waist, he lowered her down onto his waiting hardness. Merewen cried out when he buried himself to the hilt in her pulsing center. "If you want to pleasure me, then ride me, vixen. Ride me until neither of us can move."

She did just that, lifting herself up and down his shaft, slowly at first, then with increasing urgency. Her body was gripping him as tight as a fist, sending waves of sensations rippling all over her. Once again, she would explode before she'd had time to enjoy the moment to the full. Watching Wolf's burning eyes precipitated her fall.

She started to tremble and a moment later stars exploded in her skull. He groaned at the same time and the heat blooming inside of her prolonged her ecstasy.

Slowly, she came back to reality, cradled against Wolf's body, having no recollection of how she had arrived there.

"I love you, little one. "

"Oh, Wolf! I will never tire of hearing those words."

"And I will never tire of hearing you calling me Wolf. Or... Would you prefer me to ask everyone to start calling me by my real name? Is Wolf too savage for you?" he asked, cradling her closer to him.

Merewen smiled. "No, Wolf suits you, my fierce protector. Besides, you resemble the animal."

"Do I now?"

"Yes. I've heard it said that wolves mate for life and that fur of yours is so soft..." She stroked his pectoral, covered by hairs so fine they were almost downy.

"Well, I've certainly found my mate but I don't know about being soft. I'm nothing compared to you," he said dubiously. He cupped one of her breasts and moaned.

"Oh, but it is soft," Merewen sighed, running her hand over one perfect, round shoulder. "I could stroke you all day."

"Please do. You will not hear complaints from me."

And indeed she did not.

EPILOGUE
TWO MONTHS LATER

The basket was as heavy as a dead ox, or so it seemed. Merewen hoisted it onto the table with a grunt.

"You should have asked me to do that," a deep voice chided from behind her.

Ever the protector, Wolf was at her side in an instant and forced her to sit onto a stool. What could easily have annoyed her instead made her feel cherished. In the last two months, she'd had time to get to know her husband better and understood that such thoughtfulness was an integral part of him. She could choose to see it as high-handedness or accept it for what it was and enjoy it.

"Are you all right, little one? You don't look too well."

"I'm all right," Merewen assured him, placing a hand on his chest.

"Are you sure? You have not been quite yourself in the last few days and are a lot paler than usual. No less beautiful for it, mind you, but I worry all the same. I don't like to see you less than blooming."

Her heart melted. "I'm fine, but there is something I—"

"Wolf!" A voice cried from the outside. "Wolf, you will want to hear this!"

He sighed. "Forgive me, sweet? Yet again?"

"Of course." She knew he had other commitments and she did not begrudge him the time he spent helping others. In fact, she was proud of him.

Wolf brushed the side of Merewen's cheek in a silent thank you and went to open the door. Thanks to her patience, he had stopped bemoaning the constant interruptions, accepting them as a part of the life he had built in his new country.

"What is it?" he asked Sigurd.

"A ship of Icelander merchants arrived in town. One of them, a man called Ketill Einarsson asked for you."

Wolf raised an eyebrow at the name he had not heard in years. "Ketill? What did he want?"

"Oh, not much, just to tell you that your name had been finally cleared."

For a moment, he stared at his friend, unable to comprehend what he was being told. Then he looked at Merewen, who had taken his hand in hers.

"Cleared?" Could it be true?

"Oh, Wolf, what wonderful news!" Merewen smiled at him, the pallor from her cheeks replaced by the glow he had missed.

"Your old neighbor Jón Sölvasson was named as your wife's murderer," Sigurd explained. "Apparently, after you left he took over your house and started to exploit your lands. According to his son, who came forward to speak in your favor once his father was dead, he was jealous of the river running through your property and had been after your land for years. He didn't dare attack you outright but thought having you accused of murder would seal your fate just as well."

Wolf stared at Sigurd in disbelief. The man had strangled his wife in order to dispose of him! Such a pathetic reason to kill an innocent woman! He could have laughed if the man's mad greed hadn't cost Solveig her life.

He felt Merewen's hand tighten around his. She would understand all too well what he felt, considering that her brother had been murdered so that Alaric could seize their property. It seemed that they would both have to bear the pain of a loved one being sacrificed for a piece of land.

"Thank you," he told his friend. "I will go and meet with the Icelanders tomorrow."

He would ask Ketill all he could about the affair but for now he needed time alone with Merewen. Despite the smile on her face, he had detected a gleam in her eyes he could not quite account for. He knew her too well to ignore that something was preying on her mind.

When she started to unpack the basket in a blatant ploy to avoid meeting his gaze, he was certain all was not as well as she would have him believe. Heart in his throat, he waited. Was she going to announce she was ill? Once again she had gone quite pale.

"Do you intend to return to Iceland now that you are free to go?" she asked, cradling an enormous cabbage against her.

He smiled, relieved. Now he knew what bothered her. She was worried he would ask her to go and live in a land where she would always be cold. His wife was really not made for winter weather, he knew. Prizing the cabbage from her fingers, he wrapped her into his arms, engulfing her in a bear hug.

"I am not going anywhere without my wife. And if she doesn't want to go to Iceland, then I'm not going either. I'm not sure I want to live there, anyway," he mused. "I have built a life here, and thanks to you I do feel part of a community again."

"I am not saying I don't want to go ever, and see the land of your birth, but... maybe not just yet."

"I know. It is all rather sudden. Worry not, little one. I am not taking you anywhere until you are ready for it."

As he kissed the top of Merewen's head, he spotted a piece of parchment amidst the vegetables in her basket. "What's that?

"Oh, I forgot. A man gave me this at the market for you."

Wolf opened the parchment and let out such a roar that Merewen almost dropped the piece of salted pork she was unwrapping.

"Forgive me, my love," Wolf apologized. "Only..." He threw the piece of parchment onto the table and took her back in his arms. "Alaric is dead," he told her bluntly.

"Harald?" she asked after a pause.

"Yes. He finally avenged your brother, Ingrid, and all the other women the bastard hurt. He's free, don't worry, Kristján assures me that no one will be able to trace the deed back to him."

"Well, then you'll forgive my for rejoicing in a man's death."

"I will." The man had murdered her brother, almost raped and killed her, assaulted countless women. His death could not be bemoaned and in truth he was relieved not to have killed the man himself. "And now. What did you want to tell me before we were interrupted?"

She lowered her eyes to the floor.

"You will have noticed how distracted and tired I've been these last few days..." she started hesitantly.

"I have." His heart started to beat wildly.

She looked at him and gave a wan smile. "I believe I am carrying your child. I wanted to—"

He didn't let her finish. In one fluid move Wolf lifted her off the floor and wrapped her legs around his waist in a position that had become as familiar to them as breathing.

"A child with you! Oh, little one, you have made my life complete," he said in a voice full of wonder.

"I am not absolutely certain yet but I thought you ought to know about my doubts."

"Thank you," Wolf said, kissing her tenderly. It meant the world that she wanted to share everything with him. "Is that why you did not want to go to Iceland just yet?"

She nodded sheepishly. "I admit that the idea of being on a jolting boat for days on end is not one to appeal to me right now. I am rather queasy in the mornings."

"Of course," he replied, ready to burst with joy and desire. He was a free man, free to go back home, married to the woman he loved, and he was about to be a father. Life had never been better. "Can anything make this day more perfect?"

"I can think of one thing," Merewen purred, grinding her hips, pressing his hard shaft between her legs, inviting him in.

"Oh, my love, I'm torn between marching you to the village right now to shout my joy and loving you until you can't breathe," he growled.

"The sun is setting. Marching though the village and announcing your news will have to wait until tomorrow," she argued in a whisper, taking his earlobe into her mouth. "But I do need to be loved until I can't breathe."

"Well, then, your needs come first. I know how desperate for a man my wife can get."

"Not 'a man'," Merewen smiled. "You. Always."

Next Read
Soothing the Beast
Read about Sigurd and Frigyth's story

ABOUT THE AUTHOR

As far back as I remember, I have been attracted to the Middle Ages, to knights in shining armour and their ladies in spectacular dresses. Now I get to write about them, I feel like the luckiest woman in the world. Being French and married to a Brit makes each book I write extra special, as our countries share a long and sometimes painful past. But in the end, in life as well as in fiction, love conquers all!

I have published several medieval romances under my own name, including series, and also have a pen name, Judith Falcon, for spicier projects, still in historical romance.

Feel free to check my books out on virginiemarconato.com and judithfalcon.com

ALSO BY VIRGINIE MARCONATO

The Noble Norsemen

Taming the Wolf

Soothing the Beast

Wooing the Devil

Baiting the Bear